FAR FROM YOU

FAR FROM YOU

Tess Sharpe

HYPERION
LOS ANGELES   NEW YORK

Printed in the United States of America
First Hardcover Edition, April 2014
First Paperback Edition, August 2015
10 9 8 7 6 5 4 3 2 1
V475-2873-0-15135

Library of Congress Control Number for Hardcover: 2013037960
ISBN 978-1-4847-1570-3

SUSTAINABLE
FORESTRY
INITIATIVE
Certified Chain of Custody
Promoting Sustainable Forestry
www.sfiprogram.org
SFI-01054
The SFI label applies to the text stock

Visit www.hyperionteens.com

For Gramz,
who gave me all my great loves.

And for Mom,
who believed this would happen, even when I didn't.

It doesn't start here.

You'd think it would: two terrified girls in the middle of nowhere, cowering together, eyes bulging at the gun in his hand.

But it doesn't start here.

It starts the first time I almost die.

The first time, I'm fourteen and Trev's driving us home from swim practice. Mina has the windows rolled down, her hands dancing to the music, rings glinting in the late afternoon sunlight as we speed past barbed wire fences and scrabbly ranches, the mountains stretching out behind them. We sing along to the radio in the backseat, and Trev laughs at my off-key voice.

It happens fast: the screech of metal on metal, glass everywhere. I'm not wearing my seat belt, and I pitch forward as Mina's scream drowns out the music.

Then everything's black.

The second time, I'm seventeen and annoyed with Mina. We're already late, and now she's turning off the highway, onto Burnt Oak Road.

"Just one little detour. It'll be quick, I promise."

"Fine," I say, giving in easy, like always.

This is a mistake.

The first time, I wake up in a hospital room, hooked to an IV and beeping machines.

There are tubes everywhere. I claw at the one down my throat, panic climbing inside me, and someone grabs my hand away. It takes me a second to realize it's Mina beside me, to meet her gray eyes and focus enough to let her words sink in.

"You're going to be fine," she promises.

I stop fighting and trust her.

It's only later that I learn she's lying.

The second time, I remember everything. The beam of the car's brights. The shooter's eyes shining at us through his mask. How steady his finger is on that trigger. Mina's hand clutching mine, our nails digging into each other's flesh.

After, I'll trace my fingers over those bloody half-moon marks and realize they're all I have left of her.

The first time, I spend weeks in the hospital. The doctors put me back together piece by piece. Surgical scars snake their way up my leg, around my knee, down my chest.

Battle scars, Mina calls them. "They're fierce."

Her hands shake when she helps me button my sweater.

The second time, there is no hospital. There are no scars.

There is only blood.

It's everywhere. I press hard against Mina's chest, but my jacket's already soaked through.

"It's okay," I keep saying. Over and over. She stares up at me with shocked, wet eyes and takes gulping breaths. Her body shivers beneath my hands.

"Sophie . . ." My name wheezes out of her. She lifts her hand, drags it toward mine. "Soph—"

It's the last thing she ever says.

1

"So, today's the big day," Dr. Charles says.

I look across the desk. From her shiny pumps to her tasteful, "natural" makeup, there's not a hair out of place on her. When I met Dr. Charles, all I wanted to do was mess her up. Slip the glasses down her nose, crush one of those perfectly pressed French cuffs. Tear into that neat, orderly mask and get down to the grit, the chaos.

Chaos has no place in recovery, Dr. Charles would say.

But I crave it. Sometimes even more than the Oxy.

That's what happens when you're trapped by clean white walls, endless therapy sessions, and piped-in new-age music for three months. The order and rules get to you, make you want to screw up just for the messiness of it.

But I can't afford that. Not now. Freedom is so close, I can almost taste it.

"I guess," I say, when I realize that Dr. Charles is waiting for an answer. She's big on getting answers to her nonquestions.

"Are you nervous?" she asks.

"No." It's the truth. I can count on one hand how many times I've been honest with her. Including this one.

Three months of lying is exhausting, even when it's necessary.

"There's no shame in being nervous," Dr. Charles says. "It's a natural feeling, given the circumstances."

Of course, when I finally do tell her the truth, she doesn't believe me.

Story of my life.

"It is a little scary. . . ." I let my voice go reluctant, and Dr. Charles's neutral therapist mask almost slips at the prospect of a confession. Getting me to open up has been like pulling teeth. I can tell it bugs her. One time she asked me to walk her through the night of Mina's murder, and I knocked over the coffee table, glass shattering all over as I tried to get away from her—just another thing I've destroyed in Mina's name.

Dr. Charles stares like she's trying to see through me. I stare back. She may have her therapist mask, but I have my "I'm a drug addict" face. She can't ignore that, because deep down, buried underneath all the other things I am (crippled, broken, scarred, and grieving), I *am* a drug addict—always will be. Dr. Charles understands that I know this about myself. That I've accepted it.

She thinks she's the one responsible for my change from raging to recovering, but she's not. She doesn't get to take the credit for that.

So I stare her down. And finally she breaks the eye contact and looks at her leather portfolio, writing a few notes. "You've made tremendous progress in the time you've spent at Seaside Wellness, Sophie. There will be challenges as you adjust to living a drug-free life, but I feel confident that with the therapist your parents have arranged for you and your commitment to recovery, you'll succeed."

"Sounds like a plan."

She shuffles some papers, and just when I think I'm free and clear, she drops the bomb: "Before we go downstairs, I'd like to talk with you a little more. About Mina."

She looks up at me then, carefully monitoring my response. Waiting to see if I'll break her new coffee table. (It's wood this time—I guess she figured she needed something sturdier.)

I can't stop it: the way my lips tighten up and my heartbeat thuds in my ears. I force myself to breathe, in and out through my nose like in yoga, relaxing my mouth.

I can't slip up. Not now. Not when I'm this close to getting out.

"What about Mina?" My voice is so steady, I want to pat myself on the back.

"We haven't talked about her in a while." She's still watching me. Waiting for me to freak, like I have every time she's forced this. "Going home is a big adjustment. A lot of memories will come up. I need to make sure you're in the right frame of mind to deal with them without . . ." She tugs at her left cuff.

This is another of her tactics. Dr. Charles likes to make me finish her sentences. Own up to my mistakes and faults.

"Without going on an Oxy binge?" I supply.

She nods. "Mina and her murder are triggers. It's important you're aware of that. That you're prepared for the challenges her memory may bring up—and the guilt."

I have to stifle my knee-jerk response. The one that screams, *"Her murder wasn't about drugs!"*

It's no use. No one will believe the truth. No one will believe *me*. Not with the evidence in front of them. That fucker in the mask had covered his bases—he knew I'd never notice the drugs he planted on me, not after he'd shot Mina and knocked me out. My mom called in every favor imaginable to get me into Seaside to deal with my supposed relapse instead of being booked for possession.

Dr. Charles smiles at me. It's both bland and encouraging, a warring twist of pink lipstick.

This is my final test; I have to be careful with my words. They're my ticket out of here. But it's hard, almost impossible, to keep my voice from shaking, to stop the memories from creeping back. Of Mina, laughing with me that morning, both of us unaware that she'd end with the day.

"I loved Mina," I say. I've practiced it a hundred times, but this can't sound rehearsed. "And her murder is something I have to deal with for the rest of my life. But Mina would want me to move on. She'd want me to be happy. And she'd want me to stay clean. So I'm going to do that."

"And what about her killer?" Dr. Charles asks. "Do you feel ready to talk to the police about what you might know?"

"I loved Mina," I say again, and this time my voice does shake. This time it's the truth, and nothing but. "And if I knew who killed her, I would be screaming his name at the top of my lungs. But he was wearing a mask. I don't know who it was."

Dr. Charles leans back and examines me like I'm a fish in a bowl. I have to bite the inside of my lip to stop it from trembling. I keep my breathing steady, like I'm holding a difficult yoga pose and have to power through.

"She was my best friend," I say. "Don't you think I know how I screwed up? I barely sleep sometimes, thinking about what I could've done differently that night. How I could've stopped it. How it's my fault. I know all of that. I just have to learn to live with it."

This is the truth.

The guilt—it's real. It just doesn't come from the place that Dr. Charles thinks it does.

It *is* my fault. For not stopping Mina. For not asking more questions. For letting her act like a newspaper story was something to keep top secret. For following her lead, like always. For not being faster. For being crippled, unable to run or fight or do anything to protect her.

"I'd be happy to talk to Detective James again," I say. "But he doesn't think I'm the most reliable witness."

"Do you blame him?" Dr. Charles asks.

"He's just doing his job." The lie feels like glass against my gums, the words grinding through my skin. Hating Detective James is second nature at this point. If only he'd listened to me . . .

But I can't think about that now. I've got to focus. Mina's killer is out there. And Detective James isn't going to find him.

"I know going home will be hard. But I feel like you've given me the tools to handle everything way better than I used to."

Dr. Charles smiles, and relief hits me like a two-by-four. She's finally buying it.

"I'm delighted to hear you say that. I know we had a rocky start, Sophie. But our last few sessions, you've had a much more positive outlook. And that's very important, with everything that's ahead of you. Recovery is not easy, and the work never stops." She checks her watch. "Your parents should be here by now. Why don't I take you to the waiting area?"

"Okay."

We walk in silence down the corridor, past the group session going on in the rec room. That circle of chairs has been my own personal hell for the last three months. To have to sit there and *share* with people I barely know has been excruciating. I've spent every minute lying my ass off.

"They must be running late," Dr. Charles says when we get to the empty waiting room.

Right. Late.

She's either forgetting our last strained family-day session or she honestly believes the best of people.

I don't.

Which is why I wonder if my parents are late. Or if they're just not coming.

2

"Don't make me do this. Please, Mom. I don't need to go anywhere—I'm clean. I *swear!*"

"I don't want to hear it, Sophie." Mom snaps my suitcase shut and marches downstairs. I follow. I have to fight her. Make her believe me. Someone has to.

My dad's waiting for us at the front door, his coat over his arm like he's off to work. "Ready?" he asks.

"Yes," Mom says. Her heels click across the Spanish-tile floor as she takes her place next to him.

"No." I plant myself at the bottom of the stairs, square my shoulders, and cross my arms. My bad leg shakes as disappointment bears down on me from both sides. "I won't go. You can't make me."

My dad sighs and looks at his feet.

"Get in the car, Sophie Grace," Mom orders.

I say it low and slowly. "I don't need to go anywhere. I didn't relapse. Mina and I weren't out scoring. I'm clean. I've been clean for over six months. I'll take any drug test you give me."

"The police found the pills in your jacket, Sophie," Dad says. His voice is hoarse and his eyes are red. He's been crying. Crying over me. Over what he thinks I've done. "The bottle had your fingerprints on it. You were supposed to be at Amber's house, but you girls were out at

Booker's Point instead. You were buying drugs. Even if you didn't get around to taking the pills, you bought them—they didn't just magically appear in your pocket. Seaside is the best choice for you right now. Do you know how hard your mother had to fight just so you wouldn't get a drug charge on your record?"

I look desperately at each of them. Dad won't even look at me; Mom's face is frozen; she's in ice-queen mode. Nothing will crack it.

I have to try.

"I've told you before, they weren't mine. Detective James has it all wrong. We weren't out at Booker's Point for drugs—Mina was meeting someone because of a newspaper story. The police are going after the wrong people, and they won't believe me. I need *you* to believe me."

Mom rounds on me, the suitcase swinging in her fist. "Do you understand what you've put me and your father through? What about Mrs. Bishop? Do you care what she must be feeling right now? She's already lost a husband, and now she has to lose her daughter, too! Trev will never see his sister again. And all because *you* wanted to get high."

She spits out the words, and I feel like less than nothing. A speck on her shoe. Narrowing her eyes at me, she goes on, "So if you don't get in that car, if you don't go to Seaside and learn how to stay clean, I swear to God, Sophie . . ." Tears glimmer in her eyes as the anger evaporates.

"I keep almost losing you," she whispers, and her voice trembles and cracks with the weight of the words. "This is what I should've done the first time, but I didn't. I'm not going to make that mistake again." Her voice hardens. "Get in the car."

I don't move. I can't. Moving would be like admitting she's right.

Six months. Five days. Ten hours.

That's how long I've been clean, and I repeat it over and over to myself. As long as I focus on that, as long as I'm committed to making that number rise, minute by minute, day by day, I'm going to be okay. I have to be.

"Now, Sophie!"

I shake my head and grip the banister. "I can't let you do this."

All I can think about is Mina. Mina's in the ground and her killer's walking free, and the cops are looking in all the wrong places.

My dad grabs me around the waist, breaking my hold, and lifts me over his shoulder in a fireman's carry. It's gentle; Dad is always gentle with me, like how he used to carry me upstairs after the accident. But I'm done with his gentleness. It doesn't make me feel safe anymore. I pound on his back, red faced, yelling, but it doesn't stop him. He yanks the front door open, and my mother stands on the porch, watching us, her arms hugging her body like it'll protect her.

He strides down the driveway and dumps me into the car, his face stony as he slides into the driver's seat.

"Dad." Tears are slick down my cheeks. "Please. I need you to believe me."

He ignores me, fires up the engine, and drives.

3

My parents still haven't shown up. Dr. Charles keeps checking her watch and tapping her pen against her knee.

"I can wait by myself."

Frown lines mar her smooth forehead. This is not the
way things are done. My parents should have been tear-
fully embracing my new and improved, squeaky-clean self
at least twenty minutes ago.

"Let me make a phone call," she says.

I lean my head against the wall and close my eyes. I sit
and wait, wondering if she'll even let me call a cab if she
can't get hold of my parents.

About ten minutes tick by before someone taps my knee.
I open my eyes, expecting to see Dr. Charles. But instead,
for the first time in months, I feel a real smile stretch across
my face.

"Aunt Macy!" I throw myself into her arms, almost
knocking her over. My chin hooks over her shoulder as I
hug her. Macy's a few inches shorter than me, but there's
something about the way she carries herself that makes her
seem taller. She smells like jasmine and gunpowder, and
she's the best thing I've seen in what feels like forever.

"Hey, kid." She grins and hugs me back, her callused palms warm against my shoulders. Her hair, blond like mine, is down her back in a long braid. Her tanned skin makes her eyes look shockingly blue. "Your mom got held up on a case. Sent me instead."

I haven't heard from Macy the entire time I've been at Seaside, even though after the first two weeks, I was allowed letters from people other than my parents. But now she's here, and I have to bite my lip against the relief that rocks inside me.

She came. She still cares. She doesn't hate me. Even if she does believe everyone else, she *came*.

"Can we please get out of here?" I ask thickly, fighting tears.

"Yeah." She cups the back of my head, her fingers tangling in my long hair. "Let's get you checked out."

Five minutes spent signing a stack of papers, and I'm free.

I feel like running the moment I step outside. I'm half-convinced that any second, Dr. Charles will come slamming through the doors, suddenly seeing through all my lies. I want to sprint to Aunt Macy's ancient Volvo, lock myself in.

But running isn't an option. It hasn't been for almost four years, since my right leg and back got messed up in the car crash. Instead, I walk as fast as my limp allows.

"Your mom wanted me to tell you how sorry she is that she couldn't come," Aunt Macy says as she starts the car.

"And Dad's excuse?"

"Out of town. Dental convention."

"Figures."

Macy raises an eyebrow but doesn't say anything as we pull out of the parking lot and onto the highway. I roll the window down, trailing my fingers in the hot summer air. I keep my eyes fixed on the buildings blurring past me, away from her questioning glances.

I'm afraid to speak. I don't know what she's been told. The only visitors I was allowed were my parents, and they came only when they had to.

So I stay quiet.

Nine months. Two weeks. Six days. Thirteen hours.

My mantra. I whisper the days under my breath, pressing the words against my lips, barely letting them out into the world.

I have to keep adding to it. I have to stay clean, stay focused.

Mina's killer is out there, walking around, free and clear. Every time I think about whoever he is getting away with it, I want to bury myself with a handful of pills, but I can't, I can't, I can't.

Nine months. Two weeks. Six days. Thirteen hours.

Aunt Macy tunes the radio to an oldies station and changes lanes. We leave the coast behind, the scenery giving way to redwoods, then pines as we head into the Trinities. I let the air flow through my fingers, enjoying the feeling like a little kid.

We drive in silence for almost an hour. I'm grateful for it, for the chance to absorb the freedom singing in my veins. No more group. No more Dr. Charles. No more white walls and fluorescent lighting.

Right now, I can forget what's waiting for me eighty miles

past those foothills up ahead. I can trick myself into thinking that it's this easy: the wind in my hair and between my
fingers, the radio on, and miles of freedom ahead.

"You hungry?" Aunt Macy points at a billboard advertising a diner off exit 34.

"I could eat."

The diner is noisy, with customers chatting and dishes
clanging. I trace whorls of faded glitter embedded in the
Formica tabletop as the big-haired waitress takes our orders.

After she hurries away, silence overtakes us. It's like
Macy doesn't know where to start after all this time, and I
can't bear to be the person to speak first. So I excuse myself
and head to the bathroom.

I look like crap: pale and too skinny, my jeans hanging
off hip bones that used to be a mere suggestion. I splash
water on my face, letting it drip down my chin. Dr. Charles
would say I was avoiding, delaying the inevitable. It's stupid, but I can't help it.

I run my fingers through my straggly blond hair. I
haven't worn makeup for months, and the dark smudges
underneath my eyes stand out. I press my dry lips together,
wishing I had some lip balm.

Everything about me is tired and cracked and *hungry*. In
more ways than one. In all ways that are bad.

Nine months. Two weeks. Six days. Fourteen hours.

I dry my face and force myself to walk out of the bathroom, back to the table.

"Fries are good" is all Macy says, dipping one in ketchup.

I wolf down half of my burger, loving it simply because it's not rehab food and doesn't come on a tray. "How's Pete?"

"He's Pete," she says, and I smile, because that pretty much sums it up. Her boyfriend has tranquil down to an art form. "I've got some yoga flows he put together for you." She eats another fry. "Did you keep up with your practice?"

I nod. "Dr. Charles let me bring my mat and blocks. But I couldn't have the strap. I guess she was afraid I'd hang myself or something." It's a lame attempt at a joke that leaves a gaping hole of awkward silence between us.

Macy sips her iced tea, looking at me over the glass. I tear a fry in half and squish it between my fingers just for something to do.

"Anything else for you girls?" the waitress asks as she refills my water glass.

"Just the check," Macy says. She doesn't even look at the waitress, keeping her eyes on me. She waits until the woman's behind the counter. "Okay, Sophie. No more bad jokes. No more small talk. Time to tell me the truth."

I feel queasy, and for a second I'm so full of dread, I'm afraid I'll be sick.

She's the only person left who hasn't heard my truth. I'm so afraid she'll do what they all did: Blame me. Refuse to believe me. It takes every shred of strength I've got left to force out: "What do you want to know?"

"Let's start with why you supposedly relapsed two weeks after getting home from Oregon."

When I say nothing, she taps her fork against the edge

of her plate. "When your mom called and said they found drugs in your jacket, I was surprised. I thought we'd worked through all that. I could have understood your relapsing if it had been *after* Mina's murder. But this . . . not so much."

"The pills were in my jacket at the crime scene, so they had to be mine, right? Mina didn't do drugs. I'm the one with the history. I'm the one who'd barely been clean six months when it happened. I'm the reason we were out there in the first place. That's what everyone says." I can't hide the bitterness in my voice.

Macy sits back in the booth, lifts her chin, and peers at me, a sad sort of knowing in her face. "I'm more interested in what *you* have to say."

"I— You—" The words stick in my throat, and then it's like she's pulled a plug inside me. A garbled sound wrenches from my mouth, tight and incoherent with relief. "You're going to listen to me?"

"You've earned that from me," Macy says.

"But you didn't visit. You never wrote. I thought that you—"

"Your mom." Macy's mouth flattens. She has that look in her eye that she always gets before she goes off on a job. A coiled tension that's dying to leap out. "This has been hard on her," she continues. "She trusted me to get you clean, and she feels like I've failed. Plus, when I found out she'd sent you to Seaside, I may have said some things."

"What things?"

"I bitched her out," Macy explains. "And I shouldn't have, but I was angry and worried. I asked her if I could go see you or at least write, but she didn't want me involved. I love you, babe, but you're her kid, not mine. I had to respect her wishes—she is my sister."

"So you stayed away."

"I stayed away from you," Macy says. "But I didn't stay away from the case."

I sit up straighter. "What's that mean?"

Macy opens her mouth, but closes it when the waitress stops by our table, setting the bill down. "You girls take your time," she says. "Let me know if you need any boxes."

Macy nods her thanks and waits until the waitress is off taking another order before turning back to me. "Your mom had made her mind up about what happened to you. But I was the one who got you clean. I spent more time with you last year than she did. And I couldn't do anything for you while you were at Seaside, but I knew how much Mina meant to you. And I knew that if you had any information about her killer, you would have come forward, even if it got you into trouble. I couldn't shake that feeling, so I put some calls in to a few old friends from the force, asked around, got my hands on the reports, and the head detective's take on things didn't click. Even if you and Mina had been out there to score, why would a dealer leave the drugs? That's evidence.

"The killer shot Mina. He could've easily shot you, too, getting rid of both witnesses, but he chose to knock you out. That tells me it wasn't random; it was targeted. And if he planted the pills on you, that means it was planned."

Something close to relief starts to uncurl inside me.

who worked the night shift. He dragged in every known dealer in three counties for questioning, along with most of the kids in your grade, but didn't find anything to warrant further investigation. Along with a witness testimony that was—well, shaky." She fiddles with her fork, looking up at me. "Without any fresh evidence or a miraculous confession, it'll be dismissed as an unsolved drug-related murder, and that'll be it."

I feel sick inside and grit my teeth. "I can't let that happen."

Macy's eyes soften. "You might have to, babe."

I don't say anything. I keep quiet.

We get up, she pays the bill and tips the waitress before we leave the diner. I'm still silent, the idea of never knowing who took Mina away from me burning in my chest. But somehow, as always, Aunt Macy hears the words I can't say. When we're in the car, Macy reaches over and takes my hand.

She keeps it in hers the entire drive home.

It feels like a safety net.

Macy is always poised for my inevitable fall.

4

"You're a fucking sadist," I snarl at Macy.

It's been three days since my parents shipped me off to Oregon so Macy can "straighten me out," as my dad put it. Three days since I've had any pills. The withdrawal is bad enough—like my body is one giant, throbbing bruise and spiders crawl underneath my sweaty skin—but the pain, undulled and persistent, is too much to take. With the pills, I can move without it hurting too much. Without them, my back is killing me and my leg's always giving out. Every movement, even turning over in bed, sends sharp flares down my spine that leave me breathless, pain-tears tracking down my face. The pain, full-force for the first time since the accident, combined with the withdrawal is excruciating. I stop getting out of bed. It hurts too much.

It's all Macy's fault. If she'd just give me my damn pills, I'd be fine. I'd be able to move. I wouldn't hurt. I'd be okay again.

I just want to be okay again. And Macy won't let me.

I spend a lot of time staring at the cheerful yellow walls of her guest room, with its lace curtains and vintage travel posters. They make me want to puke. I hate everything about Macy's house. I want to go home.

I want my pills. The thought of them consumes me, drives everything out of my head, makes me focus with a singularity I've had for only one other thing in my life. Mina would hate me for comparing her to this, but I don't care, because I kind of hate her right now, too.

"I'm helping you." Macy barely looks up from her magazine. She's sitting in a turquoise armchair across the room, her legs kicked up on the matching stool.

"I'm . . . in . . . pain!"

"I know you are." She flips a page. "Which is why you have a doctor's appointment tomorrow. Best pain management doctor in Portland. We'll find non-narcotic options for you. And Pete's got an acupuncturist friend who's going to come to the house to treat you."

The idea twists in my gut. "You want to stick needles in me? Are you crazy?"

"Acupuncture can be therapeutic."

"There is no way I'm doing that," I say firmly. "Can't I go home, please? This is so stupid. The doctors were the ones who gave me the pills in the first place. I have *prescriptions*. Do you really think you know better than them?"

"Probably not," Macy admits. "I didn't even graduate college. But I'm in charge of you now, which means I get to do what I think is best. You're a drug addict. You screwed up. Now you get clean."

"I told you, I don't have a drug problem. I'm in *pain*. That's what happens when you get crushed by an SUV and your bones are held together by metal and screws."

"Blah, blah, blah." Macy waves it off and sets her magazine down. "I've heard it all before. Some people can handle pain meds, some can't. Considering the pharmacy your dad found in your bedroom, I'm going to say you're just a few bad days away from an OD. You think I'd let you do that? Put your mother and me through that? I don't think so. Not again.

"When you run out of bullshit excuses and admit you've got a problem, then we can talk. The sooner you admit it, babe, the sooner we'll get to the root of this. You might as well start talking—you're not going anywhere until I'm sure you're not a danger to yourself."

"I'm *fine*." I wipe the sweat off my forehead, swallowing against the constant nausea that's taken over since yesterday. God, withdrawal *sucks*.

Macy gets up and shoves a trash can in my hand. "If you're going to throw up, use this."

Her face softens, a ripple in that bad-cop facade she wears so well. She reaches over, grasping my free hand in hers, and holds on tight enough that I can't tug away. "I won't give up on you, Sophie. No matter what you do, no matter what you say, I'm here. I won't lose you. Not to this. I will get you clean. Even if you end up hating me for it."

"Great," I say bitterly. "Lucky me."

5

Harper's Bluff is nestled in Northern California's side of
the Siskiyou mountain range, a tiny town carved out of
the wilderness, sheltered by the piney mountains, surrounded by oak woodland for miles around, with a lake
that stretches out into what you trick yourself into thinking
is infinity. We've got a population just tipping twenty thou-
sand, more churches than grocery stores, American flags
flying from most of the houses, and REAL MEN LOVE JESUS
bumper stickers on every other truck on the road. It's not
idyllic, but it's comfortable.

I thought I was ready to come back, but the second we
pass the WELCOME TO HARPER'S BLUFF sign, I wish I could tell
Macy to hit the brakes. Beg her to take me back to Oregon
with her.

How can I be here without Mina?

I bite my tongue. I have to do this *for* her. It's the only
thing I can do. I stare out the window as we pass by my
high school. I wonder if they decorated Mina's locker, if it'd
been festooned with flowers and candles, notes tucked into
corners, never to be read. I wonder if her grave's the same,
teddy bears and pictures of her, beaming up at a sky she'll

never see again. I hadn't even gone to her funeral—couldn't bear to watch them put her in the ground.

As we're turning onto my street, Macy gets a call. Maneuvering the car into the driveway, she tucks the phone under her chin. "Where?" She listens for a second. "How long ago?" She shuts the car off, eyeing me. "Okay, I can be there in thirty."

"Someone jump their bail?" I ask after she hangs up. Macy's a bounty hunter, though she prefers being called a bail recovery agent.

"Sex offender in Corning." She frowns at the empty driveway. "I'd hoped your mom would be here by now."

"It's okay. I am capable of being alone in my own house."

"No, you shouldn't be by yourself right now."

"Go catch the bad guy." I lean over and kiss her on the cheek. "I promise I'll be fine. I'll even call as soon as Mom gets home, if it'll make you feel better."

Macy taps her fingers against the steering wheel. She's itching to get going, to chase down that guy and put him in jail where he belongs.

I know that feeling, that drive for justice. All the women in my family have it. Macy's is wrapped up in the chase, in hard and fast and brutal judgment, and Mom's is wrapped up in rules and laws and juries, the courtroom her chosen battlefield.

Mine is wrapped up in Mina, magnified by her, defined by her, existing because of her.

"Seriously, Aunt Macy. I'm seventeen, I'm clean, and I can spend some time by myself."

run my fingers over the red sheets. They're crinkled at the edges, which means Mom put them on herself instead of having the once-a-week housekeeper do it.

Thinking about her struggling with them in her heels and pencil skirt, trying to make it nice for me, makes my eyes sting. I clear my throat, blinking fast, and dump the contents of my bag onto the bed before going to take a shower.

I let the water stream over my head for a long time. I need to wash the smell of rehab—lemon air freshener and cheap polyester—off of me.

For three months, I've been stuck, stagnant and wait-ing, behind white walls and therapy sessions while Mina's killer walks. It hits me all at once that I'm finally free, and I jam the faucets shut. I can't stand to be inside for another second. I get dressed, leave a note on the kitchen table, and lock the door behind me. The canister of bear spray is safe in my bag.

Macy was right—I'm about to stir up some serious shit. I have no idea why anyone would kill Mina. Which means I have to be prepared for anything. For anyone.

It's getting late. But he'll still be at the park.

The good thing about growing up in a small town is that everyone knows everyone. And if you've got a routine, you're usually easy to find.

I walk to the park and get there as the guys playing soc-cer are finishing up their casual game, shirts versus skins. The sun's sinking, that dusky time where dark and light are balanced almost artificially, like an old movie, saturated with hazy color. I watch from across the street and wait until a massive, shaggy-haired blond guy in a dingy white soccer jersey and baggy shorts breaks away from the group, heading toward the bathroom, the door swinging shut behind him.

It's perfect: isolated, with nowhere for him to run. So I seize the moment.

I want to slam into the bathroom, scare the shit out of him, grind his cheek against the dirty tile with my foot until he admits the truth.

Instead, I slip in quietly and lock the door behind me once I'm sure it's just him in here.

The toilet flushes, and my stomach leaps, part anger, part fear.

He doesn't see me at first, but halfway to the sink he catches sight of me in the mirror.

"Shit." He spins around.

"Hi, Kyle."

"I thought you were in rehab."

"They let me out." I step forward, and when he moves away, a sweet feeling rushes through me. Kyle's huge, thick-necked and solid—more suited for football than soccer—and I like that he's a little scared of me, even if he's just afraid that the junkie will do something crazy.

I take another step. This time he manages not to retreat.

But he wants to. I can see the fear in that frat-boy-to-be face.

Fear means guilt.

I pull the bear spray from my purse, unlocking it and

raising it to his eye level as I step forward. "You remember that time Adam's brother accidentally got him in the face with bear spray? We were, what, freshmen? Maybe it was even eighth grade. . . . Anyway, it's one of his favorite drinking stories. To quote Adam: 'That shit stings like a fucker.'"

I tap my finger on the trigger. Kyle tenses.

"When I was in rehab, I had a lot of time to think," I say. "That's pretty much all you get to do: think about your mistakes and your problems and how to solve them. But in all that time, I never came up with the right answers to my questions.

"Maybe you can help me, Kyle. Why don't we start with why you lied to the police about the night Mina died?"

6

The day after Mina is murdered, my dad drives me home from the hospital. We're silent the whole way. I want to rest my forehead against the window to let the solidity ground me. But when I lean my temple on the glass, it presses against the arc of stitches. I wince and look to my right.

It's sunny out. A crisp February day, snow still capping the mountains. There are kids playing in the park as we pass it. It seems strange, life going on now, after everything.

Dad opens the car door for me after we pull into the driveway, but when we get into the house, I hesitate at the bottom of the stairs. He looks at me, concern in his face.

"Do you need help, honey?"

I shake my head. "I'm gonna shower."

"Remember, the detective should be here in about an hour. Do you think you'll be ready to talk then?"

They'd sedated me at the hospital. I'd been too out of it to answer questions when the police had come by.

The idea of talking about it makes me want to scream, but I say, "I'll be ready," before I labor up the stairs. I almost wish I hadn't tossed my cane when I was fifteen, because right now I could use it.

I turn the water on and undress slowly in the bathroom, peeling off my sweats and henley.

That's when I see it: a smear of red-turned-brown on my knee. Mina's blood.

I press my fingers against the spot, my nails digging into my skin until beads of fresh, bright red appear. My fingers are stained with it, and it makes my chest go tight, tight, tight.

Five months. Three weeks. One day. Ten hours.

I breathe in. The air's steamy from the shower, hot, almost sticky down my throat.

I toe off the sneakers Dad had brought me to wear home. My feet are still dirty. I'd been wearing sandals last night. Along with everything else I had on, they're probably sitting in a bag somewhere, to be tested for evidence.

All they'll find is her blood. My blood. Our blood.

My nails dig deeper into my knee. I take a breath, then another. On the third, I step into the shower.

I let the water wash away the last of her.

When I get out of the shower, I find my mother ransacking my room.

"Are there more?" she demands. There's mascara running down her face, eyes flecked with red as she rips the sheets off my bed and flips up the mattress.

I stand there wrapped in a towel, my hair dripping down my shoulders, stunned.

"What are you doing?"

"Drugs, Sophie. Are there more?" She rips the cases off the pillows, unzips them, and pokes her hand inside, clawing through the fluff.

"There aren't any drugs in here." I'm reeling from the anger that throbs off her like heat.

Mom grabs my jewelry box off my dresser, shaking it upside down.

Bracelets and necklaces tumble out, fall in a heap on the ground. She yanks my dresser drawers with enough force to pull them clean out and dumps their contents on the bed.

As she scrabbles through shirts and underwear, tears leak from the corners of her eyes, smearing more black down her face.

Mom is not an emotional person. She's a lawyer down to her bones. She likes control. Rules. The chaos she's rained down on my room is so out of character that I just stand there, my mouth open.

"Mom, I'm not doing any drugs." It's my only defense: the truth. I have nothing else.

"You're lying. Why are you still lying to me?" More tears course down her face as she throws open the closet doors. "Detective James was just downstairs. He told me they found OxyContin in your jacket pocket."

"What? No. *No!*" Shock penetrates through the numbness that's taken over me. My eyes widen as I realize that she believes him . . . as I realize what this means.

"The police talked to Kyle Miller the morning. Kyle says Mina told him that you two were going out to Booker's Point to score."

"No!" I'm on a loop, the only word I can get out. "Kyle's lying! Mina was barely even talking to Kyle. She wouldn't even pick up her phone when he called!"

Mom looks up at me from the closet, and there's shame mingling with the smeared mascara and tears in her eyes.

"They found the pills, Sophie," she says. "You left them in your jacket at the crime scene. And we all know they weren't Mina's. I can't believe this. You're not even home a month, and you've already relapsed. Which means everything Macy did . . ." She gestures wildly with one of my shoes and shakes her head. "I should have sent you to rehab. I should never have let you go to Macy. You need professional help. That's my fault, and I'm going to have to live with that."

"No, Mom. We weren't out there to score, I *swear*. Mina was meeting someone about a story she was doing for the newspaper. I'm not on drugs! I haven't taken or bought anything. I'm clean! My tests at the hospital were clean! I've got five and a half months!"

"Stop playing games, Sophie. Your best friend is dead! She's dead! And it could've been you!" She throws the shoe across the room. It thumps against the far wall and scares me so badly, my knees buckle. I crash to the floor, hands over my head, my throat choked with fear.

"Oh God, sweetie. No, no, I'm sorry." My mother's face is a study in remorse, and she's down on the ground with me, cupping my chin in her hands. "I'm sorry," she says. She's not just apologizing for throwing the shoe.

I struggle to breathe with her so close. I can't stand the contact. I push her away, scooting until my back's pressed against the wall. She stays where she is, crouched next to my dresser, staring at me, horrified.

"Sophie, please," she says. "Tell me the truth. It'll be okay. As long as you tell me. I need to know, so I can figure out how to keep you out of trouble. It'll make you feel better, sweetheart."

"I'm not lying."

"Yes, you are," she says, the ice creeping back into her voice. She draws herself up, standing straight over me. "I won't let you kill yourself. You're going to stay clean, even if I have to lock you up."

She shreds that final thread of naiveté I have. It's in pieces on the floor, with the rest of my life. My mother tears apart whatever's left, determined to find the lies, the pills—anything to prove Kyle and the detective right.

She doesn't find anything. There's nothing to find.

But it doesn't matter. Kyle's words, those pills shoved into my jacket, they're enough to convince anyone. Even her. *Especially* her.

Two weeks later, she sends me to Seaside.

7

"Seriously, Sophie?" Kyle folds his arms across his massive chest, looking from the bear spray to the door and back again. "You've lost it. Put that down; you're gonna hurt yourself. The ventilation in here sucks."

He's probably right. But I keep the can aimed right at him. "You lied to the cops about why Mina and I were at the Point. Innocent people who want their girlfriend's killer caught don't do that."

He gapes at me. "You think I had something to do with it? Are you kidding me? I loved her." His voice quavers. "Mina's gone, and it's *your* fault. If you weren't such a junkie, she'd still be alive."

My fingers tighten around the can. "If you cared about her so much, tell me why you lied."

Someone bangs on the bathroom door. I flinch, dropping the can. It rolls across the tile floor and Kyle takes advantage of the distraction, jumping for the exit.

"I won't stop," I warn him as he fumbles with the lock.

"Screw you, Soph. I've got nothing to hide."

He slams the door shut behind him. I can hear muffled voices on the outside, snatches of a conversation that starts with "Don't go in there, man" before Kyle's voice fades.

I press my hand near my heart, like that'll help it calm down. I can feel the ridges of the scar there, where the surgeons cracked my chest after the crash.

I grab the bear spray from the floor, put it in my purse, and head to the door. By now, Kyle'll be long gone. Probably off to spread the news that Sophie Winters is back home and crazier than ever.

Someone's standing at the door when I open it. I almost smack into his chest, my bad leg twists as I step back, and I falter. When a hand reaches out to steady me, I know without looking up who it is.

Dread covers me like a body, hot and heavy and fitting in all the wrong places. I'm not prepared for this. I've avoided thinking about this moment for months.

I can't face him.

But I can't walk away.

Not again.

"Trev," I say instead.

Mina's brother stares back at me, tall and broad and so familiar. I force myself to look into his eyes.

It's like looking into hers.

8

It's been four days. It seems longer. Or maybe shorter.

My parents flit around me during the day, quiet, guarded. They're planning. Preparing to go to war for me. Once my mom realizes I'm not going to tell the police what they want, she goes into lawyer mode. She spends all her time making phone calls, and Dad paces, back and forth, up the stairs, down the hallway, until I'm sure he's worn a path there.

Mom's trying to keep me out of juvie. The bottle of Oxy they found in my jacket wasn't much, but it was enough to get me into plenty of trouble—if Mom didn't have so many friends in the right places.

She's going to save me, like she always does.

She doesn't think she saved me the first time, but she did. She sent me to Macy.

The days aren't so bad, with the click of Mom's heels and the thud of Dad's footsteps. How Dad cracks open my door every time he sees it's closed, just in case.

The nights are the worst.

Every time I close my eyes, I'm back at Booker's Point.

So I don't close my eyes. I stare. I drink coffee. I stay awake.

I can't keep it up much longer.

I want to use. The constant itch inside me, the voice in my head that whispers "I'll make it all go away" flirts at the edges of me. There are parts that are starting to prickle, like blood rushing into a foot gone numb.

I ignore it.

I breathe.

Five months. Three weeks. Five days.

Two in the morning, and I'm the only one awake. I fold myself on the bench built into the dining room window, wrapped in a blanket. I watch the yard like I'm waiting for the man in the mask to charge through the gate, ready to finish what he started.

I teeter between hope and terror that he will. A high-wire act where I'm never quite sure if I want to be saved or fall.

I need to make this stop.

A light in the yard distracts me, coming from the rickety tree house nestled in the old oak at the foot of my garden. I head outside, padding across the yard in bare feet. The rope ladder is frayed, and it's hard to pull myself up with my bad leg, but I manage.

Trev's sitting there, his back against the wall, knees drawn up. His dark, curly hair's a mess. There are circles underneath his eyes. He hasn't been sleeping, either.

Of course he hasn't.

His fingers trace a spot on the floor over and over. As I climb into the tree house, I see it's the board where Mina carved her name, entwined with mine.

"The funeral's on Friday," he says.

"I know."

"My mom . . ." He stops, swallowing hard. His gray eyes—so much like hers that it hurts to look into them, like she's here, but not—shine with unshed tears. "I had to go to the funeral home by myself. Mom just couldn't deal. So I sat there and listened to that guy talk about music and flowers and if the casket should be lined in velvet or satin. All I could think about is how Mina's scared of the dark, and how messed up it is that I'm letting them put her in the ground." He lets out a tight laugh that's painful against my ears. "Isn't that the stupidest thing you've ever heard?"

"No." I grab his hand, holding tight when he tries to pull away. "*No*, it's not stupid. Remember that Snoopy night-light she had?"

"You broke it with a soccer ball." He almost smiles at the memory.

"And you covered for me. She didn't speak to you for a week, but you never told."

"Yeah, well, someone had to look out for you." He stares out the roughly framed window, anywhere but at me. "I keep trying to picture it. How it happened. What it was like. If it was fast. If she was in pain." He faces me now, an open book of raw emotion, wanting me to bleed all over the pages with him. "Was she?"

"Trev, don't. Please." My voice cracks. I want to get out of here. I can't think about it. I try to tug away, but now it's him who's holding on to me.

"I hate you." It's almost casual, the way he says it. But the look in his eyes—it turns his words into a tangle of lie and truth, bearing down on me, so familiar. "I hate that you were the one who survived. I hate that I was relieved when I heard you were okay. I just . . . *hate* you."

The bones of my fingers grind underneath the pressure of his hand.

"I hate everything" is all I can say back.

He kisses me. Pulls me forward with a sudden jerk of movement that I'm not prepared for. It's jarring; our teeth clack together, noses bump, the angle is all wrong. This is not the way it's supposed to be. This is the only way it could ever be.

I get his shirt off with little difficulty, but mine is more trouble, tangling around my neck as he gets distracted by my bared skin. His hands gentle, soft to the point of reverence, moving over skin and bone and scars, tracing the curve of me.

I let myself be touched. Kissed. Undressed and eased back onto the wooden floor scarred with the remnants of our childhood.

I let myself feel it. Allow his skin to sink into mine.

I let myself because this is exactly what I need: this terrible idea, this beautiful, messy distraction.

And if somewhere in the middle both of our faces are wet with tears, it doesn't matter so much. We're doing this for all the wrong reasons, anyway.

Later, I stare at his face in the moonlight and wonder if he can tell that I kissed him like I already know the shape of his lips. Like I've mapped them in my mind, in another life. Learned them from another person who shared his eyes and nose and mouth, but who is never coming back.

9

For a long, frozen moment, Trev and I stare at each other. I'm caught in his gaze, hungry for the slightest glimpse of her, even if it's just similar features in a familiar face.

They always looked so much alike. It wasn't just their high cheekbones and straight noses, the way their gray eyes tilted up at the edges. It was in the way they smiled when they were trying not to, lopsided. The way they both fiddled with their brown curls when they were anxious, how they couldn't stop chewing their nails for anything.

Trev is all I have left of her, a handful of echoing characteristics buried underneath what makes him Trev: the honesty and goodness and the way he doesn't hide things (not like her, not like me).

Mina had loved him so much. They'd been inseparable since their dad died, and when I came along, Trev had stepped aside to make room, though my seven-year-old, only-child self didn't understand that. Just like I didn't understand things like daddies dying and the tears Mina would sometimes shed out of nowhere.

When we were little, whenever she cried, I'd give her the purple crayon out of my box so she'd have two, and it made her smile through the tears, so I kept doing it. I stole purple crayons from everyone's crayon boxes until she had a whole collection.

And now Trev stares at me with her eyes like he wants to devour me. His hair's long, veering into mop territory, and his jaw's prickled with stubble instead of smooth. I've never seen him this scruffy. I can feel the hard edges of calluses on his palm where he's holding my arm. Rope calluses, from handling the sails. I wonder if that's where he's been spending all his time—on his boat, trying to sail away from it all.

He lets go of me, and the feelings battle inside: relief and disappointment wrapped up in a neat, bloodstained bow.

I step out of the doorway into the sunlight, and he backs away like I'm poisonous.

He sticks his hands in the pockets of his shorts, rocks on his heels. Trev is strong and tall in that way you don't really notice unless he needs to use it. It makes you feel safe, lulled into this sense that nothing bad will happen with him around.

"I didn't know you were home," Trev says.

"I just got back."

"You didn't come to her funeral." He tries to make it gentle, not like an accusation, but it hangs between us like one.

"I'm sorry."

"I'm not the person you need to apologize to," Trev says, and waits a beat. "Have you . . . have you gone to see her?"

I shake my head.

I can't go out to Mina's grave. The idea of her in the
ground, sealed forever in the dark when she had been all
light and sound and spark, horrifies me. When I force myself
to think about it, I think she would've liked to disappear in
flames, the brilliance and warmth all around her.

But she's in the ground. It's so wrong, but I can't change it.

"You should go see her," Trev says. "Make your peace.
She deserves that from you."

He thinks that talking to a slab of stone will make a difference. That it'll change something. Trev has faith in things
like that, just like Mina had.

I don't.

The belief in his face makes me wish I could tell him yes,
of course I'll go. I want to be able to do that. Once upon a
time I loved him almost as much as I loved her.

But Trev has never come first. He's always been second,
and I can't change that now or then or ever.

"You think it's my fault, too."

Unable to meet my eyes, Trev focuses on the kids playing on the jungle gym a few yards away. "I think you made
some big mistakes," he says, tiptoeing around words like
they're land mines. "And Mina paid for them."

It hurts more than I expect to hear him confirm it. Nothing like the shallow cuts my parents have left in me. This
is a blow to a heart that was never quite his, and I almost
crumble beneath his disappointment.

"I hope you're clean." He backs away from me like he
doesn't even want to share airspace. "I hope you stay clean.
That's what she'd want for you."

He's almost down the walk when I ask; I can't help myself. "Do you still hate me?"

He turns, and even from this far away, I can see the sadness written on his face. "That's the problem, Soph. I never could."

10

The morphine has worn off. The pain is all over, a sharp edge that relentlessly carves through me.

"Push," I say between cracked lips. I move my hand, the unbroken one, trying to find the button for the morphine drip.

"Here." Warm fingers close over mine, placing the pump in my palm. I push the button and wait.

Slowly, the pain retreats. For now.

"Your dad went to get coffee," Trev says. He's in a chair next to my bed, his hand still covering mine. "Want me to find him?"

I shake my head. "You're here." The morphine makes my brain fuzzy. Sometimes I say stupid stuff, I forget things, but I'm almost positive he hasn't visited before.

"I'm here," he says.

"Mina?" I breathe.

"She's at school. I got out early. Wanted to see you."

"You okay?" I ask. There's a fading bruise on his temple. He's sitting in a weird position, his leg straightened out like it's in a cast. But I can't prop myself up enough to see how bad he's hurt. Mina has a cast on her arm, I remember suddenly. The nurses and my mom had to force her to leave last night; she hadn't wanted to go.

"I'm fine." He strokes my fingers. They're pretty much the only part of me that isn't bruised or broken or stitched together.

"I'm sorry," he says. "Sophie, I'm so sorry."

He buries his face in the sheets next to me, and I don't have the strength to lift my hand to touch him.

"'S'okay," I whisper. My eyes droop as the morphine kicks in further. "Not your fault."

Later, they'll tell me that it *was* his fault. That he ran a stop sign and we got T-boned by an SUV going twenty above the speed limit. The doctors will explain that I flatlined on the operating table for almost two minutes before they got my heart started again. That my right leg was crushed and I now have titanium rods screwed into what little bone remains. That I'll have to spend almost a year walking with a cane. That I'll have months of physical therapy, handfuls of pills I have to take. That I'll have a permanent limp, and my back will cause me problems for the rest of my life.

Later, I'll finally have enough and cross that line. I'll crush up four pills and snort them with a straw, floating away in the temporary numbness.

But right now, I don't know about what's ahead for us, him and me and Mina. So I try to comfort him. I fight against the numbness instead of drowning myself in it. And he says my name, over and over, begging for the forgiveness I've already given.

11

My mom's car is in the driveway when I get home. As soon as I open the door, I hear heels, brisk and sharp against the floor.

She's immaculate, her straight blond hair in a slick bun. She probably came straight from court; she hasn't even unbuttoned her blazer. "Are you all right? Where have you been?" she asks, but doesn't pause for me to answer. "I've been worried. Macy said she dropped you off two hours ago."

I set my bag onto the table in the foyer. "I left you a note in the kitchen."

Mom looks over her shoulder, wilting a little when she sees the notebook paper I'd torn off. "I didn't see it," she says. "I wish you would've called. I didn't know where you were."

"I'm sorry." I move toward the stairs.

"Wait a moment, Sophie Grace."

I freeze, because the second Mom gets formal, it means trouble. I turn around, schooling my face into a disinterested mask. "Yes?"

"Where have you been?"

"I just went for a walk."

"You can't leave whenever you like."

"Are you putting me under house arrest?" I ask.

Mom's chin tilts up; she's ready for war. "It's my job to make sure you don't fall back into bad habits like before. If I have to restrict you to the house to do that, I will. I refuse to let you relapse again."

I close my eyes, breathing deeply. It's hard to control the anger that spikes inside me. I want to break through the ice-queen parts of her, shatter her like she's shattered me.

"I'm not a kid. And unless you plan on staying home from work, you can't stop me. If it'd make you feel better, I can call you to check in every few hours."

Mom's mouth flattens into a thin slash of pearly-pink lipstick. "You don't get to make the rules, Sophie. Your previous behavior will no longer be tolerated. If you step one toe out of line, I'll send you back to Seaside. I swear I will."

I've prepared myself for these threats. I've tried to examine every angle Mom might come at me from, because it's the only way to stay a step ahead of her.

"In a few months, you won't be able to do that," I say. "As soon as I turn eighteen, you can't make any medical decisions for me. No matter what you think I did."

"As long as you live under my roof, you'll follow my rules, eighteen or not," Mom says.

"You try to send me back to Seaside, and I'll leave," I say. "I'll walk out that door and never come back."

"Don't threaten me."

"It's not a threat. It's the truth." I look away from her,

from the way her hands are shaking, like she's torn between holding and hurting me. "I'm tired. I'm going up to my room."

She doesn't try to stop me this time.

I haven't been allowed a lock on my door since forever, so I shove my desk chair against it. I can hear Mom climb the stairs and start to run a bath.

I shove all the clothes off my bed, taking off the sheets and blankets and pillows, too. It takes me three tries to flip the mattress, both my legs shaking at the effort. Panting, I finally succeed, my back protesting all the way. I step over the pile of sheets and blankets and pull a notebook from my bag. There are loose pages stuck between the bound ones, and I shake them out on top of the mattress before going over and grabbing tape and markers from my desk.

It takes only a few minutes. I don't have much to go on— yet. But by the time I'm done, the underside of my mattress has been turned into a makeshift evidence board. Mina's junior-year picture is taped underneath a scrap of paper labeled *VICTIM*, and the only picture I have of Kyle is taped under *SUSPECT*. The picture's an old one from the Freshman Fling when all our friends went together. Mina and Amber and I are crowded to the side, laughing as Kyle and Adam are caught midshove and Cody looks on disapprovingly. We look young, happy. *I* look happy. That girl in the picture has no idea that her entire life's gonna get trashed in a few months. I circle Kyle with my Sharpie before moving on. To the side of the picture, I tape my list, the number one question: *WHAT STORY WAS MINA WORKING ON?*

In smaller letters, I add: *Killer said "I warned you." Were there threats before this? Did she tell anyone?*

I stare at it for a while, imprinting it in my head before I turn the mattress right side up and remake the bed.

I peer out into the hall, checking to make sure Mom's still in the bathroom. Then I grab the cordless—tomorrow I'll ask her if I'm allowed a cell phone—and take it into my bedroom.

I punch in a number; three rings before someone picks up. "Hello?" says a cheery voice.

"It's me," I say. "I just got out. We should meet."

12

It takes only a few days at Seaside for it to really sink in: Mina is dead. Her killer's running free. And no one will listen to me.

Nothing has ever made less sense.

So I sit in my room, on my cramped little bed with its polyester sheets. I go to Group and am silent. I sit on the couch in Dr. Charles's office with my arms folded, staring straight ahead as she waits.

I don't talk.

I can barely even think.

At the end of my first week, I write a letter to Trev. A pleading, cramped soliloquy of truth. Everything I've wanted to say for so long.

It's returned, unopened. That's when I realize I'm all alone in this.

There is no one who believes me.

So I force myself to think about it, tracing back every second of that night. I ponder possible suspects and motives, both logical and wild.

My head is filled with one sentence, an endless loop of the words he'd said right before he shot her: *I warned you. I warned you. I warned you.*

I let it push me forward, hour by hour.

I still don't talk to Dr. Charles.

I'm too busy planning.

On my fifteenth day at Seaside, my parents are called in for the first family therapy day.

My father hugs me, enveloping me in his husky arms. He smells like Old Spice and toothpaste, and for a second I let the familiarity of it comfort me.

Then I remember him throwing me in the car. The look on his face as I begged him to please, please believe me.

I stiffen and pull away.

My mother doesn't even try to hug me after that.

My parents sit on the couch, relegating me to the slippery leather armchair in the corner. I'm grateful that Dr. Charles doesn't make me sit between them.

"I brought the two of you in early," Dr. Charles says. "Because I think Sophie is having some trouble expressing herself to me."

My mother pins me to the chair with her gaze. "Are you being difficult?" she asks me.

I shake my head.

"Answer me properly, Sophie Grace."

Dr. Charles's eyebrow twitches in surprise when I say, slowly and clearly, "I don't feel like talking."

My parents leave frustrated, only a handful of words spoken between us.

Nineteen days in, I get a card. An innocuous thing with a blue daisy on it and the words GET WELL SOON in big block letters.

I flip it open.

I believe you. Call me when you get out. —Rachel
I stare at it for a long, long time.
It's weird what three words can ignite inside of you.
I believe you.
Now I'm ready to talk. I have to be.
It's the only way out of here.

13

Mom is gone by the time I wake up the next morning. On the kitchen table she's left a note and a new cell phone.

Call me if you're going to leave the house.

After I make some toast and grab an apple, I call her at the office.

"I'm going to the bookstore, then maybe get some coffee, if that's okay," I say after her assistant's transferred me over.

I can hear a printer and some chatter in the background. "All right," she says. "Are you going to take the car?"

"If I have permission." It's a deadly little dance we're doing, circling around each other with closed-lipped smiles, careful not to bare our teeth.

"You do. The keys are on the rack. Be home by four. Dinner's at seven."

"I'll be home."

She hangs up with a perfunctory good-bye. I can hear the strain in her voice.

I put it out of my head and get the keys.

Stopping by the bookstore, I buy a paperback, mostly so I'm not telling Mom a flat-out lie. Ten minutes later, I'm pulling onto the old highway, heading north, out of town and into the boonies.

There's no traffic this far out. Just a truck here and there on the narrow two-lane road that cuts between summer-bleached fields and red-clay foothills studded with oaks. I roll the windows down and turn my music up loud, like it's enough to shield me from the memories.

The house is at the end of a long dirt road riddled with potholes. I maneuver around them, making slow progress as two big chocolate Labs bound out from the back field, tails wagging.

I park in front of the house. As I get out, the screen door bangs open.

A girl my age in polka-dot rain boots and Daisy Dukes runs down the stairs, her red pigtails bouncing. "You're here!"

She gallops up and wraps her skinny arms around me. I return the hug, smiling as the dogs circle us, yelping for attention. For the first time since Macy dropped me off, I feel like I can breathe.

"I'm really glad to see you," Rachel says. "No, Bart, stop." She yanks the dog's muddy paws off her shorts. "You look good."

"You too."

"C'mon inside. Mom's at work, and I made cookies."

Rachel's house is cozy, with multicolored rag rugs scattered over the cherrywood floors. She pours coffee, and we sit across from each other at the kitchen table, bowl-sized mugs warming our hands.

Silence spreads over us, punctuated by sips of coffee and the clink of spoon against ceramic.

"So . . ." Rachel says.

"So."

She smiles, a big stretch that shows all her teeth, so genuine it almost hurts. I don't think I can even remember how to smile like that. "It's okay that it's weird right now. You've been gone a long time."

"Your letters," I say. "They were— You have no idea how much they meant to me. Being in there . . ."

Rachel's letters had saved me. Full of random facts and going off in three directions at once, they're a lot like her: scatterbrained and smart. Her mom had homeschooled her since she was a kid, which is probably the only reason we hadn't met until that night. Rachel's the kind of person you notice.

I trusted her. It had been this instant, instinctual thing. Maybe it was because she found me that night. Because she was there when no one else was, and I needed that when everything had been taken away. But that's only part of it.

There's a determination in Rachel that I've never seen before. She has conviction. In herself, in what she wants, in what she believes. I want to be like that. To be sure of myself, to trust myself, to love myself.

Rachel had stuck around when she didn't have to. When everyone else, everyone who's known me forever, had turned their backs. That means more to me than anything.

"Was Seaside bad?" she asks.

"No, not really. Just lots of therapy and talking. It was hard. To be in there and have to put everything on hold." I pause, stirring my coffee unnecessarily. "How's the telescope going?" I ask, remembering a letter mentioning some experiments.

"The refractor? Slowly but surely. I have it out at my dad's, so I'm only working on it when I'm up there. But I've got a few more projects fixing some stuff up. There's a tractor from the twenties in the backyard that my neighbor traded me. Trying to get it to work's been a pain in the ass, in that good way." With a shower of cinnamon, she takes a bite out of one of the palm-sized snickerdoodles. "I guess we should talk about what you've decided to do," she says.

"I saw Kyle yesterday."

"Run into him, did you?" Rachel asks sarcastically.

I stare at my coffee instead of her. "I might have locked him in the men's room and threatened him with bear repellent," I mumble.

"Sophie!" Rachel says, the word dissolving in a fit of laughter. "I can't believe you. You can't go around threatening people you suspect. You've gotta be subtle about this."

"I know. But he lied about me. There has to be a reason."

"Do you really think he could have had something to do with Mina's murder?"

I shrug. I've known Kyle as long as I've known most of my friends. He was my field trip buddy in first grade. It's hard to think that the boy who held my hand during the gross fish-gutting part of the hatchery tour could be a murderer. "Anything's possible. The guy who killed her planned it out. The killer had a reason for wanting Mina gone. I just don't know what that is."

"And Kyle lied."

"And Kyle lied," I echo. "There has to be a reason for that. Either he's covering for himself—or someone else."

"Did he and Mina fight a lot?" Rachel asks.

"No," I say. "That's why I don't get this. They got along. Kyle's kind of a Neanderthal, but he's sweet. He treated her like she walked on water. But even if he didn't have anything to do with her murder, he's hindering an entire police investigation. You don't just randomly lie to the police. Especially Kyle. His dad's all about the rules. If Mr. Miller found out Kyle was lying to a bunch of cops? Big trouble. His restaurant does the annual fish fry for the force every year. He's friends with a lot of them."

Rachel sighs. "I don't think you can get someone who doesn't mind lying to the police to just tell you the truth. So what's the contingency plan?"

I look down into my cup of coffee. "It might seem kind of weird, but I did have one idea."

"What is it?"

"I want to go back," I say. "To where you found me that night."

Rachel's eyes widen. "Are you sure that's a good idea?"

"It's probably a horrible idea," I concede. "But I need someone to walk me through it. Maybe it'll spur something. And you're kind of the only person who can."

Rachel presses her lips together tight, and it makes her freckles stand out even more. "Sophie . . ."

"Please." I look her straight in the eye, trying to seem confident. But I'm afraid of going. Just the idea of being there again makes my knees shake.

She sighs. "Okay." She gets up and grabs her keys from the hook on the wall. "Let's go."

Rachel's quiet as she pulls her old Chevy out onto the road, reluctance practically vibrating off her.

"I'm not gonna freak," I tell her.

"I'm not worried about that," Rachel says, and we drive in silence for a while. But twenty minutes out, she's pulling off the highway onto Burnt Oak Road and I feel like freaking a little, even though I just promised her I wouldn't.

We're not even close yet, at least a mile and a half from the Point, but suddenly everything outside the truck—the trees, the hills, even the cows in the fields—seems terrifying. Potentially fatal. My heart flutters in my chest, and I press my fingers against my scar, trace the ridges of it through my shirt, trying to calm down.

Nine months. Three weeks. Eight hours.

I don't realize I've closed my eyes until I feel the truck stop. I open them slowly.

We're here. I avoid looking at the road. I don't want to go there. I have to go there.

"I'm going to ask you one more time," Rachel says. "Are you sure you want to do this?"

I'm positive this is the last thing I want to do.

I nod anyway.

Rachel's side-eye is epic, but she shuts the engine off.

I get out of the Chevy slowly, and she follows, shading her eyes against the sun. This time of day, this far out of town, the roads are empty, no cars in sight for miles.

Just long sweeps of yellowing brush, barbed wire fences, and clusters of scrub oaks and digger pines.

"You ready?"

I nod again.

Rachel locks the truck and steps out onto the empty road, looking from side to side. Her pigtails sway every time she rocks back on her heels, and I focus on them instead of where she's standing—where she'd found me that night.

"It was a little past nine," she says. "I'd just called my mom to let her know I was almost back from my dad's. I looked away to toss my phone into my purse, and when I glanced back at the road, you were right in front of me, standing in the middle, right about . . . here."

She takes a few steps and scuffs her boot across the cracked asphalt, toeing the yellow line. I look at it . . . can't stop looking at it. Was it right there? I remember the frozen feeling. I remember wanting the truck to run me over.

"I thought I was going to hit you. I've never slammed on the brakes so hard in my life. And you just stood there. You didn't move; you didn't flinch. It was almost like you . . ." She hesitates. "You were in shock," she finishes.

I begin to walk, nervous energy filling me. I need to move, get away.

My body knows where I'm going. It's always trying to find traces of her.

Rachel follows me as the road gets steeper. Chicory and foxtails, knee-high, swish against my jeans. The red clay sticks to the soles of my shoes. I'd washed it off my feet the day after, watched it swirl down the drain with the blood and tears.

"When I got out of the car I saw you were covered in blood. So I called 911. You were bleeding pretty bad from your forehead. I tried to put pressure on it, but you kept pushing my hands away. I wanted to get you in the car or to say something, even just your name, but . . ." She hesitates again. "Do you remember any of this?"

"I remember the ambulance. I remember grabbing your hand." I keep walking. I know where I'm going now—brain, body, and heart finally in harmony. It's only a mile. The scrub oaks are sparser now as the pines take over. In just a few minutes, we'll round the curve, and there we'll be.

"When the EMTs came, you wouldn't let go. So they let me ride in the ambulance with you."

"I remember the hospital," I say. And I leave it at that.

I concentrate on my feet.

We're on the wrong side of the road, and when we reach the place where it veers off to Booker's Point, I stop and look.

The other side of the road is thickly wooded, clusters of pines jammed close together. Did the killer deliberately choose this spot? How long did he hide in the pines, waiting for us?

"You sure this is a good idea?" Rachel asks.

I take a deep breath. It's cooler up here, shaded from the glare of the sun. It'd been cold that night. I could almost see my breath in the air.

"Bad ideas are sometimes necessary." It sounds so much

like an excuse, it's such an addict thing to say, that my skin crawls.

Trying to leave the feeling behind, I walk across the road until pavement cuts off to dirt flattened by years of truck tires. I follow the crude road, disappearing into the thicket of tall pines, ignoring the way my footing falters as the ground slants up into a hill.

It's quiet, just like that night. There's a pleasant coolness under the trees. It washes over me, and I shiver.

All I can think about is how cold her skin had been.

The scar tissue around my knee aches as the trail gets steeper.

Then I turn the last bend of road, and there I am, at the top of the Point.

Just a few feet away.

Booker's Point isn't big, just a clear piece of land that fits a few cars. When I was younger, I'd hear stories about girls losing their virginity up here, of the wild parties and drug deals that went on after dark out in the boonies. But until that night, I'd never ventured out here.

Rachel hangs back, but I keep walking, across the flat stretch of road, past the straggly California poppies that grow in clumps in the dirt, until I'm standing right where it happened.

I thought it'd take my breath away. That somehow, being there again where she ended, where I'd sworn to her she'd be okay, would change something in me.

But I guess I've already been changed enough.

I move past the spot until I'm at the very tip of the Point,

"Anyone who saw you in the middle of that road . . ."
Rachel pauses, and then goes on. "Anyone who saw you the
way I did that night, they'd understand you weren't capable
of coming up with a lie—you could barely talk. And then in
the hospital . . ." She pauses again, and I know we're both
thinking about it. How I'd yelled and thrown things when
the nurse tried to make me take off my bloody clothes. I can
still feel the prick of the needle against my skin, the seda-
tive moving through me as I begged, *"No drugs, no drugs,
no drugs,"* when I really meant, *"She's dead, she's dead, she's
dead."*

"But you didn't have to stick around. At the hospital, or
after. I mean, you barely knew me."

"You went through something horrible," Rachel says
quietly. "And it isn't fair that everyone blames you. Even if
you *had* been buying drugs that night, it wouldn't matter.
The only person who's guilty is the guy who pulled the
trigger. And we'll find him. I bet you. Ten whole dollars."

She smiles determinedly at me, daring me to smile back.

I do.

14

I don't mean to steal the prescription pad.

I really don't. It never even crosses my mind until the Saturday I take Dad lunch at his office. It's hot that summer, topping 110 some days, and I should be out at the lake or something, but I like to spend time with Dad. He does free teeth cleanings for kids on every fourth Saturday, so I usually grab some takeout to share on his lunch break.

"Give me a second, sweetie?" he asks after one of his dental hygienists lets me into his office. "I've just got to check on some things. Then we can eat."

I set the bag of pastrami sandwiches on his desk, next to the burl wood clock that Mom got for him for one of their anniversaries.

He closes his office door behind him, and I sit down in his swivel chair, wincing when it leans back too far.

Dad's desk is orderly, everything in its right place. There's a picture of me and Mom, standing side by side, our shoulders nearly touching, framed in silver, and one of Dad on the sidelines, from before the accident, when he coached Mina's and my soccer team. There's a black-and-white one of me when I was eleven or twelve, my hair long and tucked behind my too-big ears. I'm smiling at something off camera, my eyes lowered, almost hopeful as my hand reaches out. For Mina, of course. Always for Mina. She'd been making faces at me while Dad took the picture. I remember how hard it was to not let my face scrunch with laughter.

I brush my fingers across the top of Dad's stash of pens, neatly grouped together by color. I pull open his top drawer. There's a bunch of Post-its, color coded again, and underneath that . . .

Prescription pads. A stack of them.

And suddenly it's all I can think about.

I'd always have enough pills. I'd never have to worry. Never have to keep count, just in case the doctors noticed. It'd be so good. So right.

The paper tickles my skin as I thumb through one of the pads like it's a flip book. I'm giddy, almost high on the mere thought of it.

I don't plan on stealing them.

But I do.

I don't even think about the trouble it could cause as I shove them in my purse.

I'm too in love with the idea of *more* and *numb* and *gone*.

15

When I hear the front door open, I think it's Mom checking on me. She came home yesterday during lunch, and we sat across from each other at the kitchen table, silent as I picked at my food and she drank a cup of coffee, shuffling through legal briefs.

I stop at the top of the stairs. I catch sight of him before he sees me, and I have a second, just a second, when I can hope.

But then his eyes fix on me and the awkwardness sparks in the air, as it has every time since he found my stash and the triplicates I'd stolen from him.

Dad isn't disappointed in me like Mom is. He doesn't have that mix of anger and fear that's fueling her. Instead, he doesn't know what to do or how to feel with me, and sometimes I think it's worse, that he can't decide between forgiving and blaming me.

"Hi, Dad."

"Hello, Sophie."

I stay at the top of the stairs, hoping the distance will protect me. "Did you have a good trip?"

"I did. How have things been? Have you settled in?"

I want to tell him everything. How Trev looks at me like he's a masochist and I'm the embodiment of pain. How Mom and I are stuck in this sick game of who'll break first. How I should go out to Mina's grave but I can't, because I'm afraid if I do, it'll make it so real that I'll slip. I'll fall down and never get up.

Once upon a time, I'd been a daddy's girl. I loved him wholly, preferred him to the point of cruelty. But that girl is gone. I rotted away what was left of her with pills and loss.

I'm not the daughter he raised. I'm not the daughter my mother wanted.

I've become something different, every parent's nightmare: the drugs hidden in the bedroom, the lies, the call in the middle of the night, the police knocking on the door.

Those are the things he remembers now. Not the time he took me to *The Nutcracker*, just him and me, and I'd been so scared of the Mouse King that I'd crawled into his lap and he'd promised to keep me safe. Or how he had tried to help Trev build me raised flower beds in the backyard, even though he kept slamming his fingers with the hammer. A dentist has no business hammering things, but he'd done it anyway.

"Sophie?" Dad asks, his voice breaking me from my thoughts.

"I'm sorry," I say automatically. "It's been fine. Things have been fine."

He stares at me longer than he should, and there are worry lines on his forehead I haven't noticed before. My eyes flick to the gray at his temples. Is there more since I last saw him? I know what he's thinking: *Is she zoning out, or is she on something?*

I can't bear it.

Nine months. Three weeks. Three days.

"I was going out to my garden." I gesture toward the backyard, feeling stupid.

"I've got some work to do." He hesitates. "I could do it out on the deck? If you'd like the company?"

I almost say no, but then I think about those worry lines and the gray in his hair, what I've done to him. I shrug. "Sure."

We don't speak for the hour we stay out in my garden. He just sits at the teak table on the deck and goes through his files while I dig and root rocks out of the soil.

It feels like what I used to think safe was.

I know better now.

16

For three weeks, Macy plays hardball: no phone, no computer, nothing until I start talking to the shrink she sends me to, until I follow the schedule Macy's given me, until I finally admit that there's something wrong.

The only order I've obeyed is doing yoga with Pete. Pete's nice; I like him. He's quiet; he doesn't pester me with questions, just helps me through the poses he's shown me, the ones adjusted to my problem areas. That first week, I'd heard him on the phone, deep in conversation with my old physical therapist. The next morning, he'd dropped a mat on my bed and told me to meet him in the brick two-room studio in the backyard. The bamboo floors were cold underneath my bare feet, and Pete had some sort of cinnamon oil in a diffuser so it smelled like Christmas.

I won't admit it to Macy, but I like that hour every morning. After years of dulling all my senses with anything I could get my hands on, it's weird to focus positively on my body. To pay attention to my breathing and the way my muscles stretch, to let my thoughts go, to push them away so I can *feel*—feel the air and movement and the way I can make my bad leg bend and make it do what *I* want for once.

Sometimes I falter. Sometimes my leg or back wins.

But sometimes I can go through an entire sun salutation without

one mistake or wobble, and it feels so amazing to be in control, so sin-
gularly powerful, that tears track down my face and something close
to relief surges through me.

Pete never mentions the tears. When I'm done, we roll the mats up
and head into the house, where Macy's making breakfast. My cheeks
are dry and I pretend it never happened.

But the feeling, the memory, it lingers inside me. A spark waiting
for enough fuel to spread.

One night, when Macy's off chasing down another idiot trying to jump
bail, Pete knocks on my door. I'm allowed to keep it closed, but there's
no lock, something I've hated since I got here.

Macy never knocks. She says I haven't earned it.

"Come in."

Pete holds up an envelope. "Something came for you."

"I thought the warden said no contact with the outside world."

"Just don't rat me out."

"Seriously?" I can't believe he's going to give it to me. But he places
the letter at the foot of my bed and ambles out of the room, whistling.

"Pete," I call. He turns and grins. His front teeth are a little
crooked, and there are acne scars pitting his cheeks, but his eyes are
big and green and sweet, and I suddenly understand why Macy looks
at him like he's the best thing she's ever seen. "Thank you."

"Don't know what you're talking about," he says, his smile wide
and innocent.

I look down at the letter. My name, above Macy's address, is written in loopy purple letters.

Mina's handwriting.

I tear the envelope open, almost ripping the letter in my hurry.

I unfold the notebook paper, my heart pounding like I've been holding a pose for too long. The words are written in pencil, which is
weird, because she's stockpiled purple pens for as long as I can
remember.

> Sophie—
> I know you're still mad. I'm not sure you'll even read this.
> But if you do . . .
>> Please get better. If you can't do it for yourself, do it
> for me.
> Mina

I press my fingers under the smudge the word *me* is written over,
trying to make out the word she'd erased. I trace two letters, the
shadowy, barely there curls of a *U* and an *S* she didn't quite erase: *do
it for us.*

When Aunt Macy gets home, peeking into my room without
knocking, I'm still sitting there with the letter in my lap.

"Sophie?"

When I don't answer, she walks in and sits next to me. I keep my
eyes on the letter. I'm not strong enough to look at her.

"You're right. I'm a drug addict. I have a problem."

Macy lets out a long breath, an almost soundless exhalation of
relief. "Okay," she says. "Now look me in the eye and say it."

When I don't, she reaches over and grabs my hand, squeezing
hard. "You'll get there."

I believed her. I put in the work. I followed the rules from then on,
talking to the therapist, starting up my mental calendar, making days

turn into weeks and then months. I struggled and fought and won.

I wanted to make myself better. For Mina. For me. For what I thought might be waiting when I got home.

But this is the thing about struggling out of that hole you've put yourself in: the higher you climb, the farther you have to fall.

17

I call Trev three times over the next week, but he won't answer. After the third unanswered call, I switch gears and go by the *Harper Beacon* office, only to be told that Tom Wells, the head of the internship program, is out of town.

With my parents still watching me so closely, I spend most of my days in my garden, among the redwood beds Trev built for me.

After the crash, Mina had insisted I needed a hobby and presented me with a preapproved list. I'd chosen gardening to get her off my back, but then, as usual, she'd taken it to extremes. She'd shown up the next day, Trev in tow with lumber, hammer and nails, bags of soil, a box of seedlings, and foam knee pads so I wouldn't hurt myself.

I like the feel of dirt between my fingers, nursing delicate plants into strength and bloom. I like watching things flourish, like the swath of colors I can grow, bright and alive. It hurts to get up and down, but the pain's worth the effort. At least I have something pretty to show for it.

After a full day of weeding, removing rocks and clay soil from the neglected beds, I spend another filling them with fresh, rich compost. Midweek, I've got the first two beds in good enough shape to think about planting. I run my fingers compulsively over the worn wood, making lists in my head of flowers that'll thrive this late.

Mina had painted hearts and infinity symbols on the outsides of the beds, adding to them when she'd sit out here with me: her favorite quotes surrounded by stars, a pair of crooked stick-figure girls holding hands and faded red balloons. I brush my dirty fingers over the wood to touch what she'd touched.

"Sophie."

I look up from my spot on the ground. Dad's on the porch, dressed in his regular blue button-down and tie. His tie is crooked, and I want to reach out and fix it, but I can't.

"You have your first therapy appointment with Dr. Hughes in an hour," he says. "I moved some appointments so I can drive you. You should clean up."

I let go of the wood and follow him into the house.

Dr. Hughes's practice is in one of the older neighborhoods, on a block where most of the houses have been turned into offices. Dad parks the car in front of the blue-and-white sign with Dr. Hughes's name on it. The little one-story Craftsman is painted the same color as the sign, cheerful against the lighter blue sky.

I'm surprised when my dad gets out of the car after me. "You're coming in?"

"I'll sit in the waiting room."

"I'm not going to ditch therapy."

His mouth tightens, his hand drops from the car door. "I'll pick you up in an hour, then."

I'm almost at the door when he stops me in my tracks.

"We just want you to be better. That's why we sent you away. You know that, don't you?"

I don't look at him. I can't give him the confirmation he wants. Not without lying.

I was already better.

The office is full of comfortable-looking furniture and Norman Rockwell prints on the walls. A receptionist looks up with a smile from the papers she's filing. "Good morning."

"Hi. I'm Sophie Winters. I have a twelve thirty appointment."

"Come with me, please."

She brings me to a large room with a desk, an over-stuffed couch, and a few leather chairs. I take a seat on the couch as she closes the door behind her. My shoulders sink into the cushions, half of my body lost in brown suede.

Dr. Hughes comes in without knocking. He's an older man, with dark skin, a neat silver goatee, and square black glasses. He's short—I'd be taller than him if I were standing up—and his sweater-vest is stretched snugly over his round stomach. "Hi, Sophie." He sits down at his desk and spins in his chair to face me with a smile. His eyes are kind underneath his glasses. He radiates thoughtfulness. Just as a good therapist should.

It makes me want to run.

"Hi." I burrow deeper into the couch, wishing it'd just swallow me up.

"I'm Dr. Hughes, but feel free to call me David. How are you feeling today?"

"Fine."

"I've talked to Dr. Charles on the phone about you, and I have her notes and your medical history. I've also had several sessions with your parents."

"Okay."

"How are you adjusting?"

"It's fine. I'm fine. Everything is—it's all fine."

He taps his pen against his notebook, watching me. "Dr. Charles said you'd be a hard nut to crack."

I sit up straighter, on guard. "I don't mean to be."

David leans back in his chair, his eyes crinkling as his lips twitch. "I think you do," he says. "I think that you're an intelligent young woman who is very good at keeping secrets."

"Got that from a few notes and, what, an hour-long talk with Dr. Charles?"

He grins. "Now that's more like it. Dr. Charles is excellent at what she does. But as soon as you stopped resisting therapy at Seaside, all you did was tell her exactly what she wanted to hear—what she expected to hear from an addict on the verge of relapse."

"I am an addict."

"It's good that you acknowledge that," David says. "That's important. But at the moment, I'm more concerned with the trauma you suffered. What jumped out at me, from Dr. Charles's notes, is how you sidestep the subject of Mina every time she's brought up."

"No, I don't."

"You didn't break a coffee table when Dr. Charles asked you about the night Mina was killed?"

"My leg makes me clumsy; it was an accident."

David raises an eyebrow. I've done something that's made him take notice, and I'm not sure what it is. It makes heat prickle down my back. I'm not going to be able to play him like Dr. Charles.

"Why don't you tell me about Mina?" he asks.

"What do you want to know?"

"How did you two meet?"

"Mina moved here after her dad died. The teacher sat us next to each other in second grade."

"Did you spend a lot of time together?"

I don't answer immediately.

"Sophie?" he prompts gently.

"We were always together," I say. I can't keep it out of my voice. That choked-up emotion bleeds through, makes it waver. I look away from him, my nails digging into my jeans. "I don't want to talk about Mina."

"We're going to have to talk about Mina," David says quietly. "Sophie, you were put into an environment designed to get you clean right after you experienced a major trauma and loss. While I understand what motivated your parents to do that, it might not have been the best thing for you in terms of processing your grief.

"Most of your therapy at Seaside was focused on your problems with addiction. I don't think you've been given the space or the tools you need to deal with what happened to you and Mina the night she was killed. But I can help you with that, if you let me."

Anger surges inside me, stampedes through my veins at

his words. I want to hit him. To throw the stupid tasseled pillows on the couch at him.

"You think I haven't *dealt with it*?" I ask. My voice is horribly low. I'm about to cry. It builds in the back of my eyes, threatening to break through. "She died scared and in pain, and I felt it—when she went, when she left, I *felt* it. Don't you dare tell me I haven't dealt with that. Every day, I deal with it."

"Okay," David says. "Tell me how you do that."

"I just do," I say. I'm still breathing hard, but I will myself not to cry in front of him. "I have to."

"Why do you have to? What's keeping you motivated?"

"I have to stay clean," I say.

The answer would've worked with Dr. Charles, but not with this guy. My quick search before Dad had driven me over had pulled up four articles Dr. Hughes wrote about PTSD and its effects on teenagers. Mom and Dad have done their homework. With my addiction tackled, now they're setting out to fix me completely. A New and Improved Sophie. Whole and mended, with no jagged edges or sharp points. Someone who doesn't look like she knows how death feels.

"I don't think you're telling me the whole truth," David says.

"You a human lie detector?"

"Sophie, you can trust me." David leans forward intently. "Anything you say here, any secrets you choose to share, nobody else will know, and there'll be no judgment from me. I am here for you. To help you."

I glare at him. "You already got me to talk about it when I didn't want to," I say. "That doesn't really breed trust."

"Getting you to open up isn't tricking you. It's about your having a safe outlet to talk. You have to share with someone or you'll burst."

"Is that in your professional medical opinion?"

He smiles, dispassionate, with no edge to it, no pity, no judgment. It's a nice change from everyone else. "Absolutely," he says wryly. He pushes the box of tissues across the coffee table at me. I take a few, but instead of patting my eyes, or blowing my nose, I twist them in my hands.

"This won't happen again," I tell him. "Don't start expecting it."

"Whatever you say." He nods and smiles. I look away.

18

On the morning of my sixteenth birthday, I wake up with a purple Post-it note stuck to my forehead. I pull it off, wondering how in the world she'd managed to stick it there without waking me up.

> *Congratulations! As of 5:15 this morning, you are officially sixteen. Proceed to your closet for part one of your surprise.*
> *—Mina*
> *P.S. Yes, you have to wear what I picked out. No arguments. If I leave it up to you, you'll just wear jeans. Please, go with me on this for once. The color is perfect.*

I shuffle to my closet and pull it open. She's bought me an entire new outfit. It's not a surprise, considering how much she complains about my fashion sense. I rub the soft jersey dress between my fingers. Its dark red color is nice, but it's too short.

I pull it out of the closet anyway and see the note she's taped to it.

No arguments!!!

Rolling my eyes, I layer two camisoles underneath the dress to cover the scar on my chest and pull on a pair of leggings and knee-high boots. I'm putting the finishing touches on my makeup when there's a tap on my door.

"You awake, birthday girl?" my dad calls.

"Morning, Dad. Come on in."

He pushes open the door, a big smile on his face. "That's a pretty dress," he says. "Is it new?"

"Mina," I explain.

Dad grins. "Speaking of Mina . . ." He hands me an envelope. "She sneaked in this morning. Wanted me to give you this. You girls have plans today?"

I nod. "You and Mom have me tonight," I promise.

"Good," Dad says. "I've got to get to the office. Your mom had to go in early. But there's a surprise downstairs for you." He ruffles my hair. "Sixteen," he says. "Can't believe it."

I wait until I hear his car pull out of the driveway before I do my morning lines of Oxy.

I'm sure he wouldn't believe that, either.

Go to the Old Mill Bridge and walk to the middle.

—M

Mina loves birthdays. Trev and I have been trying to top her for years, always failing. For my thirteenth birthday, she'd gotten my dad to help her in an elaborate ruse involving a flat tire, a clown, and a skating rink full of balloon animals. She'd spent an entire year saving for and planning Trev's eighteenth. I'd helped her decorate his sailboat so it looked like it'd been shipwrecked. We filled it with presents, and then sailed it out to one of the little islands dotting the lake. She'd arranged for Trev to borrow a friend's boat and texted him coordinates, sending him on a quest to find his treasure, with little chests of foil-wrapped chocolate coins marking each stop.

Now it looks like I'm in for another surprise of my own.

The Old Mill Bridge has long been closed to car traffic, with a newer, shinier version built down the river. I brush my fingers over the moss-covered bricks, looking for something that doesn't belong.

The flash of bright color grabs my eye—a red balloon tied to one of the stone columns. I walk up and untie it, but there's no note. I look around, expecting to see her leap out from somewhere, bounding toward me, all smiles and trickery and delight.

"Mina?" I call. I search the ground. Maybe the note fell.

But I find nothing.

My phone rings.

"You forget something?" I ask after I pick up.

"Pop the balloon," she says, and I can hear the smile in her voice.

"Are you watching me?" I ask, looking around. I go to the edge and peer down the bridge, trying to find her. It feels good to lean on the solid stone railing, take the weight off my bad leg for a second.

"I've got binoculars and everything," Mina says, lowering her voice, trying to make it sound dangerous and failing when she bursts out laughing.

"Stalker. Where are you?" I peer behind me, trying to spot her.

"I had to make sure no one took the balloon! I had your dad text me when you woke up."

"You could just show yourself," I suggest. I look down over the railing and finally spot her on the north side, down the trail near the riverbank. She's a blur of yellow, her dress bright against the gray railing. She waves.

"Pop the balloon first, then I'll come up," she says.

I dig my keys out and jab the longest one into the balloon. It pops, and something small and silver falls to the ground, skittering across the pavement. I chase after it, bending down on my good knee to pick it up where it's spun to a stop.

For a long moment, I'm silent, the ring in my hand, the phone against my ear.

"Soph? Did you get it?" Mina asks.

"Yeah," I say. "Yeah, I . . ." My thumb swipes over the ring, over the word engraved on it. "It's beautiful," I say. "I love it."

"It's like mine," Mina says. "We match."

"Yeah," I say. "We match."

I press my thumb against the word, let it imprint on my skin.

Forever.

19

Dad drops me back off at home. He stays at the curb, the car idling until I'm safe inside the house. I wait until he's gone, then I get in my car and drive to Sweet Thyme Nursery.

I try to distract myself among the rows of plants, leaning too hard on the cart as I push it along. I breathe deep, gulping in the scent, rich and earthy and green, and it loosens something inside my chest that's been there since I stepped inside David's office.

After paying for my marguerite daisies and organic soil, I smile and shake my head at the girl at the counter who asks if I need help. The cart's heavy, but I put my weight into it, gritting my teeth as my muscles spasm.

By the time I get to my car, my leg's hurting enough that I'm steeling myself to go get someone to help me load the bags of soil into the trunk. Someone honks behind me, and I pull the cart out of the way.

"Hey, Sophie, is that you?" Adam Clarke peers out at me from his pickup. I've known him, like nearly everyone else at my school, for most of my life. He'd dated our friend Amber for almost a year, and she used to go on and on about how he looked like a country music video version of a Disney prince. Pair the worn baseball cap, his shit-kicker

cowboy boots, and a fondness for Wranglers and John
Deere T-shirts with his green eyes, straight nose, and perfect smile, and Amber had a point.

"Hi, Adam."

He looks from my trolley of soil down at my leg, and
understanding filters through his face. "You need help?"

When I finally was allowed back to school after the
crash, Mina had assigned all our friends jobs to make sure
my comeback went smoothly. There'd been a calendar with
color blocks and code names and everything. Amber had
been my bathroom buddy because Mina had a different
lunch period than we did. Cody was in charge of remind-
ing me when to take all my medications, because he was
the most punctual. And because they were the biggest and
in all my classes, Adam and Kyle had carried my stuff for
me and made sure I didn't fall down.

I'd hated Mina's little army of helpers at first, but after
the fourth time I got the stupid walker I used back then
stuck in the handicapped stall, I knew better than to refuse
the help. I learned to be grateful for Amber and how she'd
slam the bathroom door shut if anyone tried to come inside.

"That'd be great. Thanks, Adam."

Adam pulls his truck up next to my car and hops out.
"Planting a garden?"

"Yeah, gives me something to do." I pop my trunk open,
and he grabs the first bag of soil, placing it inside. "What
are you doing here?"

"Mrs. Jasper buys venison from me and Matt. She makes
jerky out of it."

"Good season this year?"

Adam smiles, pushing his baseball cap back, black hair curling against his forehead. "Yeah. It's been great for Matt. He's been getting healthy." He hefts another bag easily over his shoulder, dumping it in my trunk.

"What about you?" I ask, because I don't want the conversation veering to me. "Are you going for the soccer scholarship still?"

"Trying." He grins. "Pretty much the only way I'm gonna get out of here. But Uncle Rob thinks I've got a good chance. He's been on my ass about it. Making me run suicides."

I wince in sympathy. "I remember he used to have us do those. My dad thought we were too young. They used to argue about it."

"I forgot you played soccer."

"I lasted a season, and then swimming took over. And after that, you know . . ." I shrug.

Adam reaches out and squeezes my arm, and it takes an effort not to flinch. If I don't see it coming, I tend to jump when people touch me now. I'm sure David would have loads to say about it.

"I know things have been tough. But it'll get better," he says earnestly. "You just need to stay clean. You know, my brother went through the same thing. He relapsed, too. He really screwed up, stole money from our mom—she almost lost our house because of it. But my uncle got him on the right track. Matt made amends, and he's doing really good on the program now. Healthy, like I said. He and my mom are even talking again. So I know if you take it seriously, stick close to your family, you'll be okay. You're strong, Soph. Just think about all the stuff you've gotten through."

"That's really nice," I tell him. "Thank you."

Adam smiles. "So, listen, I'm glad I ran into you. Kyle mentioned that you two kind of got into it last week."

"Is that what he's saying?" I ask, trying for casual.

"Look, I know you guys have had your problems. But really, Soph, that fight he had with Mina—"

"What fight?"

"I thought that's what you guys were . . ." He stops abruptly, red creeping along his cheekbones. "Um, maybe I shouldn't—"

"No, you can tell me," I say, maybe a little too quickly, because it makes his straight black brows scrunch together, forming a solid line.

"Look, Kyle's my best friend—" he starts.

"And Mina was mine."

Adam sighs. "It's not a big deal," he says. "They just— they had a fight the day before she died. Kyle came over to my place shitfaced afterward. He wouldn't tell me what it was about, but he was really upset. Dude was crying."

"Kyle was crying?" I can't even picture giant, lumbering Kyle in tears.

"It was weird," Adam admits, shaking his head.

"Did he say anything? Tell you why they were fighting?" She hadn't been taking his calls that day. What had they fought about that would drive him to cry on his best friend's shoulder? Was it enough to make him want to kill her?

"He was so drunk, I could barely understand half of it. He just kept saying that she wouldn't listen to him and his life was over. I think it's hard for him, you know, because they fought and he never got to say he was sorry."

"Yeah," I say, but now I'm the one with the furrowed brow, absorbing this information.

"I shouldn't have brought it up," Adam says when the silence has stretched out too long. He grabs the two bags of soil left in the cart and dumps them in the trunk for me, brushing his hands against his jeans. "I'm sorry."

"No, it's okay," I say. "Thanks for telling me. And thanks for helping me with all this dirt."

"You have someone to help you unload at home?"

"My dad'll do it."

"Text me sometime," Adam calls out as he hops into his truck. "We'll hang out."

I wave at him as he drives off. I get into my car and press hard on the gas, like if I drive fast enough, I can leave all the questions behind.

When I get home, I leave the bags of soil in the car and head into the house. After I take a shower, I do what I've been dreading. I've put off searching Mina's room for too long. If Trev won't answer my calls, I'll have to trick him. But that means I have to wait until my dad's home so I can use his phone. So I force myself to grab a cardboard box and go upstairs to my room to start filling it with her things. They're my ticket inside the house.

Through the years, her clothes and jewelry had mixed

with mine. I have the folders full of newspaper clippings and printouts of online articles that she'd page through while we'd lie on my bed, listening to music. Books, movies, earrings, makeup, and perfume, they all mingled until they weren't mine or hers anymore. Just ours.

Everywhere I look, there she is. I can't escape her if I try.

I take my time choosing what to put in the box, knowing that Trev will thumb through every book, every article, as if they hold some deeper meaning, a message to comfort him. He'll place her jewelry back in the big red velvet box on her dresser, and the clothes back in her closet, never to be worn again.

I'm sliding the last book into the box when I hear my dad open the front door.

I go downstairs. "Good day?" I ask.

He smiles at me. "Yeah, honey, it was okay. Did you stay here the rest of the day?"

"I went to the nursery and got some more soil. And some daisies."

"I'm glad you're still gardening," Dad says. "It's good for you to be out in the sun."

"I was gonna call Mom and see what she wanted to do for dinner, but my phone's charging upstairs. Can I borrow yours?"

"Sure." He digs in the pocket of his charcoal trousers, coming up with it.

"Thanks."

I wait until he's disappeared into the kitchen before going out onto the front porch. I call my mom first, just so

I'm not lying, but it goes to voice mail. She's probably in a meeting.

I punch in Trev's number.

"It's Sophie," I say quickly when he answers. "Please don't hang up."

There's a pause, then a sigh. "What is it?"

"I have some of her things. I thought maybe you'd want them. I can bring them by."

Another long pause. "Give me a while," he says. "Around six?"

"I'll be there."

"See you then."

After I hang up, I get antsy. I can't go back inside. I can't just sit upstairs, next to the scraps of her I've dumped in a box. I go around back to my garden, because it's the only distraction I have left.

Dad's pulled the bags of soil out of the car and lined them up next to the beds for me already. I wave at him from the yard, and he waves back from the kitchen, where he's washing dishes.

I collapse in an awkward heap on the ground, reach out, and dig through the soil of the last neglected bed, rooting out stones and throwing them hard over my shoulder. The summer sun pounds down, and sweat collects at the small of my back as I work. Bent at this angle, my leg is killing me, but I ignore the pain.

I tear open a bag of soil and heft it over the edge of the wood, spilling new dirt into the bed. I dig my hands into the moist soil over and over, letting it filter between my fingers, the rich smell a little bit like coming home. I mix it deeper and deeper into the bed, turning up the bottom soil, combining old and new. The tip of my finger brushes against something smooth and metallic, buried deep. I grasp it and pull a tarnished, muddy silver circle out of the ground.

Astonished, I lay the ring on the flat of my palm, brushing off the dirt.

It's hers. I remember she thought she'd lost it at the lake last summer. Mine is in my jewelry box, locked away, because it doesn't mean anything without its match.

I curl my fingers around the ring so tightly, I'm surprised the word stamped into the silver doesn't carve its way into me the way she did.

20

THREE AND A HALF YEARS AGO (FOURTEEN YEARS OLD)

"Get up."

I pull the covers over my head. "Leave me alone," I moan.

I've been home from the hospital for a week and I haven't left my bedroom. I've barely left my bed, the walker just another reminder of how much everything sucks. All I do is watch TV and take the cocktail of pain pills the doctors keep giving me, which leaves me so fuzzy, I don't want to do anything, anyway.

"Get *up*." Mina yanks at my blankets, and I can't fight her with just one hand, my other still in a cast.

"You're mean," I tell her, rolling slowly over to my other side, smashing my extra pillow over my head instead. The effort it takes just to roll over makes me groan. Even with the pills, everything hurts, whether I'm still or moving.

Mina plops down on the bed next to me, not bothering to be gentle. Her weight jostles the mattress, making me rock back and forth. I wince. "Stop it."

"Get out of bed, then," she says.

"I don't want to."

"Too bad. Your mom says you won't leave your room. And when your mom starts calling *me* for help, I know there's a problem. So—up! You reek. You need to shower."

"No," I groan, smashing the pillow into my face. I have to use that stupid shower chair for old people with bad hips. Mom's hovered outside the door each time, basically worrying herself into a fit about whether or not I'll fall. "Just leave me alone."

"Yeah, right, that's *really* gonna work on me." Mina rolls her eyes.

I still have the pillow pulled over my head, so I feel, rather than see, her get up off the bed. I hear the sound of water being turned on. For a second I think she's turned the shower on in the bathroom, but then the pillow I'm holding is yanked out of my hands and, when I open my mouth to protest, Mina dumps a glass of cold water over my head. I shriek, jerking up way too fast, and it hurts, oh shit, *it hurts.* I'm still not used to how I can't twist and move my spine like I used to. But I'm so angry at her that I don't care. I push up on the bed with my good arm, grab the remaining pillow, and hurl it at her.

Mina giggles, delighted, dancing out of the way and then back, tilting the empty glass in her hand teasingly at me.

"Bitch," I say, yanking my dripping hair out of my eyes.

"You can call me whatever you want, smelly, as long as you shower," Mina says. "Come on, get up."

She holds her hand out, and it's not like anyone else who's offered themselves to me as a temporary cane. Not like Dad, who wants to carry me everywhere. Not like Mom, who wants to wrap me in cotton and never let me go anywhere again. Not like Trev, who wants so desperately to fix me.

She holds her hand out, and when I don't take it immediately, she snaps her fingers at me, pushy, impatient.

Just like always.

I fold my hand in hers, and when she smiles, it's sweet and soft and full of the relief that can only come after a lot of worry.

21

The Bishop house has pink shutters and white trim, and an apple tree's been growing tall in the front yard for as long as I can remember. I walk up the porch stairs carefully, the rail taking most of my weight as I balance the box on my hip.

Trev opens the door before I can knock, and for a second I think my plan will fail, that he won't invite me in.

But then he steps aside, and I walk into the house.

It's strange to feel unwelcome here. I've spent half of my life in this house and know every nook and cranny: where the junk drawer is, where the spare Oreos are stashed, where to find the extra towels.

And all of Mina's hiding places.

"Are you okay?" Trev's eyes linger on the way I'm favoring my good leg. "Here." He takes the box from me and forgets himself for a second, reaching back for my arm.

He remembers at the last moment and stops, snatching his hand away. He rubs it over his mouth, then looks over his shoulder into the living room. "You want to sit?" he asks, the reluctance in his words ringing through the room.

"Actually, can I use your bathroom first?"

"Sure. You know where it is."

Like I'd expected, his attention's already fixed on the box of Mina's things. He disappears into the living room, and I go down the hall. I pause at the bathroom door, opening and closing it for effect, and tiptoe through the kitchen to the only bedroom on the ground floor. Mina had liked it that way. She'd always been restless at night, writing until dawn, baking cookies at midnight, throwing rocks at my window at three A.M., luring me out for mini road trips to the lake.

Her door's closed, and I hesitate, worried about the sound. But it's my only chance, so I grab the knob and slowly turn it. The door opens and I slip inside.

When I thought up this plan, I worried that I might make it all the way here, only to find all her things boxed up or gone already.

But it's worse: everything is the same. From the lavender walls to that girly canopy bed she'd begged for when she was twelve. Her cleats are next to her desk, stacked haphazardly across each other, as if she's just toed them off.

The room hasn't been touched. Mina's bed's still unmade, I realize with a horrible swoop of my stomach. I stare at the rumpled sheets, the indentation in the pillow, and I have to stop myself from pressing my hand into where her head had rested, trailing my fingers through sheets frozen in the curled shape of her last peaceful night.

I have to hurry. I drop to the floor and crawl on my stomach under the bed, my fingers scrabbling for the loose floorboard. My nails catch at the wood and I lift it up and away, pulling myself farther beneath the steel framework.

My fingers search below the floor, past some cobwebs, but I don't feel anything hidden in the nook. I dig my phone out of my pocket and shine it down into the space under the floorboards.

There's an envelope tucked in the corner underneath the loose board, way in the back. I reach down in the gap of space to grab it, crumpling the paper in my hurry. I'm putting the floorboard back when I hear Trev call my name from the hallway.

Shit. I snap the board into place and push myself out from underneath the bed. I have to bite hard down on my lip when my leg twists the wrong way getting up and pain stabs down my knee. I want to lean against the bed for a second, deal with the pain, but I don't have the time. Breathing fast, I shove the envelope in my bag without opening it.

"Soph? You okay?" Trev's knocking on the bathroom door.

I duck out of Mina's room, closing the door quietly behind me before hobbling into the kitchen and grabbing a glass from the cupboard.

Footsteps. I glance up at him as I turn the faucet on and fill up the glass. I swig the water, trying not to look suspicious. "Water's supposed to help with the muscle cramps," I explain, rinsing out my glass and putting it in the sink.

"Still doing the all-natural stuff?" he asks as we make our way into the living room. I sigh in relief; he doesn't notice that I'm out of breath. One of her books from the box lies open on the coffee table.

"It wasn't like that, was it?" Trev asks.

I shake my head. It had been the opposite, and he's known that all along, but when I confirm it, I can see how it breaks him.

"Did she say anything?"

I wish I could lie to him. Wish I could say that she gave a proper good-bye, that she made me promise to watch out for him, that she said she loved him and her mom, that she saw her dad waiting for her on the other side with open arms and a welcoming smile.

I wish it had been like that. Almost as much as I wish it had been over instantly, so she wouldn't have been so scared. I wish that any part of it could have been peaceful or quiet or brave. Anything but the painful, frantic mess we became in the dirt, all breath and blood and fear.

"She kept saying she was sorry. She . . . she said it hurt." My voice breaks. I can't continue.

Trev covers his mouth with his hands. He's shaking, and I hate that I agreed to this. He can't handle it. He shouldn't have to.

This is mine to bear.

It would be so easy to drown all of this with pills. The urge snakes through me, it's right below my skin, waiting to lash out and drag me down. I could make myself forget. I could snort so much that nothing would matter anymore.

But I can't let it take over. Whoever did this has to pay.

Nine months. Three weeks. Five days.

"I tried, Trev. I tried to get her breathing again. But no matter what I did—"

"Just go," he says tightly. "Please, go." He stares straight ahead.

There's a crash that makes me turn around before I can get to the front door. He's kicked the coffee table over, spilling the contents of the box onto the floor. He meets my eyes, and I throw the words at him to break him, because I want to in that moment. Because he made me talk about it. Because he looks so much like her. Because he's here and so am I, but she's not—and that's so unfair, I can barely breathe through it.

"Still can't hate me, Trev?"

22

"What do you think of Kyle Miller?" Mina asks. We're making the hour-and-a-half drive to Chico, where Trev's working on his bachelor's in business. Mina likes to drag me with her on these monthly trips. I never put up much of a fight because it's usually nice to see Trev. Mina had wanted to leave early, so I haven't had a chance to take anything extra and it's making me jittery. I wish I hadn't said I'd drive, but I hate being the passenger, especially for long distances.

We pass by another roadside fruit stand, a crooked sign marked CLOSED FOR WINTER teetering in the wind. Miles and miles of walnut and olive orchards whiz by us on both sides, the branches stark and black against the pale gray sky. Tractors rust in the empty fields, along with the faded FOR SALE signs on the wire fences that have been hanging there forever.

"Soph?"

"Huh?"

"Stop zoning out. Kyle Miller? What do you think?"

"I'm driving. And why are we talking about Kyle Miller?" I don't know why I'm playing dumb. When Mina gets bored, she toys with boys.

"I dunno. He's sweet. He used to bring us brownies when you were in the hospital."

"I thought his mom made those."

"No, Kyle did. Adam told me. Kyle bakes. He just doesn't broadcast it."

"Okay, the brownies were good. But he's not smart or anything." I wonder if that's the point. That he won't be smart enough to notice. I'm always worried Trev will.

"Kyle's not dumb," she says. "And he's got those big brown eyes. They're like chocolate."

"Oh, come on," I snap, too on edge to hide my annoyance. "Don't tell me you're gonna start dating him just because he looks at you like he wants to be your love slave."

She shrugs. "I'm bored. I need some excitement. This year has been blah. Trev's gone, Mom's got her charities. Not to mention the biggest thing to happen in school all year was homecoming court."

"The look on Chrissy's face when Amber hit her over the head with the scepter was worth the week in detention."

Mina snickers. "You're the one who broke her crown."

I don't bother to hide my grin. "I didn't mean to step on it! That float was totally unstable. And I was already at a disadvantage."

"Uh-huh, I believe you, Soph," Mina says. "Homecoming was fun. Detention, not so much. But I don't want fun. Or detention. I want something interesting to happen. Like when Jackie Dennings disappeared."

"Don't wish that! That's twisted."

"Abductions and unsolved cases generally are," Mina says.

"Please tell me you aren't getting into that again. The first time was creepy enough."

"I'm not being creepy. *Something* bad happened to her."

"Stop being so morbid," I scold. "Maybe she ran away."

"Or maybe she's dead."

My phone trills, and Mina picks it up, turning the alarm off. "Pill time?"

"Yeah. Hand me my case?"

She grabs it from my purse but doesn't give it to me. She looks at me out of the corner of her eye, turning the case over and over, the pills clacking together inside.

"What?" I ask.

"Sophie." That's all she says. One word, but she can infuse it with such frustration, such worry.

We are experts in each other. It's one of the reasons I've been dodging the inevitable confrontation, because if she asks me outright, she'll know my answer's a lie.

"I'm fine," I say, with as much truth as I can muster. "I just need my pills." My skin crawls under her scrutiny. I'm sure she can look right through me, see the drugs floating through my system.

I focus on the road.

She tilts the case back and forth in her hand. "I didn't realize they still had you on so many."

"Yeah, well, they do." It's like I'm on the edge of a cliff that's crumbling, the ground beneath my feet breaking free, slipping from me. I keep glancing at the case in her hand. She's not handing it over.

What am I going to do if she doesn't?

"Maybe you should think about getting off them. Do a tapering thing or something. It's been forever, and that stuff isn't good for you."

"I think my doctors would probably disagree." I can't keep the edge out of my voice, the warning. Won't she just drop it already?

But she won't. She hears the warning and breezes past it, because that's the way Mina is.

"Seriously, Soph. You've been acting like . . ." She huffs out a breath. She won't say it out loud. She's afraid to. "I'm *worried* about you. And you won't talk to me."

"It's nothing you'd understand." She can't. She came out of the accident with a broken arm and a few bruises. I'd come out with metal for bones and a dependence on pain pills that had morphed into a hunger I couldn't—didn't want to—ignore.

"Why don't you try explaining it to me, then?"

"No," I say. "Mina, drop it. Okay? Just give me my pills. The rest stop's coming up."

She chews on her lip. "Fine." She tosses the case into my lap and folds her arms, staring out the window at the rows of bare trees that blur by faster as I press hard on the gas.

We drive the rest of the way in silence.

The party Trev takes us to later that night is crowded. The apartment's too warm with bodies, the smell of beer mealy in the air. I lose Mina in the crowd about twenty minutes in, but we've barely spoken since we argued in the car, so it doesn't really matter.

That's what I keep telling myself.

The music's awful, some top-forty hit blasting so loud it makes my head ache. I want nothing more than to get out of here, walk to Trev's apartment, lie down on his couch, close my eyes, and fade out for a few hours.

I weave my way through the crowd, narrowly avoiding an ass grab by some frat boy wearing his baseball cap turned sideways. I sidestep him and slip out onto the empty balcony. Fishing a few pills out of my pocket, I down them with what's left of my vodka.

It's cold outside, but quieter, with the rumble of the crowd and the thump of the music muffled. Buzzed from the vodka, I press my elbows against the railing, waiting for the foggy feeling of the high to smooth all the sharp edges away.

The balcony door opens and closes. "There you are," Trev says. "Mina's looking for you."

"It's nice out here," I say.

Trev walks up next to me and leans against the railing. "It's freezing." Taking off his coat, he drapes it over my shoulders. The smell of pine and wood glue curls around me.

"Thanks," I say, but I don't gather the edges of his coat against me. I can't lose myself in him like I do with her.

"You two fighting?" Trev asks.

"A little."

"You know, it's easiest to forgive her for whatever she did. She'll just bug you until you do."

"Why do you think it's her fault?"

Trev smiles. "Come on, Soph. It's you. You don't do anything wrong."

I shiver, thinking about the extra drugs stashed all over my room. About the lines I snorted this morning before we drove here. About the pills I just took. About all the pills I pop, off schedule, like secret candy. "It's not her fault. It's nothing. It'll be fine."

I hug myself. The Oxy is starting to kick in, that numb, floaty feeling mixing with the buzz of the alcohol, and I nearly drop the cup.

Trev frowns and takes it from me, setting it on the ground. "Maybe this wasn't a good idea, bringing you two. I don't want to give your mom more reasons to hate me."

"She doesn't hate you," I mutter, even though we both know it's a token, that I'm lying. "And I can hold my own. Mina's the bad drunk."

"Oh, trust me, I know." Trev's easy smile unravels the tightness in my chest that's been there since Mina confronted me in the car. He's only trying to help; he doesn't know.

He doesn't see me the way Mina does.

I face him and lean back against the balcony railing. The movement makes his coat slip off my shoulders, and the light from the apartment illuminates my skin. I'm wearing a shirt cut so low you can see the edge of my scar if you're at the right angle. I tug at the neckline automatically, but it's useless. Trev's eyes flicker down, turning serious and studying, blatantly staring.

His smile disappears and he closes the space between us in a step. His hand cups my shoulder, pulling me forward. I feel, rather than see, his coat puddle to the ground. The fabric hits the back of my legs on the way down, and I wish that I'd wrapped myself in it.

"Trev?" I question, and my voice wavers. I've mixed too many pills with vodka; this isn't a good idea. He's way too close.

"Soph." His thumb presses over the line of the scar that cuts my chest in uneven halves, physical in a way he's never, ever been with me. He has to be drunk—he'd never do this sober; he's always so careful about touching me.

"God, Sophie." He sucks his cheeks in, biting at them. "This is where . . ."

His hand flattens against me, covering the worst of it. His palm curves in the space between my breasts, his callused fingertips resting lightly on the scar, rising and falling with each breath I take.

My heart thuds, pounding beneath my skin, greedy for the contact.

"I don't know why you forgave me," he says, words thick with emotion and beer.

"I was the moron who didn't put on my seat belt," I say, like I've said every time he's brought this up.

"I was so scared when you didn't wake up," Trev says. "I should've

"How did your appointment go?" Mom asks.

"Fine," I say.

"Do you like Dr. Hughes?" Dad asks. I wonder if they've made some prearranged agreement to go back and forth with their questions.

"He's okay."

"I realize you've never had a male therapist," Mom says. "If that's a problem . . ."

"No," I reply. "Dr. Hughes is fine. I like him. Really." I take a bite of roast chicken, chewing it for an unnecessarily long time.

"We should talk about college soon," Dad says. "Make a list of universities you're interested in."

I put my fork down, my appetite lost. I'd hoped to have a few more weeks before we got into this. After all, school doesn't even start for two more months.

"You're on track to start senior year in August," Mom assures me, mistaking the look on my face.

I push my peas across my plate, afraid to swallow anything. There's a lump in my throat the size of Texas. I don't have time to think about this. I have to concentrate on finding Mina's killer.

What's on that thumb drive?

"And the independent study you completed at Seaside was all very good work; your teachers were impressed," Mom continues, a rare smile on her face.

"I'm not worried about that," I begin.

"Is it the applications? We can find some way to explain those months you spent away. And if you center your personal essay around the accident, and overcoming all that you had to just to walk again, I'm sure—"

"You want me to play the gimp card?" I cut in, and she flinches like I've slapped her.

"Don't call yourself that!" she snaps.

I have to stop myself from rolling my eyes. Mom is the one who took the accident the hardest. Dad had driven me to physical therapy and done all the research on my surgeries. He'd carried me up and down the stairs that first month, and when I was still in the hospital, he'd read me a story every night, like I was still in second grade. He got to take care of me all over again just when I was supposed to be taking care of myself. And Dad is good at taking care of people.

Mom is good at fixing things, but she can't fix me, and she can't handle that.

"It's the truth." The words are harsh, aimed to shatter her ice-queen armor. Make her finally stop longing for the girl I was to return. "I am a gimp. And a junkie. And you think it's partly my fault Mina got shot, so I guess we should add *accidental killer* to that list, too. Hey, maybe I can write my personal essay on *that*."

She goes red, then white, and then almost purple. I'm fascinated, arrested by her anger as the expression in her eyes melts from concerned to enraged. Even my father puts down his fork and rests his hand on her arm, like he's wondering if he's going to need to stop her from lunging at me across the table.

"Sophie Grace, you will show respect in this house," she

finally spits out. "To me, to your father and, most impor-
tantly, to yourself."

I toss my napkin onto my plate. "I'm done." I push myself
up, but my leg shakes and I have to hold on to the table for
longer than I'd like. Limping, I make my way out of the
dining room. I can feel her watching me, the way her gaze
absorbs each uneven step, each moment of clumsiness.

When I get upstairs, I almost drop my bag, I'm in such
a hurry to get at the thumb drive. I grab it, flip open my
laptop, and plug the drive into the port, tapping my fingers
against my desk.

The folder appears on my desktop, and I double-click it,
my heart thumping in my ears.

The alert *Enter Password* flashes on-screen. I type in
her birthday first. Next I try Trev's, then mine, then her
dad's, but no use. I try names of old pets, even the turtle
she got when we were in third grade that died the week
she brought it home, but nothing works. For over an hour,
I type in every word I can think of, but none of them will
open the drive.

Frustrated, I get up, passing by my dresser, where I've
set Mina's ring next to mine. I pick it up, tilting it, the word
winking at me in the lamplight.

I whirl back around, suddenly hopeful, type *forever* into
the dialog box, and press Enter.

Incorrect Password.

Bottled-up anger, twined with the lingering hurt of my
mother's words, floods through me. "Goddammit, Mina," I
mutter. I throw the ring, hard. It bounces off the wall and
onto the carpet near my bed.

Almost as soon as it falls, I'm on my knees, wincing at the pain, but scrambling to scoop it up. My hands shake as I slip it on.

They don't stop until I go over to my dresser and the second ring—mine—joins hers on my thumb.

24

After the party, I'm drunk and still high, lying on the floor of Trev's living room next to Mina, each of us tucked into a sleeping bag. I can hear his roommates' snores all the way down the hall.

The floor is hard, with thin carpet that has mysterious stains I don't want to think about, in this apartment full of boys. I'm restless, shifting back and forth, staring at the beer caps pressed into the ceiling. My eyes are heavy, but I don't let them shut.

Mina's awake, but she's pretending not to be. She can't fool me; years of sleepovers have taught me when she's faking.

"I know you're awake."

"Go to sleep" is all she says. She doesn't open her eyes, doesn't even change that annoying exaggerated slow-breathing thing she's doing.

"You still mad?"

"C'mon, Soph, I'm tired."

I play with the zipper on my sleeping bag, jerking it up and down, waiting for her to answer me, knowing she might not.

"Is your back okay?" Her eyes pop open in concern as she breaks her self-imposed silence.

"I'll be fine."

I won't, though. I'll wake up stiff tomorrow. My good leg will be numb, but the bad one will ache like a bitch where the scar tissue is tight in my knee.

I should take another pill. I deserve it.

"Here, have my pillow." She leans over and tucks it underneath my head. "Better?"

"You haven't answered my question," I remind her.

Mina sighs. "I'm not mad at you," she says. "I already told you, I'm *worried*."

"You don't need to be," I insist.

It's the wrong thing to say. I can see real fear in her. It bothers me more than I'd like to admit, makes me want to hide, to numb myself further from this, from her.

"Yes I do," she hisses, sitting up, half out of her sleeping bag. She grabs my arm, pulling at me until I do the same. Then she's leaning into my space so fast that I'm startled into letting her.

"You're taking too many pills. You're hurting yourself." She swallows and seems to realize, suddenly, how close we are. Her fingers flex around my arm, tightening and loosening, then tightening again.

"Sophie, please," she says, and I can't tell what she's asking here. She's too close; I can smell the vanilla lotion she rubbed into her hands before we went to bed. *"Please,"* she says again, and my breath catches, because there's no denying what she's asking for now.

Her eyes flicker down to my mouth, she's pulling me toward her, and I'm breathless, so caught in the anticipation, in the *oh my God, this is actually happening* feeling that spikes through me, that I don't hear the footsteps until it's almost too late.

But Mina does, and she jerks away before Trev comes down the hall. "You two still awake?" He yawns, walking into the kitchen and grabbing a bottle of water from the fridge.

"We were just going to sleep," Mina says hastily, lying back down.

She won't look at me, and I can feel my cheeks redden. My entire body's gone hot and heavy, and I want to squirm deeper into my sleeping bag and press my legs together tightly.

"Night," Trev says. He leaves the kitchen light on so Mina doesn't have to be in the dark.

Mina doesn't say anything. She settles in her sleeping bag next to me and tucks one hand under her head. For one long moment, we stare at each other.

I'm afraid to move. To speak.

Then Mina smiles, just for me, small and real and on the edge of wistful, and her other hand slips into mine as she closes her eyes. Her silver rings, warmed from her skin, are smooth against my fingers. The scent of vanilla swirls around me, making blood rush beneath my skin, and the hot pull inside my stomach twists and revels in the contact.

When I wake the next morning, our fingers are still tangled together.

25

"Thanks for coming." I step aside to let Rachel into the house.

"Sophie, was that the—" My mother catches sight of Rachel, with her flaming hair, the mustard-yellow sweater she's buttoned wrong, the chunky skull pendant dangling from the bike chain around her neck. "Oh," she says.

"Mom, you remember Rachel."

"I do." Mom smiles, and it's almost genuine, though her eyes linger on Rachel a moment too long. I wonder if it's Rachel's appearance or if Mom is remembering that night. Rachel had stayed by my side until my parents showed up. I hadn't really given her a choice; I wouldn't let go of her hand.

"How are you, Mrs. Winters?" Rachel asks.

"Well. And you?"

"Fabulous." Rachel grins.

"There's something wrong with my computer. Rachel's gonna check it out for me."

"Bye!" Rachel says cheerfully, following me up to my room. When we close the door behind us, she tosses her purse on my bed, collapsing next to it. "Okay, I've only got forty minutes. I have to drive to Mount Shasta to spend time with my dad. It's his birthday."

"Can you hack a thumb drive in forty minutes?"

A smile tugs up the ends of her red-painted lips. "No way. I'm good with taking computers apart and putting them back together. Code is another monster. It'll take me a while."

I hand over the drive. "I appreciate your trying. My method involved entering as many passwords as I could think of."

"Probably not the most effective approach."

"Agreed."

"So how did it go, talking to Mina's supervisor at the *Beacon*?" Rachel asks, grabbing a pillow to prop her chin on. She tucks a leg underneath her, the other dangling off my bed.

"He's out of town, but he's coming back next week. I'm going to go back then to talk to him."

"And obviously getting inside the house went smoothly," Rachel says, holding up the drive, wiggling it in the air.

I shrug. "Trev hates me."

"I really doubt that," Rachel says.

"He wants to," I say. "And he should. He would. If he knew the truth."

Rachel shifts on my bed, turning the thumb drive over in her hands. But she looks up to meet my eyes when she says, "The truth?"

I don't say anything else, because when you hide, it's instinctual. It's something you have to train yourself out of, and I never trained myself out of this secret, even when I wanted to.

"Soph, can I ask you something?" She looks me in the eye, and there's a question there.

The question.

I can look away and stay quiet. I can say no. I can be that girl, hiding from the truth, denying her heart.

But it'll eat at me. Through me. Until there's nothing real left.

I twist our rings on my thumb, and they bump against each other, trading nicks and scratches earned through the years.

"Sure. Ask away."

"You and Mina, you two were . . ." She switches tactics, suddenly so blunt, just like her letters, starting in one direction and veering off into another midsentence. "You like girls, don't you?"

My cheeks heat up, and I pick at the hem of my comforter, trying to decide how to say it.

Sometimes I wonder what my mother would think, if she'd try to sweep it under the rug, add it to the ever-growing list of things to fix.

Sometimes I wonder if my dad would mind that someday he might walk me down the aisle and give me away to a woman instead of a man, gaining another daughter instead of a son.

Sometimes I wonder what it would've been like if I had been open from the start. If we'd never had to hide. How much would it have changed things if we'd been honest?

I'll never know. But I can be honest now, here, with Rachel. Maybe it's because she met me at the worst moment of my life. Maybe it's because she stuck around, even after.

Maybe it's because I don't want to be afraid anymore. Not of this. Because compared to everything else—the addiction, the hole that losing Mina left inside me, the guilty knot that Trev twists me into—being hung up on this isn't worth it. Not anymore.

Which is why I say, "Sometimes."

"So you like guys, too."

"It just depends. On the person." I'm still fiddling with the comforter, wrapping the loose strands of thread around my fingers.

She smiles, open and encouraging. "Best of both worlds, I guess."

It makes me laugh, the sound bursting out of me like truth. It makes me want to cry and thank her. To tell her that I've never told anyone before, and to tell it and have it be accepted like it's no big deal feels like a gift.

26

"Come on. Open the door." Mina knocks for the third time.

I'm locked in the bathroom, trying to smear enough foundation to cover the scar on my neck. I'm failing. No matter how hard I try, a shadow shows through.

It's been almost six months since the crash, and the idea of going to a dance, the irony of going to a dance when it still hurts to move too fast, makes me want to scream and yell *no, no, no* like a toddler. But my mom was so excited when Cody asked me, and Mina talked endlessly about dresses, and I couldn't bring myself to say no to anyone.

But now I don't want to leave the bathroom. I hate how twisted and uneven I am, how I have to lean hard on my cane with every step.

"Soph, if you don't open this door in the next five seconds, I'll break it down. I swear I will." Mina knocks harder.

"You couldn't," I say, but I smile at the thought of her, five-foot-two, a hundred pounds soaking wet, trying.

"I can! Or I'll go get Trev—I bet he could break it down."

"Don't you dare get Trev." Every time I'm alone with him, he wants to apologize—to *fix* me.

I can almost see her triumphant expression through the door. "I will! I'll go get him right now." I hear exaggerated footsteps—Mina stomping in place outside the door. I can see the shadow of her feet.

I toss the tube of foundation into my makeup bag and wash my hands off. The elaborate curls that Mina coaxed into my hair skim my bare shoulders. "I'll be out in a second." I tug the neck of my dress higher. The red silk is pretty—it makes my skin look milky instead of sickly pale—but Mom had to take it to a tailor to get lace added to the deep V neckline so it would cover the worst of the scarring.

It'd taken forever to find something with sleeves. We must have tried on at least fifty dresses, sharing the same fitting room as my mom waited outside. Mina had fussed with me, helping me step in and out of the heaps of tulle and satin. She'd grabbed my hand and steadied me, and when she'd let go (holding on a second too long, my skin against hers, half-dressed in the tiny room), she'd blushed and stammered when I asked her if she was all right.

My leg is killing me. I'd left my cane in the bedroom, and I need it now, even though I don't want to look at it.

I take the orange bottle out of the beaded clutch that Mina had insisted I buy along with the dress. I shake out two pills.

She knocks again. "Come on, Sophie!"

Make that three. I down them with water from the tap, tucking the bottle away.

I open the door, and red silk swishes against my legs, a foreign, almost pleasant feeling floating above the mess of scars.

Mina beams. "Look at you." She's already dressed, wrapped and draped in silver fabric, all shimmer and tanned skin. Mrs. Bishop is going to freak when she sees how low her Grecian-style dress is cut. "I was right—the red is perfect."

She spins around. Her curly hair is looped up in a headband of silver leaves, little tendrils falling over her bare shoulders as she rummages around in the blankets on her bed. She grabs something, hiding it behind her. "I have a surprise!" She's practically vibrating in her eagerness.

"What is it?" I ask, playing along because she's so happy. I always want her to be happy.

She holds it out triumphantly.

The cane she's clutching is painted scarlet to match my dress. Mina has glued red and white crystals all along it. They twinkle and catch the light. Velvet ribbons stream from the handle, spirals of silver and red, twisting and swinging in the air.

"You tricked out my cane." I reach for it, and my smile is so wide, I feel like it's going to split my face in two. I press my hand against my mouth, like I need to hide it, hold it in, and I do, because the tears are there, down my face, probably messing up all my makeup. I don't care, because she does something that no one else can: she makes my life pretty and good and full of sparkles and velvet, and I love her so much in that moment that I can't contain it.

So I say it because I mean it. Because I have to, there is no choice, standing there with her: "I love you."

It's there, just for a second. I see the flicker in her eyes, and she does so well to cover it, but I *see* it, before she hugs me and whispers against my ear, "I love you more."

27

Rachel leaves for her dad's, promising to call me as soon as she gets the thumb drive open. I start my morning yoga practice, but I pushed myself too much yesterday. After my knee buckles for the fourth time in warrior pose, I roll up my mat and put it away.

It's important to know when you're beat.

My jeans are still on the floor where I tossed them last night, and when I pick them up, the envelope the thumb drive had been in falls out of the pocket.

There's a piece of notebook paper folded inside that I hadn't noticed last night. I unfold it and see unfamiliar handwriting:

Please, babe, just answer the phone. We have to talk about this. All I want to do is talk. I promise. Just answer the phone. If you keep ignoring me you're not going to like what happens.

I turn the note over, but it's not signed.

It doesn't matter. It has to be from Kyle.

If you keep ignoring me you're not going to like what happens.
I read the sentence over and over again, stuck on it, like it's on an endless loop in my head.

"Sophie?"

I look up from the paper in my hand. Dad's standing in my doorway, frowning.

"Sorry. Yeah?"

"I was just saying I'm heading out," he says. "I've got an early lunch with Rob. Your mom already left. Sweetie, are you okay? You look pale. I could cancel—"

"I'm fine," I say, but my ears are ringing. Already, I'm cycling through the possible places Kyle would be right now. "I just pushed myself too much. My knee hurts."

"Do you want some ice?"

"I'll get it," I say. "You don't have to cancel, Dad. Go to lunch. Say hi to Coach for me." I need Dad out of the house. I have to find Kyle. Where would he be right now? At home?

"Okay," Dad says. "You'll call me if it gets bad?"

I smile, which he seems to take as a yes.

I wait, Kyle's note crumpled in my fist, until Dad drives off in his sedan. Then I pick up my phone and punch in Adam's number. I pace across the room as it rings.

When he finally picks up, I can hear laughter and barking dogs in the background. "Hello?"

"Adam, hi. It's Sophie."

"Hey, what's up?"

"I was wondering if you knew where Kyle'd be right now," I say. "I found a necklace of Mina's that I think he gave her. I wanted to give it to him to make up for being such a bitch last week. I wasn't sure where or when he was working this summer."

"Yeah, he's probably at work," Adam says, and someone

says his name, followed by more male laughter. "Wait a second, guys," he calls. "Sorry, Soph. He's at his dad's restaurant, not the diner, the seafood place out on Main . . . the Lighthouse."

"Thanks."

"Yeah, no problem," Adam says. "Hey, give me a call next week. The team's having our bonfire out at the lake. We'll hang out."

"Sure," I say, not taking it seriously. "I've got to go. Thanks again."

I drive too fast, gunning it as the yellow lights switch to red, barely pausing at stop signs, careening around corners. Our downtown isn't much because our town isn't much. The good and bad parts are kind of squished together, the courthouse and the jail a block apart, the liquor store kitty-corner to the Methodist church. A handful of restaurants, a diner tucked across the railroad tracks, and a few pay-by-the-week motels that are a breeding ground for trouble. I slow down only when I see the Capri M-tel, the blue-and-pink neon sign with the missing O.

The Lighthouse is right next to it, so I park quickly and bang through the doors, not caring if I'm drawing attention. Kyle is leaning on the counter, watching the basketball game on the flat-screen on the far wall.

The restaurant is almost empty, just a few tables full. I march past them and up to Kyle as his mouth tightens.

"I need to talk to you."

"I'm at work." He glares at me through his floppy blond hair. "If you go psycho in here—"

"Take a break to talk to me, or you'll find out how psycho I can get."

He glances around at the people at the tables. "Come on," he says, and I follow him through the kitchen and out the back way, behind the restaurant, where there's a fenced-in area for the Dumpsters. It smells awful out here, like grease and fish and garbage, and I breathe through my mouth, trying to block it out.

"I can't believe you." Kyle rounds on me as soon as the door closes and we're alone. "What's your problem?"

I hurl the note at him, slapping my palm on his chest. "Want to explain that?"

He grabs it from me, scanning it. "So what?"

I fold my arms and plant my feet. "Tell me what you and Mina fought about the night before she died."

Kyle is the definition of an open book. He's crap at hiding his emotions, and his mouth drops for a second before he remembers to close it. "It's none of your business."

"It is when you're leaving Mina threatening notes right before she gets murdered!"

"Bullshit," Kyle says. "This wasn't a threat. I just wanted her to call me back."

"You threatened her. 'If you keep ignoring me you're not going to like what happens.' Who says that to their girlfriend?"

Kyle goes red, his puppy-dog eyes hardening. "Shut up. You don't know what you're talking about."

"Then explain it to me. Tell me what you guys were fighting about."

"You need to leave it alone," he warns.

"Not gonna do that."

"Fuck you." He starts toward the door, and I plant myself in front of him and push him hard. He's over six feet and thick with muscle, but it feels good to shove him. As he stumbles, I move toward him again, but he recovers his balance and grabs my wrists easily. "Stop it, Sophie." Then he lets go of me and steps back, holding his dinner plate–sized hands out in front of him. "You're gonna hurt yourself."

I lunge for him again, but he darts out of the way. I come down too hard on my leg and nearly fall.

"You're such a pain in the ass," he mutters as he grabs my arm to steady me.

"Tell me," I insist. I'm panting, adrenaline ricocheting through me. "Why were you fighting?"

"Don't," he says. "Just don't."

"What did she tell you that made you so angry? What were you threatening her with?" With each question, I push him, and he just takes it. I'm right in his face, inches away, standing on my tiptoes. I have to grasp the chain-link fence behind him to stay steady. My leg is shaking, but I try to ignore it. I won't fall in front of him. "She cared about you. She even let you sleep with her! Why would you—"

"Shut up!" he yells, and I gasp, flinching at the raw note in his voice. His brown eyes shine, like he's about to cry. "*Shut up.* There's only one of us here who was fucking her, and it sure as hell wasn't me."

28

"We are so late," Amber says, grabbing her soccer bag out of her mom's car.

Mina glares at her, pulling the walker out of the backseat and unfolding it for me. "Chill out," she says sharply.

"Coach is gonna kick our butts. We have to warm up."

I nudge Mina. "Go. I can get to the bleachers by myself."

"No," she replies.

"Amber, go," I tell her. I don't want her to be pissed at me for making her late. She hadn't even wanted me to come, but Mina insisted.

Amber nods, taking Mina's bag with her.

"I've got it," I insist when Mina doesn't go with her.

Mina looks over her shoulder. The girls are already on the field; she'll get in trouble if she doesn't hurry. "Hey!" she shouts, waving across the parking lot. "Adam! Kyle!"

"Mina—"

"If you want me to go, then you let Kyle and Adam help you," she says to me.

I roll my eyes and grab the handles of the walker, heaving myself up, leaning on it. The doctors are making me use it for an extra month before I can switch to the cane. I can't believe I'm actually looking forward to a cane, but I am.

The boys come over, and once Mina's reassured they won't let me fall off the bleachers, she tears off toward the field, her hair streaming behind her.

Kyle looms over me. His jeans are an inch too short—he's already bigger than everyone else in our grade and hasn't shown any signs of stopping. He keeps a hand hovering behind my back during the torturous minutes it takes to get to the bleachers, like he's afraid I'm going to just pitch over at any moment.

"Where's your dad today?" Adam asks as I sit down on the bottom bleacher. "Uncle Rob's short a coach."

"Emergency root canal," I say.

"Is that even a thing?" Kyle asks.

"I guess so. You guys can go sit up at the top, if you want. I'm fine here on my own."

"Better view from here," Kyle says with a grin.

It makes me smile back. I dig in my purse, coming up with a bag of M&M's, and we pass it back and forth as we turn our attention to the soccer field.

The girls are getting ready to start, warming up on the side of the field. Mina's dark, curly head is bent as she touches her forehead to her knee, stretching her legs out.

"Aren't you helping Coach out?" Kyle asks Adam.

"In a sec," Adam says. "He doesn't need me till they start."

Kyle's eyes stay on Mina, watching her stretch her arms above her head, reaching up, up, up, like she can touch the sky. She's the smallest on the team—but when she's on the field, it's like she's ten feet tall, full of strength and speed.

"You're getting good moving around." Adam pulls his baseball cap off, sticking it in his back pocket.

"Almost ready for a cane," I say. "Go me."

"Hey." Kyle frowns. "You should be proud. Mina says you work your ass off in physical therapy."

"Is that what Mina says, Kyle?" Adam asks, and he grins at me conspiratorially as Kyle's face reddens.

"Your parents bugging you about college yet?" Kyle asks, like he's desperate to change the subject.

"They're making noises. But it's kind of early."

"Maybe for you," Adam says. "I've gotta start thinking scholarships. I can't go anywhere without help. And I'm not gonna get any prizes for my grades."

Kyle laughs. "Hell, no," he says. "You're gonna get one for being the best goalie NorCal's ever seen."

Adam grins, standing up. The girls are starting to gather on the field. Our team's in blue, the Anderson Cougars are in red. "Well, here's hoping. I don't want to be stuck here forever. I should get down there before Uncle Rob gets too pissed. See you later, Soph."

With Adam gone, Kyle and I turn back to the field, our attention honing in on Mina like a magnet to metal.

The team is lining up for the kickoff, and Amber says something that makes Mina toss her head back and laugh, her curls bobbing against the gray sky. She play-pushes Amber, who pushes her back, laughing, too.

I watch Kyle watch her out of the corner of my eye. "You really like her, don't you?"

He jerks, the tops of his ears turning red. He doesn't meet my eyes, but looks down at his hands, digging into his jeans. "Is it that obvious?"

"Kind of."

He laughs. "Way to make a guy feel better."

I shrug.

I don't say what I'm thinking. I don't tell him how lucky he is, that he can just sit there and admit it, sheepish, but unashamed. Like it's his right. Like it's okay, because she's supposed to belong to someone like him, instead of someone like me.

29

"I don't know what you're talking about," I say, but my voice shakes. I can feel the panic rise inside me: Kyle *knows*.

"Shit, Sophie, give me a little credit," Kyle says. "She told me."

My stomach lurches. Saliva floods my mouth, a hot, slick rush that I can't contain. I gag, moving past the Dumpsters, and manage to get to an empty trash can before I start to throw up, coughing and spitting.

Big hands grab clumsily at my hair, pulling it back as the rest of my breakfast comes up. I jerk away from him, my skin flashing hot and cold, goose bumps breaking out everywhere. Finally I straighten up, wiping my mouth with my hand, my eyes damp with tears, my throat raw. He steps away from me again, leaning against the chain-link fence, his hands in his pockets.

"Kyle . . ." I start, and then I stop, because I don't know what to say. I hate that he knows. It's different with Rachel, with someone safe, someone who didn't know Mina.

The smell of vomit curls inside my nose, making the queasiness roar back to life, and I press my fingers to my mouth, swallow convulsively, and breathe through pursed lips until it passes. I back away from the trash until my shoulders are pressed against the chain-link fence that separates the restaurant's back lot from the Capri M-tel. I can see people on the second level, walking back and forth from the ice machine.

"I was so pissed. I yelled at her. I shouldn't have, but I did. I made her cry, I . . . I said some really shitty things. And then she wouldn't take my calls the next day, she wouldn't listen to me, so I left her that note. I just wanted to tell her I was sorry. But she wouldn't pick up, and then the next thing I know, Trev's on the phone telling me that she'd been killed." He takes a step back, like he needs the distance as much as I do. "I fucking hate you sometimes," Kyle says. "Every time I see you, I get so pissed at you. Whenever you're around, I think about her telling me, the look on her face . . ." He lets out a shuddering breath. His Adam's apple bobs under the collar of his polo shirt. "She was so relieved. Like she'd wanted to say it forever. And I was just—I was *shitty*. All I did was make her cry."

"This is why you lied to the police." It's crazy, and I'm furious that all of this, the months I spent trapped at Seaside, was because of this. Because she'd trusted him, of all people, with her—our—biggest secret. Because he was mad at being tossed over for another girl.

I hit him, a hard smack across his chest that feels better than it should. "You screwed up everything!" I burst out. "I spent three months in rehab for a drug addiction I'd *already* kicked. My parents think I'm a hopeless junkie and a liar! Everyone in this town thinks I'm the reason Mina was out at Booker's Point. Trev won't even look at me. Not to mention that by giving the police false information, you probably helped the murderer get away with it."

"There *were* drugs," he insists. "I didn't make it up. I heard the police had found pills. Who else would they belong to? I didn't want to explain to the detective why I was calling Mina so much that day, so I told him that Mina had said you two were going out to the Point to score and that I tried to stop her. I thought it'd get you in trouble."

I want to hit him again, but I hold back this time. "Yeah, well, you thought right. The only problem is the drugs weren't mine. Whoever killed her planted them on me."

His eyes narrow. "You've really been clean this whole time?"

"Do you want me to swear it on her grave?" I ask. "Because I will. We can go there right now."

"No," he says, too quick, and I realize I'm not the only person who has a problem visiting Mina's grave. "I—I believe you."

"Oh, great," I snarl. "That makes me feel so much better. Thanks a lot."

He stands there, and now more than ever, he's like a massive, slobbery puppy. He sticks his big paws inside the pockets of his cargo shorts, biting his lower lip, staring at his feet. "Look, I'm sorry for lying . . . even though I didn't think I was totally lying," he says. "But you did sleep with my girlfriend."

"I didn't sleep with her while she was your girlfriend!"

"Whatever."

"Seriously," I say. "Look at me." He scuffs his foot on the pavement, and I snap my fingers in front of his face until he meets my eyes. "You don't get to be pissy to me about this," I tell him. "Whatever she told you . . ." I let out a breath. I can't think about what she told him, about herself, or about the two of us. Every time I do, I feel everything slipping out of my control, my footing in the gray area precarious.

Nine months. Three weeks. Six days.

I tap the numbers against the skin of my wrist, a heartbeat to build on.

"She liked girls," I continue when I've got a hold on myself. "She only liked girls. The guys were a cover. I'm sorry, but that's just the way it was."

"I know that," he says quietly. "I know," he says again, his face crumpling.

The back door of the restaurant bangs open. "Kyle," calls a man in a spattered apron. "We need you."

Kyle ducks his head so the guy can't see how undone he is. "Just a sec," he mumbles. The guy nods and heads back inside.

Kyle stares up at the sky, and I give him a moment of silence to get himself together.

"I've got to get inside," he says. He wipes at his cheeks and clears his throat before pushing past me.

"Kyle, Mrs. Bishop can't find out about this." I hate how small my voice gets, that I'm practically begging.

What looks like sympathy flickers across his face before he looks away. "She won't find out from me. I promise."

He's doing it for Mina and for himself, not for me, but I don't care, as long as it stays a secret.

Mina had constructed her cage a long time ago, built by shame from the beliefs she was brought up with. She may have told Kyle. But she never wanted anyone else to know.

I plan on keeping it that way.

30

My phone buzzes. It's two A.M. and I'm half-asleep, but as soon as I see it's Mina, I answer.

"What?"

"Look out your window."

I get out of bed. Mina's parked across the street, leaning against a familiar blue F-150.

"You stole Trev's truck? You only have your permit."

"I *borrowed* it. And no one's gonna catch us. Come on, let's go."

I pull my shoes on and sneak downstairs. I'm in pajama pants and a tank top, but it's a warm night and I don't care. Mina beams when she sees me coming out the door. "Where's the cane?" she asks as I get into the passenger seat. "You have another three weeks—"

"I'm getting better without it," I interrupt. "It's fine. I need to get used to walking. Even the guys at PT said so."

"Okay," Mina says, but she doesn't sound convinced.

We roll down all the windows and head to the lake, singing along to the radio. Taking the back road, we head toward a spot only locals know, where we've spent hundreds of lazy hours over the years, swimming and soaking up the sun.

The lake stretches out in front of us and Mina pulls over, parking in a turnout by the side of the road. When we get out of the car, I can hear the soft lapping of the water against the rocks below. The moon's high in the sky, shining off the water. We've been coming to this spot since we were kids, but it was easier to navigate the trail down to the shore back then.

Mina helps me down the tricky stretch to the little beach. We strip down to our underwear, and there is nothing self-conscious about her when she tosses her shirt onto the rocks. I follow suit, slower, more carefully. Mina walks into the lake, waiting until she's hip-deep before slipping under. She comes up with a splash, her dark hair flying everywhere as she beams at me in the moonlight.

The water is cold—almost too cold—against my skin, and goose bumps prickle on my arms as I wade in after her. My toes dig into the muddy bottom for better traction, but once I get deep enough, I can lift my feet and let the water buoy me back and forth, weightless, almost painless.

Mina floats on her back, staring up at the sky. "I heard something today," she says.

"Hmm?" I float next to her, letting the water support my body.

"Amber said she saw Cody buying condoms at the drugstore last week."

I reach my arms above my head, pushing through the water, away from her.

I'm not fast enough. She jerks forward, off her back, splashing everywhere as she treads water, facing me. "You didn't!" When I don't say anything or look at her, she says, "Oh my God, you *did*."

"So what if I did?" I ask, and it comes out way more defensive than I intend. Cody and I had been dating for months; it had seemed like the thing to do. I just didn't want to tell anyone afterward.

She should know how good I am at pretending. It's all we do. It's all I do. I pretend that I don't hurt, that I want Cody, that I don't want her, that I'm not taking too many pills, that my virginity had been important.

It hadn't been. It only means something when it's with the right person. And I couldn't have her.

"I can't b-believe . . ." Mina stutters. "Oh my God."

"It's not a big deal," I mumble.

"Yes it *is!*" She says it so quickly, and I can hear the catch in her voice.

Like she's about to cry.

"Mina." I start to swim over to her, but she turns from me, dives deep. She glides under the water, and when she surfaces I can't tell if it's tears or lake water dripping down her face.

We never talk about it again.

A week later, Mina and I are at a party at Amber's when Amber way-lays me, walking across the crowded deck with a self-satisfied smile on her face.

"Why didn't you tell me?" she demands, twirling her sun-streaked hair around her finger. We're outside. Amber's house is next to the river, and I've been zoning out, staring at the ducks riding the current downstream.

"What?"

"You mean Mina didn't tell *you?*" Amber's eyes widen. "Maybe I shouldn't say anything. . . ."

"Amber, out with it," I snap. I can be a bitch when I need to be. And no matter how much Amber would like it to be her, *I'm* Mina's best friend.

"Mina's totally sleeping with Jason Kemp."

"What?" I can feel blood drain from my face. I have to tighten my hold on my cup so I don't drop it.

I look for Mina immediately, instinctively. When our eyes meet across the deck, I understand: she planned it, she wanted it this way, she'd just been waiting for me to find out—and I hate her for it.

It's the most vicious thing she's ever done to me, but really, how can I blame her?

Two weeks after that, two weeks of her hanging off Jason's neck, of them making out *everywhere*, of that gleam in her eye, the way she's pushing at me, punishing me, I finally can't handle it anymore. I'm sobbing as I crush the pills.

I've been on the edge of this for months, gulping down too many, numbing myself to the pain. Numbing myself to her. This is the inevitable next step down, the evolution of my fall.

It's like a roller coaster, the dip and slide searing through me, going straight to my head. The buzz—fleeting, but oh so good—floods me, and I'm reaching for more before it vanishes completely. Anything to erase her from me.

But some marks, they don't fade. No matter what.

31

When I get home, I stare at the evidence board on my mattress because I can't think about anything else. I take Kyle's picture down, rip it in half, and toss it on the floor, barely resisting the urge to stomp on it a few times.

"Sophie?" My mom knocks on my door. "Your dad said your knee was hurting. I came home to check on you."

"Just a second." I scramble to push my mattress down. My sheets are in a tangle on the floor, and I don't have time to do anything but pile them on the bed, shoving Kyle's torn picture under my pillow and throwing myself on top of the mess. "Come in."

She frowns when she sees me, flushed and guilty-looking. Knowing Mom, she probably has a numbered list of things to watch out for when it comes to her junkie daughter.

"What are you hiding?" she asks.

"Nothing," I say.

"Sophie."

I sigh, reach next to my bed, and grab the shoe box stashed underneath my nightstand. I flip it open, spill the contents onto the comforter. Photos spread everywhere. "I was looking at pictures."

My mom's face softens, and she picks up a photo, one of me and Mina, our arms wrapped around each other, neon-green swim caps clashing horribly with our pink tie-dyed racing suits. "This was before your growth spurt," she says.

I take the photo from her, trying to remember when it was taken; some sunny day during swim practice. Mina's missing a front tooth, which means we must've been about ten. She'd pitched headfirst off her bike that summer, racing me. Trev had run all the way home with her in his arms, and later I found him checking her bike to make sure it was safe.

"That was before a lot of things," I say. I put the photo back into the box, grabbing up others, shoving them out of sight.

"I want to talk to you." Mom sits down on the edge of my bed, and I keep on putting the photos away to give myself something to do. I pause at the photo of Trev and me, standing on the deck of his boat, sticking our tongues out. There's a pink blur on the side of the photo: the edge of Mina's finger, obscuring the lens.

"I shouldn't have said what I did about your college essay," Mom continues. "I'm sorry. You should be able to write about anything you'd like."

"It's okay," I say. "I'm sorry I yelled at you."

She takes another photo, this one of me, fat and happy in the lap of Aunt Macy. "You know," she says quietly, "my mother died of an overdose."

I look up, and I'm so surprised she's brought it up that I drop the stack of photos. "I know," I say, bending over quickly to pick them up, grateful I won't have to look at her right away.

Mom rarely talks about my grandmother. My grandpa lives on fifty acres of wilderness, in a house he built with his own hands. After the crash, he'd clapped his hand (a little too hard) on my shoulder and said, "You'll get through this."

It'd been almost an order, but I'd felt comforted by it, like it was a promise at the same time.

"I was the one who found her," Mom says. "I was fifteen. It was one of the worst moments of my life. When your father searched your room . . . when I realized that you could've followed her down that path . . . when I realized that someday I might walk into your room and you wouldn't be breathing . . . I knew I'd failed you."

It's unimaginable, the words coming out of her mouth. She *had* failed me, but only after I'd recovered. She'd refused to see the changes in me, the things I'd overcome and accepted about myself—the ones she never could. She'd stood there, stone-faced to my begging and tears, my heart still a fresh wound pouring out grief and shock, and she'd seen it all as guilt and lies.

I hate it, but there's a part of me, the sliver that's not consumed by Mina, that can understand why she and Dad didn't believe me. Why they shoved me into rehab and practically threw away the key. They wanted any way to keep me safe.

I understand.

I just can't forgive them for it yet.

32

Adam's back field is crowded with people. School's finally done and his mom is out of town, leaving him and his brother to throw a party that everyone from two counties seems to have shown up for.

After waiting forever for the bathroom and a much-needed pill break, I head outside to find Mina and Amber. I stumble down the deck steps and I tell myself it's because of my leg.

It's not.

"Hey, Sophie, careful." Adam hurries over from the cluster of kegs and coolers at the end of the deck, grabbing my arm. He leads me over to the picnic table, where Amber is sitting next to a tray of Jell-O shots.

"Having fun?" she asks me as Adam slips his arm around her waist.

"Yeah," I lie. It's sweltering, and I'd rather be home than out here, getting drunk and bitten by mosquitoes. I've already had a few drinks, but I take the little plastic cup Amber hands me, and we tap them together before popping them back. Fake cherry and vodka slide across my tongue, and I swallow hard.

"Where's Mina?" Amber asks.

"Not sure," I say.

"I saw her in the house earlier with Jason," Adam says. He squeezes Amber's waist, pulling her closer as music suddenly booms through the yard. "Oh, you gotta dance with me, babe." And Amber grins at me as I wave them off.

I abandon the Jell-O shots and go back into the house, weaving my way around the crowd of older people, Adam's brother holding court among them. They are definitely Matt's friends, if the smell of pot coming off them is any indication.

I'm walking through the kitchen and into the living room when I hear it.

"Screw you, Jason!"

I walk in on the tail end of the confrontation. Mina's smack-dab in a crowd of people, swaying on heels planted in the brown plush carpet. She's right up in her boyfriend's face, and Jason clutches his red plastic cup, looking miserable. People are staring, and I catch Kyle's eye from across the room. I mouth, *How long?*

He shrugs and raises his eyebrows like, *Need some help?*

I shake my head. They've been fighting on and off for a week now, so I'm used to it. I walk over and grab her arm. She's shaking, wobbly in a too-many-Jell-O-shots way, and she stumbles against me in her heels.

"You're such a jerk!" She lunges at him, and I grab her by the waist, struggling to stay balanced and restrain her at the same time. It's kind of hard considering I'm bordering on drunk and just snorted two lines in the bathroom.

"I'm done, I'm done!" Mina says. It's more for my benefit, so I don't end up falling, because I will if she keeps this up. She rolls her eyes when she realizes the room's gone silent, everyone staring at her. "Let's go," she huffs, and she stalks out of there, with me following, as usual.

"Um, Jason still has your keys," I say as I try to catch up with her. She's already halfway across Adam's yard, heading toward the winding dirt road that leads to the highway.

"I took care of it," she says. She stops, turns, and waits for me. When I reach her, she loops her arm in mine.

Out here, away from lights and cloud cover, the stars shine amazingly bright, and Mina tilts her head up to look at them, a smile on her face.

"I am *so* breaking up with him," she announces. "And I don't want to talk about it anymore."

I stumble, kicking up clouds of dirt with my boots, navigating around tufts of prickly star thistle and blue cornflowers. "Whatever you want," I say, but inside I am glowing, triumphant.

"Come on, Soph. I told him we'd be at the end of the road." She skips ahead, shaking her hips to the strains of music floating from the house. I grin, following after her.

"Who did you call?"

"Trev."

I stop. "You didn't."

"Of course I did." She tugs me forward, knocking her hips against mine. The moon is bright, and I'm messed up enough to let my eyes linger on the curl of her hair, the dark ripple against her pale skin. I can smell vanilla underneath the pine and almost-rain scent in the air.

"He'll freak when he sees we're drunk."

"I don't care. He'd freak more if we ditched Jason and drove drunk. You know how he gets about you and cars."

This is true. Trev is morbidly afraid of something else happening to me. Even years later, he watches me in that way I've gotten used to, part fear, part want, all protectiveness. Occasionally I'll turn, meet his gaze. Sometimes he doesn't look away, and I catch a glimpse of what all the other girls see in him, what they want from him.

"Becky's probably with him," I say. "She hates me."

Mina laughs, a little too long. She always was a lightweight. "She

really does; you should hear her talk about you. Girl's got a mouth
on her."

"Trev's girlfriend talks to you about me?" I ask, surprised through
my Oxy-vodka haze.

"Well, not to me. I heard her on the phone one day after you left.
I took care of it."

"What was she saying?" I stagger to a stop and face her. "What do
you mean you took care of it?"

Mina sighs, dropping her arm from mine and leaning against
a fence post. She bends down and plucks a cornflower, twirling it
between her fingers. "It doesn't matter." I watch her tear off the blue
petals, one by one—*She loves me, she loves me not*—before tossing the
stem on the ground. She spins in a lazy circle, her short skirt flaring up.

"Anyway, everyone knows you and Trev will end up married with
babies and stuff," Mina says with a smile, but I can hear it: the bitterness underlying her slurred words. "And Becky wants him for good.
She can't admit the only person he wants is you."

"But I don't want Trev," I say.

Sometimes I wish Trev knew that he was caught in the middle of
this; then I wouldn't feel so guilty. But he can't imagine it, because
Mina hides behind her secrets and I wither away my soul with pills,
and we are Just Fine, Thank You. Reckless girls dancing down dirt
roads, waiting to be saved from ourselves.

"We'd be sisters if you married Trev," Mina says, and her lower
lip sticks out like she's pouting at the thought of it. Like Trev's taking
away a toy she wants.

The idea horrifies me, makes me want to vomit. "You're not my
sister."

Mina blinks, and her eyes glint in the moonlight. I want to lean forward, press my lips against hers. I need to know what her mouth tastes like—sweet, maybe, like strawberries.

I'm almost messed up enough to do it, emboldened by her fight with Jason and how high I am. I step toward her, but my knee gives out, the pain sharp and sudden, and it makes me falter. I pitch forward with an "oomph," and Mina catches me halfway. But I've got four inches and twenty-five pounds on her, and we end up tangled in the dirt, laughing. Giggles fill the air as truck headlights wind down the road toward us.

"There you two are." Trev leans out the window as he cuts the engine. "I heard you shrieking all the way down the road."

"Trev!" Mina beams at him, and her hands squeeze my waist in a way that makes my stomach leap. "You came! I'm breaking up with Jason. He's an ass."

"And you're drunk." He gets out of the truck and hauls her up, gently setting her on her feet. He brushes dirt off her shoulders before crouching down next to me. "You fall, Soph?"

"I'm okay." I smile and he smiles back, the concern in his face retreating. He waits until I hold my hand out for him to pull me up.

"Steady," he says when my leg wobbles and I lean into him. Trev is solid, warm. Mina giggles and presses into his other side until he's got two armfuls of us. We hold on to him. Put him between us like our barrier against the truth.

But her hand finds mine behind his back and our fingers lace together, the click of our rings a secret sound only we understand.

Some barriers, they're made to be broken.

33

"You're quiet today," David says halfway into our second therapy session on Monday. "What are you thinking about?"

I look up from my place on his couch. I've been twisting the rings on my thumb, tracing the grooves of the letters like they're a key to a lock I haven't found yet. "Promises," I say.

"Do you keep your promises?" David asks.

"Sometimes you can't keep them."

"Do you try?"

"Doesn't everyone?"

David smiles. "In a perfect world. But I think you're well acquainted with the unfairness of real life."

"I try to keep mine. I want to."

"Did Mina keep her promises?"

"Mina didn't need to. You always ended up forgiving her, no matter what she did."

"You care about her a lot."

"Way to state the obvious, David."

David's eyebrow twitches, his pleasant smile dropping at my hostility before settling back to neutral. "You forgave her a lot, too."

"Don't talk about her like you knew her," I say. "You didn't. You won't."

"Not unless you tell me."

I don't talk for a long time, just sit there, and he doesn't force me to continue. He folds his hands together and sits back in his chair to wait me out.

"She was bossy," I say finally. "And spoiled. But really thoughtful. And smart. Smarter than everyone else. She could bullshit her way out of anything by just smiling. She was a bitch when she needed to be and she'd never apologize for it. She's the first thing I think of when I wake up, the last thing I think of when I go to sleep, and the only thing I think about in between."

I stare at the framed diplomas on the wall, the award David got from some organization for homeless youth, another from an abused women's group. By the time he speaks, I've practically memorized the entire wall.

"That makes her sound like an addiction, Sophie."

I keep staring at the wall. I can't look at him. Not now.

"I don't want to talk anymore today."

"Okay," David says. "We'll sit here just a few minutes longer, in case you change your mind."

When I get into the car, my phone vibrates. I'd turned it off during my session, but now I see that Rachel has left me a message.

I call my voice mail and freeze in the act of turning my keys in the ignition, listening to the message play: "It's me. I got the drive open. You need to call me. I think I know why Mina was killed."

34

"We're lost," I insist.

"No, we're not." Mina navigates Trev's truck down the dirt utility road we've been on for the past thirty minutes. It's dark outside, and the Ford's brights cut through the forest as we rock back and forth on the rough road. "Amber said off Route 3, down the second road to the right."

"We're totally lost," I say. "No way there's a campground out this far. There's nothing here but trees and deer."

Mina sighs. "Okay," she says. "I'll turn around. Maybe we missed a turnoff or something."

The trees are too thick to get a signal, so I can't call Amber to tell her why Mina and I are so late to join her and Adam at the campground. Mina backs the truck up slowly—the road we're on is cut out of the mountain, hugging a cliff that's so steep, I can't see the bottom in the darkness. The wheels skirt close to the slope and Mina bites her lip in concentration, her knuckles white against the wheel. After a few false starts, she finally gets us turned around, but we only get a half a mile before a *thunka-dunk, thunka-dunk* reverberates through the cab, and the ride gets even bumpier.

"Crap." Mina slows to a stop. "I think we have a flat."

I grab the flashlight from the glove box and follow her out of the truck, shining the beam on the tire.

Mina frowns. "Do you know how to change it?"

I shake my head and look down the road. It's at least three miles back to the highway. I rub absently at my leg, thinking about how much it's gonna hurt, walking that far.

Mina pulls her phone out and stomps around, trying to get a signal. I don't tell her it's useless, because she's got that determined look on her face and she keeps throwing glances at my leg, like she knows the hurt I'm anticipating. I lean against a big piece of slate that's embedded in the mountain looming over us like a gray giant, and wait for her to admit defeat. It's August, but it's still cool at night, and I like the little shiver that goes down my back, the prickle of goose bumps over my skin. It's nice being out here in the forest; loud in its own way, the rustle and cracks in the undergrowth—hopefully a deer instead of a bear—the groan of the branches in the wind punctuated by the steady crunch of Mina's boots against the road. I close my eyes and let the sounds fill me.

"You don't have any signal?" Mina asks hopefully after about five minutes of walking back and forth, waving her phone around.

"Nope. We should start walking," I say. "It's not like we're blocking a main road. We'll get Trev to come change the tire in the morning."

"Don't be stupid. I can't make you walk that far. I'll go get help and come back for you."

"I'm being stupid? You're the one who failed the wilderness skills part of Girl Scouts. You'll probably get eaten by a bear. You go, I go."

"It's a road. I can't get lost following a road. And anyway, you couldn't walk that far," she says.

"Sure I can."

"No way," she says, her mouth set mulishly.

"You can't tell me what to do. I'm coming."

"No!" Mina says.

"Yes," I say, starting to get annoyed. "What is up with you? Stop treating me like I'm—"

"Weak?" she finishes for me. "Disabled? Hurt?" Her voice rises with each word, trembling and high-pitched, like they've been stuck in her forever, now finally free.

I jerk back from her, like she's hit me instead of just telling the truth. Even though she's standing ten feet away, I need more distance from her. I stumble, achingly aware of my clumsiness in that moment. "What the hell, Mina?"

But I've inadvertently unleashed something in her, and she keeps talking, the words spilling out in the night. "If you walk that far, you'll use it as an excuse to take more of those stupid pills. And then you're gonna be all dopey and zoned out, like you *always* are lately. I know you're in pain, Soph; I know that. But I also know *you*. You're hurting yourself, and either no one else has noticed or they're not saying it. So I guess I'm going to say it. You need to stop. Before it becomes a problem."

Panic and relief twine inside me. Panic, because she knows, and relief, because she doesn't realize how bad it is. She thinks I'm still at the edge of the hole, ready to throw myself off, instead of in it so deep that I can barely see her at the top.

There's still time to fix this.

To lie my way out.

I don't even think about taking her seriously, because I'm *fine*. I've got it under control, and it's none of her business.

It's partly her fault.

"Please, Sophie, I need you to hear me," she says. Her eyes are wide and concerned in the glare of the headlights, and I stifle a wild urge to tell her, for a second, about how far I've gone, what I've done, what I've become.

But then the love she has for me—whatever kind that is—will be gone. I know it. How could she love me when I'm like this?

"You're right," I say. "I'll talk to my doctors about it, okay?"

"You will?" she asks, and she seems so small. She's tiny, of course, but right now she *sounds* it. "Really?"

"Really," I say, my stomach turning at the lie. I tell myself I will ask them, that I'll do it for her.

But deep down, I know I won't.

I can't.

She gallops back to hug me. The scent of vanilla floods me, the smell of damp and green from the forest mingling with it to make the best perfume. Her hands are warm, looped around my waist, her face pressed into my neck as she breathes, the relief pouring off her.

She heads off into the night with a flashlight and a water bottle, and I stay obediently in the truck like a good girl.

I wait until she's out of sight before fishing out the container of pills in my bag.

I shake out four and swallow them dry.

35

I can't get hold of Rachel. After a half hour of pacing my bedroom, I toss the phone (six unanswered calls, five texts, three messages) in my purse and head downstairs. She must be at her house. I'll go there.

But when I pull my front door open, Kyle is standing on my porch.

"What are you doing here?" I want to push past him, get him out of my way, out of my sight.

What had Rachel found? Why isn't she calling me back?

"I want to talk to you," Kyle says.

"Now is really not a good time." I step outside, lock the door behind me, and head down the porch stairs.

"You ambush me twice, and now you don't have five minutes?" He follows me down the driveway, so close it makes the back of my neck flush with anger.

"You lied to the police, sabotaged a murder investigation, and got me locked up in rehab—all because you were jealous. Forgive me if I'm still pissed at you."

I open the car door and he slams it shut, making me jump. I look up, and for the first time, I see the circles under his bloodshot eyes.

I remember what Adam had said about Kyle crying the night before Mina died. How thick Kyle's voice had gotten when he'd revealed that she'd told him the truth.

He had loved her. It made me queasy, but I didn't doubt it. And I understood too well the frustration, the evisceration, of loving and losing her.

"I have to go. If you want to talk, get in," I say, against my better judgment. "If not, get out of my way."

He glances at my purse. "You're not gonna spray me in the face with that bear repellent, right?"

"In or out, Kyle. I don't care." I climb in the car, turning the key. He sprints to the other side and opens the door, throwing himself in as I hit the gas. "Put on your seat belt." It's an automatic order that's given to anyone who gets in my car. Trev does it, too, a tic that neither of us can break.

After a few minutes of silence, Kyle's leg jiggling up and down, I roll my eyes and switch the radio on. "You choose," I say.

He turns the dial as I speed down the street, heading toward Old 99, east of town.

"So where are we going?" he asks, settling the radio on the new country station and looking out the window.

"I have to meet someone. You'll stay in the car."

Kyle rolls his eyes.

"You gonna tell me what you want?" I pass an old lady in a Cadillac crawling twenty miles below the speed limit and press harder on the gas as we turn down Main to get to the on-ramp. We pass the old brick building City Hall's been in since the town was founded back in the gold rush days. Hanging over the entryway there's a banner advertising the upcoming Strawberry Festival. Mina used to make me go, play those stupid rigged carnival games, eat way too much shortcake.

"I really didn't mean to get you in trouble," Kyle says.

"If you're gonna lie to me, you might not want to do it to my face."

"Okay, I did want to get you in trouble," Kyle admits. "But that was only when I thought you were *already* in trouble. I wouldn't have done it if knew you were being set up. I think I screwed up. Because . . . if it wasn't about drugs, that means it was something else, right?"

"Duh."

I turn onto the highway. This time of year, Old 99 is a gray line cutting through a sea of yellowed grass and barbed wire fences, speckled with the dark green of scrub oaks. Cows dot the fields, dirt roads branch off the highway, tumbledown barns and ranches are set away from the cars' searching headlights. It's peaceful. Time seems to move slower.

I know how deceptive that can be.

"And it wasn't a mugging," Kyle continues. "I know he took your purses and stuff, but if it was a mugging, why would he shoot just one of you? Why would he shoot anyone, if he got what he wanted? Why wouldn't he take the car? Why would he leave you alive? Why would he plant drugs?"

He's really been thinking about this. I wonder if the circles under his eyes are a result of staying up too late to page through articles about Mina's death. If he has a copy of the police report, like I do. If he has it memorized yet.

I have to stop myself from rolling my eyes. "That's what I've been saying for months. But, weirdly, people haven't been listening to me."

"I told you I screwed up," Kyle says quietly. "I apologized. I explained why."

"It's not that easy," I say. "You helped derail the entire police investigation. You helped lock me up in rehab, where I got to sit and think about how Mina's killer was walking around free and clear, with nobody looking for him. An apology can't change any of that. We're not in first grade anymore. Admitting you screwed up is not going to fix it or catch the killer. So all I can do now is pick up the pieces and try to put them together myself."

"I want to help."

A squirrel dashes out onto the road, and I jerk the wheel to avoid it, overcorrecting into the next lane. For a horrible second, I think I'm going to lose control of the car and crash.

"Shit, Sophie." Kyle's hand is on the wheel, and he's half leaning over me, pulling the car off the road, onto the shoulder as I bring the car to a shaky stop.

I whimper, bite at the inside of my mouth, trying to get my lips to stop trembling as I twist the key and the engine shuts off. I suck air in through my nose.

"Hey." Kyle frowns and pats my shoulder clumsily. Weirdly, it makes me feel better. "We're okay. It's fine."

I'm gripping the wheel so hard my knuckles are white. My lungs are tight; my heart hammers inside my chest. I'm not getting enough air. I want to sag against the wheel, press my face against the cool glass of the window, but I can't do that in front of him. I won't. So I just focus on breathing. In and out. In and out.

When I've finally gotten myself back to normal, Kyle asks quietly, "Should I drive?"

In and out. In and out. Two more deep breaths, and I release my death grip on the wheel. "I'm fine," I say.

I turn the engine back on and push on the gas, kicking up dirt clouds as I turn back onto the road.

In and out.

In and out.

36

All week, I look forward to my call to Mina. I'm only allowed to have two nonparental calls a week. It sucks, but I'm following Aunt Macy's rules. So when Trev's number appears on my phone instead of Mina's, I feel a flash of disappointment.

"Hey," I say, trying to sound cheery. "Aren't you busy with school?"

"I needed a break. And I wanted to see how you are; it's been a while."

Months, in fact. "Things are good," I say as I pick at the quilt spread across my bed. It has hand-tied squares, and I like to twirl the strands of silky embroidery floss between my fingers.

"Yeah?"

"Yeah, you know, therapy, admitting my mistakes, my failings, basically examining all the bad parts of me. It's been a ball."

"Sounds like it. What about the pain? Is it . . . Are you handling it?"

"It hurts," I say. "All the time."

I can hear his intake of breath over the phone, ragged and too quick, and I wonder if I've been too honest with him. If he still blames himself for all this.

Of course he does. Trev wouldn't know what to do if loving me wasn't wrapped up with some form of guilt.

He and Mina have that in common.

"I've been worried about you," he says.

"I know." I lie back on my bed, sink into the safety of my pillows as I cradle the phone against my cheek. "I'll be okay."

"Mina misses you."

"I miss her." Can he hear it? The truth in those three little words?

"Do you know when you'll be home?"

"Probably not for another few months. It's hard, adjusting to no pain meds. I don't want to . . ." I stop.

"What?" Trev asks.

"I just—I can't. Not right now." I know he doesn't get what I'm talking about. How much it hurts. How hard it's been. How I've been forced to look at the worst parts of myself. The ugliness on the surface is nothing compared to what's inside me.

I am not the same. I've gone hollow, scooped my insides out. The constant fear that it's too late, that I'll mess it up, slip back down into that hole, no way out, gnaws at me. I understand now how weak I am.

"I'll get better. I'm getting these cortisone shots in my back that help, and believe it or not, I'm doing yoga, and I actually like it."

"Yoga?" he asks. Something eases inside me, hearing the laughter in his voice. "I'd think that'd be a little slow for you."

"Things change, I guess."

"Guess so."

Another pause. I stare up at my ceiling, at the glow-in-the-dark stars Macy stuck up there. "Is Mina there?" I ask. "She was supposed to call."

"I know," Trev says. "She asked me to call and tell you she'll talk to you on Tuesday. She's all distracted. Mom and I are officially meeting this new boyfriend of hers."

Cold shock spears through me. I sit straight up, so fast that my back flares painfully in protest. "Boyfriend?"

"Didn't she tell you? Of course she didn't. Mina and her secrets."
Trev's words are full of fondness. "He's that blond one who follows her
around like a puppy. Kyle."

"Kyle Miller," I croak. I think I'm going to be sick. I almost drop
the phone, but force myself to keep listening.

She never said anything. This entire time, all these months, I'd
been thinking . . .

Oh God. This is Jason Kemp all over again. But it's so much worse
this time.

"Yeah, that's it. Is he still a good guy? Or am I gonna have to scare
him off?"

"Um . . ." What do I say? He's a man-whore. The biggest asshole in
the world. A chronic cheater . . . any wild lie to get him away from her.

"Soph?"

"He . . . he's okay, I guess," I stutter. "Kind of a jock. He's always
had a crush on her. I guess she's decided to finally give him a chance."

Macy knocks on my open door, peering in. She taps her watch,
and I nod to show I'm finishing up. "I have to go," I blurt out. My eyes
burn. Any second I'll start crying, and I'm desperate to hang up before
he catches on. "Trev . . . does she seem happy?"

"Yeah," he says, unaware what that one word does to me.

"Good, that's—good. Anyway, I should go. Thanks for calling."

"I'll call again," he says. "And I'll see you when you get home."

"Of course."

I never want to go home now. I want to stay here forever. Hide
from what's waiting. I'm so angry and hurt, the memory of her touch
still fresh on my skin after all this time. I don't even know what to do.
I put my phone away and sit on my bed.

I want to use.

The thought slips through me, tantalizing, kissing across my body. It beckons me. *Just one more time. It'd feel so good, it'd make you forget, it'd make it better.* And I want to so badly.

Three months. One week. One day.

I can't.

I won't.

But, oh, do I want to.

37

"Are you really gonna make me stay in the car?" Kyle asks as we drive down the dirt road leading to Rachel's house. I park behind her mud-spattered Chevy and get out, trying to ignore how my legs are still shaking.

"No," I say reluctantly. "Come on."

He follows me up the porch steps, and I knock hard on the door. The impatience that I've kept at bay leaps to life again.

What has she found?

Rachel doesn't answer, but I hear the rumble of an engine in the distance, so Kyle and I walk around the house to the back field. The dogs are lying on the deck, panting in the heat. Rachel's riding an ancient mower, cutting swathes of long, summer-bleached grass in the yard. She waves when she spots us, cutting the engine and hopping off, walking toward us.

"Who's this?" she asks when she gets close to the porch.

"Kyle."

Rachel raises an eyebrow. "Seriously?"

"I think he's on our side now," I say.

"That's right," Kyle says. "Hi." He holds his hand out to

her, and she takes it, frowning.

"You're gonna have to fill me in later, Sophie," she says.

"Will do," I say, trying to conceal my impatience. "Now what did you find out?"

Rachel wipes her forehead, clearing the sweat beading at her temples. "Come inside. I've got it all set up. It's better if you see it."

She leads us into her living room, where she's got a laptop sitting on the wagon-wheel coffee table. She clicks and taps for a few seconds, then flips the switch of the projector she's got rigged next to it. On the wall opposite us, her desktop appears.

"I've got to say, your girl? She was thorough." Rachel clicks on a file labeled *TL*, and my eyes widen as the first thing I see is: *September 28: Jackie Dennings disappears while jogging on Clear Creek Road (approx. 6PM). Mother calls police when she doesn't return by dinner (approx. 8PM). Police recover pink sweater at the side of Clear Creek Road (approx. 9PM).*

I scan the rest of the page.

It's a time line.

My chest is tight with triumph. I'd been right. Mina chasing after a story got her killed.

"What is this?" Kyle asks.

"They're Mina's notes," I say as Rachel clicks on the arrow, revealing another date on Mina's time line: *September 30: Matthew Clarke (Jackie's boyfriend) is brought in for questioning.* "This is the real reason we were out at Booker's Point. Rachel, are all the files on the drive about Jackie Dennings?"

"Yeah." Rachel minimizes the time line and brings up more files, newspaper articles, their headlines blaring *Community Searches for Missing Girl*; *Six Weeks, No Sign of Local Girl*; and *Two Years Later, Dennings' Disappearance Still a Mystery.*

"Fuck," Kyle says.

"What?" I ask.

"Last year, Mina asked me to get my brother to give her Amy Dennings's phone number. Tanner and Amy are friends."

"Jackie's little sister?" I ask.

Kyle nods. "You remember when Jackie disappeared? We'd just started freshman year. There were all those vigils."

"Trev was upset," I say. "He and Jackie were in the same class."

I look at the article Rachel's projector beams onto the wall. Jackie Dennings's face smiles at me, her straight blond hair brushing her shoulders, blue eyes full of warmth.

What had Mina found that made her chase after this so recklessly?

"What else do the notes say?" I ask Rachel.

"Jackie Dennings has been missing for almost three years," Rachel says. "They never found any trace of her. No sightings. She's just . . . *gone*. I don't mean to sound all dire or anything, but she's almost definitely dead. And Mina thought so, too." Rachel taps on the keyboard for a few seconds, and the newspaper articles disappear, replaced with a map of the county. There's a big circle drawn around the northwest corner, and when I look closer, I see that right at the center of the circle is Clear Creek Road, where Jackie disappeared.

"Was she looking for places where Jackie's body might be?" I ask, feeling sick to my stomach.

"Well, yeah," Rachel says. "I mean, I don't know if she was going off in the woods with a shovel, but she mapped it out. Estimated how far whoever took Jackie would be able to get before the police put up roadblocks. Mina's theory was that Jackie got abducted on Clear Creek Road and then taken to a second location, killed there, and dumped."

"West of town, he had half the Trinities to choose from." I shake my head.

"And the lake's only ten miles away," Rachel says. "The ideal place to dump a body. No one's gonna be finding it."

"So you're saying that whoever took and probably killed Jackie Dennings three years ago killed Mina, too?" Kyle asks.

"Well, if she was meeting someone for a story, it was most certainly *this* story," Rachel says. "And she was interviewing people connected to the case. There are three audio files of her interviewing Jackie's family members and the boyfriend. That's probably why she wanted Amy's number from you, Kyle. Amy's interview is on the thumb drive."

My breath catches in my throat and something twists inside me, a weird mix of dread and wonder. "There's . . . her voice . . . It's Mina talking?" I ask.

Rachel reaches over and squeezes my hand. "Do you want me to play them?"

A sickening heat floods me, half want, half protest.

I'm not ready.

"No," I say quickly. "No. Please. Don't."

There's an exhalation of breath behind me, a relieved sigh from Kyle.

"She had a lot of material," Rachel says. "I swear she saved every article ever written about Jackie. And her suspect list is so detailed—she was good at this."

"Too good," I say. "She got too close. She was gonna figure it out. And he stopped her so she wouldn't tell."

"There's one thing," Rachel says. "I think the killer tried to warn her. Tried to get her to back off."

"What?" Kyle and I say at the same time.

"Seriously, look." Rachel brings forward Mina's time line again, paging forward. "The time line's huge; it spans years. The most recent entry is December, just a few months before Mina was killed. Look at what it says."

December 5: Warning note received. Sender's been tipped off (Accidentally? On purpose?)

December 20: Note #2 received. Going to lie low for a while. Just to be safe.

I'm paralyzed for a moment with anger, consumed by it.

Why did she have to be so secretive all the time? She should've known better. Should've known she wasn't invulnerable. I hate her for being so reckless. For not bothering to think about all of us, left in her wake.

"That's what the killer meant," I whisper. "That night. He said 'I warned you' before he shot her."

"She was getting threatening notes and she didn't tell us?" Kyle looks bewildered. "She would've told the police,"

"I can take care of myself," Kyle mutters.

"It's not a good idea," I say hastily, more for Trev's sake than Kyle's.

"But—"

"Drop it, Kyle," I say. "Rachel, what else have you got?"

"Not much. I'll make copies of all this for you both. You guys knew her, the way she worked and thought; you might be able to see something I didn't."

"We can meet again in a few days," Kyle suggests. "Compare notes?"

"Sounds good," Rachel says, looking at me for my consent.

I nod. "Yeah. Sounds good."

38

"We're gonna be late," Mina says.

I zip up my boots and pull my jeans down over them. "We've got twenty minutes. Chill."

She collapses on my bed, scattering throw pillows everywhere. She's wearing a hot pink dress that's so short, her mom would throw a fit if she saw it—which, of course, is why Mina changed into it at my house. There are little beads on the three-quarter-length sleeves, and they keep catching the light, like she's twinkling.

She props herself up on her elbow, her hair spilling over her shoulder, a dark mass of brown curls against the pink. "Are you sure you want to wear those jeans? You should wear the black skinny ones. Tuck them into your boots."

"I can barely breathe in the skinny ones."

"But you look so good in them."

I size her up, suspicious of her sudden interest in my clothes. "Is there something about tonight you're not telling me?" I ask. There's nothing Mina loves more than a surprise. "Why do I need to be dressed up? You're not planning a welcome-home party, are you? Mina, I hate that sort of thing."

"Which is why I stopped myself," Mina says. "It's just burgers with Kyle and Trev. I already told you."

I shoot her a look. "Okay, but I think you're acting weird."

"And I think you should change."

"Not going to happen."

"At least put on some lip gloss."

"What's with you?" I ask as I pull my sweater on. "It's just Trev and your boyfriend." Every time I call Kyle her boyfriend, it gets easier. I've been practicing it in front of the mirror.

"You're so pretty." Mina gets up from the bed to paw through my jewelry box. "And you spend half of your life dressing so *boring* because you think it'll make people notice you less."

"Maybe I don't want people to notice me."

"That's my whole point." Mina holds a pair of silver hoops up to her ears in front of the mirror, turning her head back and forth before discarding them. "You want to hide. It's unfair to yourself."

"I'm not the one who wants to hide, Mina," I say, and she fumbles and drops the necklace she's picked up.

"I'm going downstairs," she says flatly. "We should leave soon."

Trev and Kyle are already sitting in a booth when we get there. Angry Burger is busy, packed with college students home for the weekend, a big group shooting pool in the corner, Corona bottles stuffed with lime wedges clutched in their free hands. They haven't updated the music on the jukebox in forever; it's always twangy, old-school country, heavy on the banjo.

Mina slides into the spot next to Kyle while Trev gets up from the chipped oak booth.

I've been home from Oregon for a week. This is the first time I've seen him, and I'm surprised at how happy I am. Trev is simple. Easy. Exactly what I need tonight, after days of Mina's doublespeak and guarded glances.

He hugs me, and it's comforting, like Trev always is.

"Good to see you, Soph," he says, and I can feel the rumble in his chest where it's pressed against mine.

"How's school?" I ask him as we sit down. I'm determined to focus on Trev instead of Kyle and the way he's got his arm slung across the back of the booth behind Mina like he owns it. Owns her.

"Busy," Trev says.

"Trev's been building a boat," Mina puts in.

"Another one?" I ask.

He'd rebuilt a trashed catboat after the accident, and sometimes I'd go to the dock to keep him company. It was the only time, still fresh from the crash, that I could be around him and not feel assaulted by the weight of his guilt. His focus, for once, had been on fixing something other than me.

It took him months, repairing the smashed hull and broken spars. When he'd finally finished, he took us out, just him and me and Mina, for her maiden voyage. I'd watched him brush his fingers over his boat like he was touching a holy thing and I'd understood him in a way I never had before. Realized that he and I were cemented together, almost as much as Mina and I.

"You should see the line of girls at the docks every weekend," Mina says, snickering. "They loll around frying in the sun and watch him— it's ridiculous. If he took his shirt off, I think they'd have a collective fit. Disgusting." She flicks water at Trev, sticking her tongue out.

Trev rolls his eyes while Kyle laughs. "Right on, man."

"Brat," Trev says to Mina.

"You should go out there, Soph. Scare 'em off." Mina nudges me with her foot underneath the table, and all the easy energy, the comforting familiarity of Mina and Trev's teasing, dissipates in a second.

I can't stop the way I go white, can't stop Trev noticing my reaction. I wonder if he sees the way she looks at me, how every shred of her attention is on me, the bitterness in her smile, desperate and so damned scared. Can he even understand what she's doing to me—to all of us?

And because she's Mina, she just *won't stop.*

"Kyle and I need a couple to double-date with. It's perfect. Wouldn't that be fun, baby?"

"Sure," Kyle says.

I can feel Trev's eyes on me, but I can't rip my gaze away from her as I say, "I'll be right back."

Not a ripple on her face. She keeps looking at me like that until I'm half-ready to launch myself across the table at her.

"Good idea. We should freshen up." She slings her purse over her shoulder and throws a smile at Kyle. It's her Fine, Just Fine smile. Kyle can't tell she's bullshitting, but I can—and so can Trev, who frowns as he tries to figure out why I'm so upset, why she's so triumphant.

She saunters across the restaurant toward the ladies' room like she doesn't have a care in the world. Like she didn't just try to set me up with her brother, like she isn't screwing with me (and with him) in the worst possible way.

Mina likes to play with fire.

But I'm the one who gets burned.

39

Kyle and I are silent on the drive back to my house.

When I park in my driveway and reach for the door handle, he doesn't get out. He stares at the dashboard, hands in his lap. For a long, uncomfortable moment, all I want to do is leave him there. But then he starts talking.

"I told her I loved her," he says. "A week before she . . . I told her I loved her and she started crying. I thought she . . . It was stupid. I'm stupid. I thought I knew her. But I didn't." He looks at me, those puppy-dog eyes so miserable, it hurts even though I'm still mad at him. "How does that even work, Sophie? To love someone so fucking much and not even really know her?"

I don't know how to answer that. I'd loved her. The real her. The half version she'd shown to the world and the scared parts that ran from me as much as they reached for me. Every part, every dimension, every version of her, I knew and loved.

I think about when we were younger. Even back in middle school, Kyle was on the outskirts, watching, entranced as I was with her. Waiting, and finally getting, only to be crushed.

I understand why he hates me. It's the exact reason I hated him those months before. He took her away from me. And then she got taken away from both of us. Neither of us won in a game he didn't even know he was playing.

Because of that kinship, I can put aside my anger. I can be kind. She would've wanted that.

"Mina trusted you. She told you. That means something. It means everything."

He stares at me like he's seeing me for the first time. The misery is still sharp in his eyes, but there's something else now, too, a kind of searching look that makes me want to run. "You know how everyone has, like, a dream? For their life, I mean?"

I nod.

"Mina was mine."

I reach out—I can't help it—and squeeze his shoulder. "Mine, too."

After Kyle leaves, I go inside and up to my room to download the files Rachel gave me.

Mina's time line is a thing of beauty compared to the makeshift one stuck to the underside of my mattress—it's years long, with a detailed suspect list and precise notes on each person involved.

I don't think I'd ever talked to Jackie Dennings. My freshman year had been overshadowed by the crash, but even if it hadn't, our paths probably wouldn't have crossed. She'd been a junior and class president, and popular, so to me she existed just as a pretty blond girl that I knew of, more an idea than a person. And then one day that pretty blond girl was on a Missing poster, and they were plastered everywhere. The Dennings family had even put up billboards on the highway, but no tips ever led anywhere.

According to Mina's notes, Jackie was a good student and star athlete, a loving sister and daughter. She'd even been headed to Stanford on a full soccer scholarship. The only ripple in her good-girl image was the boyfriend.

When Jackie disappeared, Matt Clarke had been the number one suspect. A history of drug abuse, a few citations for public intoxication and bar fights, with only a shaky alibi from another known drug user didn't help him any, but the police search of his truck and house had turned up nothing.

My cursor hovers over the link that'll open the audio file of Mina's interview with Matt. I need to click it. I have to listen to it.

But I can't bring myself to click. Sitting here alone in my room, her voice would be like hot metal against skin, burning through the layers until there's nothing left to brand.

I'm not strong enough.

Ten months. Two days.

The next day, both my parents are out of the house by eight, off to meetings and appointments. I set out the mat on my bedroom floor and go through my regular asanas, but I can't focus—or rather, unfocus. Now that I have something to go on, the urge to track down and interrogate everyone who ever knew Jackie is fierce.

But I can't do that. Jackie had a little sister and parents and people who love her, who miss her. Who might object to someone snooping around.

I'm not Mina. I'm not good at making people comfortable or getting them to talk. Even before the crash, it wasn't one of my talents.

I'm finishing up my practice, sitting in lotus pose, breathing long and slow, when the doorbell rings.

I check the window before going downstairs. Trev's F-150 is parked outside my house, and my first instinct is to change. I'm in shorts and a tank top. It's stupid. It's not like he hasn't seen me in less; in nothing at all.

The bell rings again.

I take a deep breath and walk down the stairs.

"I need to talk to you," he says as soon as I open the door. He brushes past me, not waiting to be invited in.

He turns, trapping me against the door, and stares me down. "Kyle stopped by last night," he says.

Shit. I should've made Kyle promise not to go to Trev.

"He told me the drugs weren't yours. That he lied about Mina telling him that you two were going to score. That you've been telling the truth this whole time. That Mina was investigating Jackie Dennings's disappearance, and that's why you were at the Point."

I cross my arms, planting my bare feet on the Spanish tile. It's cool, solid, and I tilt my chin up and meet his eyes.

"Is that what Kyle says?"

Anger darkens his face. "No, Sophie, you don't get to do that. I just spent eight hours tearing my sister's room apart

with Kyle, trying to find some threatening notes he's claim-
ing she got. Don't pull that shit with me. Not about Mina.
Tell me the truth!"

"I tried," I spit out. "I wrote you when I was at Seaside.
I explained everything. But you sent the letter back
unopened. You didn't seem interested in the truth then." I
can't hide the resentment in my voice. I don't want to.

He looks down, disarmed for a moment. "There were
drugs at the scene. The pill bottle had your prints on it.
Detective James was sure it was a drug deal. What was I
supposed to think? You'd lied to us for years. *Years*, Sophie.
Just six months away to get clean, and I'm supposed to forget that?"

"I don't care that you didn't believe me," I say. "Not
anymore. Not after everyone else turned on me. I care that
you didn't believe in *her*. She *never* would've taken me anywhere to get drugs. And you should've known that—you
should've known her!"

My voice rises with each word, until I'm yelling at him,
jabbing my hand in the air with each sentence.

"Don't you . . ." He steps toward me, then thinks better
of it and backs away instead, until he's right up against the
front door.

I hold my ground. It's been months since he sent the
letter back, but my anger feels fresh, pushed down and
ignored.

"You let me down," I say. "And you let her down by
believing that she'd allow me to relapse like that—like she'd
even help me score. Are you kidding me? She's the one who

ratted me out the first time. What the hell were you thinking?" I'm yelling, my voice rising and rising, like my rage
has no limits.

This time, he doesn't back away. He stands up straight,
and sweat trickles down my spine when he glares at me. "I
was thinking that I didn't know who the hell you were anymore," he says. "You lied to us for years. You pretended to
be fine, and we fell for it. I fell for it. And it started to make
me wonder what else you were lying about. When you
went to Portland, Mina spent the next two months just . . .
wrecked. I'd never seen her like that. Not since Dad . . ." He
rubs a hand over his mouth, his shoulders pressing hard
into the door, steeling himself.

"I tried to tell myself she was worried, she missed you.
You two were always your own little dastardly duo. Like
sisters. But that's the thing, isn't it? You and Mina. You
weren't sisters. And you weren't just friends, were you?"
He's searching my face, looking for a hint of the truth.

He knows.

Ohgodohgodohgod, too late, too late, too late.

"Were you in love with Mina?" he demands, and I can
hear it, the dread in his voice. "Was she in love with you?"

I don't know how to answer that last question. I wish
I did.

"Kyle told you."

"Jesus Christ," Trev breathes, and I realize that Kyle
hadn't said anything—instead I've just confirmed it, this
long-ignored fear, the deeply buried *what-if* in Trev's mind.

He's gone pale beneath his deep summer tan. He leans

against the front door like he needs it to hold himself up. I wish we'd done this in the living room so he could sit down—so *I* could sit down. My legs are trembling, and my palms are slick with sweat.

"Jesus Christ," he says again, shaking his head, staring into space like I'm not even there. "This entire time . . ." He looks back at me. "Why didn't you ever tell me?"

"It was none of your business."

"None of my . . ." He lets out an incredulous half laugh. "You know I love you. Don't you think you should've mentioned that you don't like guys? This whole time, I've been telling myself you just needed . . ." He trails off. "Never mind. It doesn't matter. Not anymore." He shakes his head once and turns away, going for the door.

"Hey." I catch his arm.

It's a mistake to touch him. I know it instantly. There's no excuse. No fresh shock of Mina's death. No drunken night and flimsy shirt.

It's just him and me. The two left standing. He is the only other person who misses her the way I do, who shares half my memories of her, who's loved me the exact opposite way she did: steadfastly and openly.

He doesn't pull away. He can't, so I have to. For both of us.

"You didn't make it up," I say firmly. "You and me. There's chemistry. Or whatever you want to call it. There've been times, moments with you . . . You didn't make it up, Trev. I promise you."

"But you're into girls."

"I'm not gay; I'm bisexual. There's a difference."

"And Mina?"

My silence answers for me, and then he does, too.

"It was Mina this whole time, wasn't it?"

I give him the only thing I can: the cold, hard truth. The one that'll rewrite every memory he has—of him and me, her and me, the two of them, all three of us: "It'll always be Mina."

40

The bathroom is empty. Mina is in front of the mirrors, rifling through her makeup bag.

I stand there, furious and enraged and every other angry word I can think of.

She won't even look at me. Just starts applying lip gloss like we really are in here to freshen up.

"What are you doing?" I demand.

"I'm putting on lip gloss," she says. "Do you think it's too dark for me?"

"Mina!"

She flinches. The tube falls out of her hand and onto the brown tile floor. Wide eyes meet mine in the mirror before she looks away.

"What are you doing?" I ask her again.

"Nothing," she mutters.

"Nothing? You're trying to set me up with Trev."

"What's wrong with that?" she asks, quick and defensive, like I've insulted her brother. "Trev's sweet and he's good and he's honest. He'd be a great boyfriend."

"He's *Trev*," I say, which should explain everything.

"He loves you; you know that."

Of course I know that. It's why what she's doing is so twisted. She is not this stupid—but she is exactly this smart. If I'm with Trev, I'm off-limits in a way that'll keep her from crossing any line. It's the only thing that'll stop her. Stop us.

I want to scream at her. I want to apologize to Trev, because there might have been something between us if Mina hadn't ruined me for anyone else. I want to run out of here and slam the door behind me so hard the tiles crack.

I want to press her between the sinks and run my tongue along her collarbone.

"Why are you doing this?" I step toward her, and she backs away, but I just keep coming until her shoulders knock against the mirror. I use that stretch of height I have over Mina to my advantage. I get in her space and stay there. I've never done this before, the aggressive thing. The initiation part has always been the guy's job, but now it's different. I'm different. I can do anything. I can be anything.

I can draw the back of my finger down the soft skin of her neck and let the sound she makes twine deep in my stomach and stay there.

So I do.

"Sophie." It's a warning, a gasp. "I just—I want things to go back to normal. Things need to go back to normal."

"They can't," I say.

She licks her lips. "We can't do this."

"We can," I say.

"But Trev . . ." She trails off. "My mom. Everything. It can't work. You and me—it's not right. You and Trev is right. It's normal. Every-one expects it. I'm trying to help."

"You're trying to hide," I say.

"I can hide if I want."

"I'm saying you don't have to."

She jerks out of my hold. "Of course I do!" she bursts out. "What do you think? That everything's going to be fine if I tell my mom I'm a lesbian? She'd call in an army of priests to start praying. How do you think Trev will feel when he figures out the girl he's been in love with forever screwed his little sister? And everybody at school—do you remember what happened to Holly Jacobs? Do you want *DYKE* spray-painted on your car? Because that's what's waiting for us, Soph. Hiding is safe. Choosing Trev is safe."

There are tears in my eyes, down my cheeks. There's nothing to say to convince her. We don't live in a big city. Mina doesn't come from a family where such things are accepted. She's right, her mother *would* call in a priest. And Trev—no matter what happens, Trev will always get hurt.

Nothing I say will change her mind. Years of loving her taught me that. I hate how trapped she is, how trapped she's made me.

"Trev loves you," she says in the horrified quiet that hangs between us. "He'd be good for you."

"I love Trev," I tell her. "I love him enough that I can't do that to him. I can't use him to hide because it's safe or because you want me to."

"Be smart, Sophie," she says, and I hear more warning than pleading in her voice. A wariness that's never been there before. "Choose him."

I walk away from her—it's almost easy, like another person is controlling me—but when I get to the door, I turn back. She stands at the mirror, watching me through the reflection, and I meet her eyes.

"I'll choose you," I say. "No matter how hard it is. No matter what people say. Every time, I'll choose you. It's up to you to choose me back."

As I close the door behind me, I hear her start to cry.

41

Trev is quiet, leaning against the front door for an endless stretch of time.

There is nothing either of us can say.

There is nothing left to say.

There is just the truth, finally out in the open. I can see the weight of it settling on him, dragging him down. I hate that I've done this, hurt him this much, but at the same time, an undercurrent of relief pulls at me.

He's all I've got left—my best friend by default. The quiet, steady presence in my life that's been there for so long, I'd be lost without him. I've taken advantage of that steadiness so many times, and I hate that I can't stop now.

He comes alive suddenly, like he'd been frozen by the truth I've thrown at him. He straightens against the door and starts talking fast, a staccato burst of sound from a grim mouth: "If it was never about drugs, I have to tell my mom. The police—"

"No, absolutely not."

"But if you think you have a lead—"

"I have *nothing*," I say. "I have Mina's notes on an almost three-year-old cold case. I don't have any evidence that proves she was being threatened. I can't go to Detective James and be like, 'Hey, here's a break in the investigation you think I'm hindering.'"

"But if Kyle explains that he lied, they'll have to believe you."

"No, they won't. There were drugs at the scene. My fingerprints were on the bottle. As far as Detective James is concerned, I'm a liar who's still covering for her dealer. Some notes that Mina wrote about Jackie's case aren't going to change that. But figuring out who was sending Mina threatening notes *will*. Whoever got rid of Jackie killed Mina—and I'm going to find him."

"Are you crazy?" Trev asks. "Mina died because she got too close to figuring it out. And now, what, you want to launch an investigation? Do you have a death wish or something?"

I step even further away from him, a flinch I can't control. He's too wrapped up to notice the hurt I'm throwing off. Or maybe this is what I've pushed him to, this kind of heart twisting that once was Mina's specialty.

"I'm doing this for Mina. Do you really think Jackie's still alive, after three years? That bastard in the mask killed her. And then he killed Mina because she was too close to finding him out. He has to pay."

"Yes, he does. But that's what the police are for. You're gonna get hurt if you keep this up," Trev grits out.

I take a deep breath. "I'm not Mina. I'm not going to keep secrets. I've got Kyle and my friend Rachel helping out. But to get the police to listen to me, I need proof Mina was looking into Jackie's disappearance, that she was being threatened because of it. You and Kyle didn't find the killer's warning notes, did you?"

Trev shook his head.

"So I have to put together a list of people who knew Mina was investigating Jackie and then narrow it down to the likely suspects."

Trev runs his hands through his hair. "This is insane."

"What else am I supposed to do? I can't sit around and hope that the cops will figure it out. I understand that you're trying to move on or whatever, but I can't do that. Not yet."

It's exactly the wrong thing to say to him—I know it before the words are out of my mouth. His gray eyes widen, and his cheeks flush beneath his tan.

"Move on?" He spits out the words like they're poison. "She was my baby sister. I practically raised her after Dad died. I was supposed to be there when she got what she wanted out of life. She was supposed to be the aunt to my kids, and I should've been an uncle to hers. I wasn't supposed to lose her. I would've done *anything* for her."

"Then help me!" I snap at him. "Stop yelling at me and *help* me already. I'm doing this with or without you, but I'd rather do it with you. You understood her."

"I guess I didn't understand her at all," Trev says, and it hits me all over again that Trev didn't just lose Mina. He lost me, too—this shining, bright idea of a me that never was.

I want to touch him, to comfort him somehow, but I

know better. I settle for going toward him a few steps, close enough to touch.

"You understood her," I say. "As much as anyone could, you did. She loved you, Trev. So much."

Trev had been Mina's favorite person. Her second confessor, after me. I think, if I hadn't been at the center of this, she would've told him the truth about herself.

Maybe he would have made it easier. If she could have basked in his acceptance, it might have given her enough strength to break free.

I don't know. I can't ever know. Thinking about it is masochistic, like the hours I spent in rehab, spinning a perfect version of our lives, where she tells everyone and it doesn't matter, a future filled with prom dresses and slow dances and promises that never get broken.

When he looks at me, I feel exposed. For the first time since I've come downstairs, I'm acutely aware of how little I have on. How bright the hall lights are, and how my scars shine white and pink.

There's a clicking sound, and Trev steps forward, away from the front door just as my dad opens it.

There's a long, uncomfortable moment when Dad's eyes flick over my face, tear-stained and too red, to settle on Trev, looking just as bad.

"Trev," Dad says, and it's like he's seven feet tall instead of five foot eight.

"Mr. Winters," Trev says.

I shift from foot to foot, clenching my fists at my sides to keep from scrubbing at my face.

"Sophie, is there a problem here?" Dad asks, still not taking his eyes off Trev.

"No," I say. "Trev was just leaving."

"I think that's for the best," Dad says.

Trev nods. "I'll just— Well, good-bye, Sophie. Bye, sir."

The door's barely shut behind him before Dad is turning to me, opening his mouth. "Just a second," I tell him, and I slip out the front door after Trev before Dad can stop me.

He's already walking down the path.

"Trev!" I call.

He turns.

From where I stand at the bottom of the porch steps, it's like an ocean between us, this new knowledge that stretches us so far from each other.

"The interviews," I say, lowering my voice. "The ones that Mina did about Jackie. They're recorded."

His eyes widen, and he takes a step toward me almost automatically.

"I can't listen to them alone," I confess.

Trev nods. "Tonight?" he asks.

Relief, sweet and simple, rushes through me.

He's always giving me what I can't ask for.

"Tonight," I say.

42

"I can do it myself," I say, clutching the bottle of vitamin E oil.

"No offense, but your hand still looks like raw hamburger."

Mina is not patient or soft. She grabs the bottle, ignoring my protests. It's normal, her being bossy and my falling into line, so I shrug my robe off one shoulder as she settles behind me on my bed.

I bite my lip, looking down at the carpet. I can feel her eyes on my shoulder where metal dug into the skin, mangling it. Her fingers don't linger as she gently smooths the oil over my scars with determined efficiency. "This stuff smells like my grandma." She gets up and moves to my front.

"Lavender," I explain. "Mom got it at that natural health food store in Chico. Here, let me." I try to grab the bottle away from her, but she dangles it out of my reach. "Nice," I say. "Way to taunt the gimp."

"I dare you to call yourself that in front of your mom. She'll flip." Mina smiles wickedly at me.

"She'd probably just send me to the shrink for another six months."

"She means well. That whole week you were in coma-land, she was freaking out. Soap-opera style. It was intense." Her fingers trace over the top of my shoulder, the new rough landscape that my body has become.

"She keeps acting like things are going to go back to normal."

"Well, that's stupid," Mina says. "Things are different. But it doesn't mean they have to be awful."

"I feel awful, sometimes," I whisper. "I mean, look at me." I hold my arms out, my robe slips all the way off my shoulders, and the scar on my chest, a raw split of skin, is even uglier in the light. "I'm gross. And it's not like things are going to change. She needs to realize that."

"Oh, Soph." Mina practically deflates. She sits down next to me. "What happened to you was horrible," she says. "Beyond horrible. And it isn't fair or right that Trev and I came out of it fine and you . . ." She trails off. "But *gross*?" She presses her hand against my heart. Her thumb brushes up against the edge of the scar on my chest. "This isn't gross. You know what I think when I see this?"

I shake my head.

Her voice drops. She's whispering, a secret for just the two of us: "I think about how strong you are. You didn't stop fighting, even when your heart stopped. You came back."

The unspoken "to me" hangs between us. We both hear it, but neither of us is brave enough to say it.

"You don't . . . you don't ever wish they hadn't saved you, right?" Mina asks. She's staring hard at her hand, like she can't bear to be looking in my eyes if I give the wrong answer.

I can't tell her the truth. She'd be almost as scared of it as I am.

"Of course not," I say.

The truth?

I don't know.

Maybe.

Sometimes.

Yes.

43

When I get back into the house, Dad is waiting in the hallway.

"What was that about?" he asks.

"Nothing," I say.

"Sophie, you've been crying." He reaches out, and I move away when his hand makes contact with my cheek. "Did Trev say something—"

"We were talking about Mina," I interrupt. "I got sad. Trev wasn't—I was just sad." I rub at my arms, stepping farther away from him. "What are you doing home? Did you forget something?"

"Your shots are today," Dad says. "Didn't your mother tell you?"

"Oh. She did. I forgot."

"I thought I'd take you."

I can't stop the hesitation that passes over me, and I can tell he's hurt by it. It's the barest flash in his lined face, but it's there.

I remember, suddenly, all those days he took off work so he could drive me back and forth to physical therapy. How he'd sat in the lobby doing paperwork while I bullied my body into working better. How he'd always wrapped his arms around me afterward.

"Sure," I say. "I'd like that."

On the drive to the doctor's office, we talk about ordinary things. About the soccer team that Dad's dental office sponsors, how he's thinking about retiring from assistant coaching because Mom wants him to take swing dancing classes with her.

"Have you thought any more about college?" Dad asks as we pass the post office.

I glance at him. "Not really," I say.

I can't. Not yet. There are things I have to do first.

"I know how hard it's been for you, honey," he says. "But this is an important time. We need to start thinking about it."

"Okay," I say. Anything to get him to stop.

Dr. Shute's office is in a brick building across from the railroad tracks, and Dad pauses a second before getting out of the car, like he's sure I'll snap at him the way I did when he took me to therapy with David. So I stand outside the car, wait until he gets out, and we're both quiet as we walk inside.

He stays in the lobby when the nurse leads me back, and I have to bite my tongue to keep from asking him to come with me. I tell myself I don't need him to hold my hand, that I'd learned how to handle getting the shots solo at Seaside. I've learned to depend on myself. I sit down on the exam table and wait.

The door opens, and Dr. Shute pops her head in the

exam room and smiles at me, her red glasses hanging on a beaded chain around her neck. "It's been a while, Sophie." After a minute of small talk and a rundown of my pain level, she leaves so I can get undressed. I take my shirt off, lying facedown on the exam table in my bra. The table is cool against my belly through the crackly paper, and I dig into my jeans pocket and come up with my phone as Dr. Shute knocks and comes back inside. I page through my music and put in my earbuds, letting the sound warp my senses. I press my forehead into the cradle of my arms, concentrating on my breathing.

"Let me know when you're ready," Dr. Shute says. She knows the deal, knows I can't stand to see the long epidural needle, knows how freaked out it makes me—that even after all this time, after all the surgeries, I can't handle a stupid needle sinking into me.

I'll never be ready. I hate this. I'd almost prefer another surgery.

"Okay, do it," I say.

The first one goes into the left side of my spine, in the middle of my back, where the pain is the worst. I breathe in and out, my clenched fists crumpling the paper liner set over the exam table. She moves down, three more on my left side, ending deep in my lower back. The long needles pierce through me, the cortisone pushes into my inflamed muscles, buying me some time. Then four on the right side. By the time she's moved to my neck, I'm breathing hard, the music fuzzy in my ears, and I want it to stop, please, stop.

I want Mina holding my hand, brushing my hair off my face, telling me it'll be okay.

On the way home, Dad pulls into Big Ed's drive-through and orders a chocolate–peanut butter milk shake. It's exactly what I need at that moment, and tears well up in my eyes when he does it without being asked. It's like I'm fourteen again. I never thought I'd want to go back there, to the days of physical therapy and canes, floating on a cloud of Oxy, but I do. Because then, at least, she'd been alive.

When Dad hands over the shake, he meets my eyes, not letting go of the cup. "Are you okay, honey?" he asks, and I want to hide inside the concern in his voice.

"I'll be fine," I say. "Just stings a little."

We both know I'm lying.

44

"I hate you!"

I duck just as a shoe comes flying out of Mina's room, closely followed by Trev.

"Jerk!" Another shoe sails down the hall, and Trev barely looks at me as he stalks past, his face stormy. He yanks the back door open and charges outside, leaving the door swinging on the hinges.

I can hear Mina muttering angrily underneath her breath, and I peek around the corner, knocking lightly on her open door. She whirls around, and my chest tightens when I see she's been crying.

"What's wrong?" I ask her.

"Oh." She brushes the tears away. "Nothing. It's fine."

"Um, bullshit."

She flops on the bed, on top of a pile of papers scattered across her comforter. "Trev's a jerk."

I sit down next to her. "What'd he do?"

"He said I was being too *open*," Mina snarls.

"Okay," I say slowly. "You're gonna have to fill me in more than that."

Mina rolls over to her side, freeing up some of the papers she's lying on. She grabs a stapled stack, handing it to me. "It's my personal statement for the *Beacon* internship. I asked him to read it, and

because he's an *asshole*"—she shouts the last word so he can hear it—
"he told me I shouldn't submit it."

"Can I read it?" I ask.

Mina shrugs, throwing an arm over her eyes dramatically. "Whatever," she says, like it doesn't matter, which means, of course, that it does.

She's quiet for the five minutes that it takes me to read. The only sound in the room is the rustling of paper when she shifts on the bed.

When I finish, I stare at the last sentence for a long time, trying to think of what to say.

"Is it that bad?" Mina asks in a small voice.

"No," I say. "No," I say again, because she looks so unsure, and it makes me want to curl up next to her and tell her she's wonderful until she stops. "It's beautiful." I squeeze her hand.

"It's supposed to be about what shaped me," Mina says, almost like she needs an excuse. "It was what I thought of first. Trev said he'd proof it for me. I didn't think he'd get so mad."

"Do you want me to go talk to him?"

Her gray eyes, still red and puffy, light up. "Would you?"

"Yeah. Be right back."

I leave her in her room and walk outside to the shed in the backyard that Trev's converted into a shop. I can hear the rhythmic scrape of sandpaper against wood as I walk up to the doors.

Trev's hunched over his workbench, sanding a pair of triangle trellises for my garden. I watch for a moment, his broad fingers moving confidently over the cedar, smoothing the rough edges. I step forward into his domain, breathing in the smell of sawdust and the sharp bite of motor oil.

"I don't want to talk about it, Soph," he says before I can speak. He keeps his back to me, moving to the other side of the trellis. The sandpaper rasps against the wood, motes of sawdust floating up in the air.

"He was her dad, too. She should be able to write about him."

Trev's shoulders tense underneath the thin black cotton of his T-shirt. "She can write whatever she wants. Just not . . . about that."

"I didn't know. She never told me," I say haltingly. "That you two were with him when he died."

"Yeah, well, we were." I hate how flat his voice is, like it's the only way he can actually admit it. "Happened kind of fast."

I don't know what else to say. It makes me ache to think of ten-year-old Trev playing ball with his dad and watching him drop from a brain aneurysm between one pitch and the next.

"I didn't realize how much she remembered," Trev says hoarsely. His back is to me, which might be the only reason he's still talking. "I told her to look away. She was good about listening to me when we were little. And she never talked about it afterward. I thought she blocked it out or something . . . hoped she did."

"She didn't. So you guys need to talk about it."

"No."

"Yes." I know I'm crossing a line here. Spurred on by Mina, unheeding in her shadow.

He finally turns around, holding on to the sandpaper like a lifeline.

"Trev," I say softly. "It's been years. If you never have before . . . you have to."

He shakes his head, but when I hug him, he falls into me like I've cut him off at the knees. I hold on tight, press my palms flat against his shoulders, two points of warmth seeping through his shirt.

When I look up, over his shoulder, I can see Mina standing on the porch, watching us.

I hold out my hand, beckoning, beseeching, and she steps forward hesitantly, off the porch, one step, two, steadier now, until she's in front of me, wrapping her arms around Trev's waist as I pull back.

"I'm sorry," he whispers, or maybe it's her, or both of them who say it, and I move away, out of the shed, toward the house.

Like a silent guard, I sit on the porch, the indistinct murmur of their voices blending with the crickets and night noises, and I wish that things were easy.

45

I'm supposed to rest after I get my shots, but when Dad goes back to work, I drive downtown to the *Harper Beacon* office. The newspaper is in a slant-roofed, mustard-yellow building from the seventies that's next to the best—and only—Mexican restaurant in town. The air is fragrant with cilantro and carne asada as I push through the swinging doors.

The guy at the reception desk points me to the right when I ask him about internships, and I make my way down a winding hallway with framed front pages on the walls, their headlines blaring. The hall leads to a room neatly divided into a dozen or so gray cubicles, the overhead lights bathing everything in a sickly blue sheen.

I make my way through the maze of cubicles. Every few seconds, a phone rings or someone's printer screeches. There's a low hum of computers and voices. I can just picture her standing in the center of it all, that smile on her face as the buzz washed over her.

This had been Mina's first step toward what she always wanted. To become a part of the world outside of our dusty little town, "to *contribute*," as she used to put it.

Instead, she'd been reduced to a handful of stories written *about* her instead of *by* her.

"Mr. Wells?" I tap on the cubicle wall with his name on it.

"Just one second," he says before I can move into the cube. All his focus is on his computer screen as he types, giving me time to look him over.

He's younger than I thought he'd be. Only a few years older than Trev, so maybe twenty-three or twenty-four. His button-down shirt is half-tucked into his jeans, and he's wearing black Chucks. He's cute in a rumpled sort of way, like he spends a lot of time running his hands through his brown hair, thinking big thoughts.

Mina had liked him. A lot, actually. Half of our conversations when I was in Portland had been about her internship and Mr. Wells and how much he was teaching her about digital media and what a great journalist he was.

She hadn't mentioned he was cute.

Probably on purpose.

"Okay, hi," he says. He spins around in his chair and looks me up and down. "Internship apps, right? Jenny has them, she's right over—"

"I'm not here about an internship," I interrupt. "I'm here because of Mina Bishop."

The easy cheer in his brown eyes dims. "Mina," he repeats sadly, and sighs.

"I'm Sophie Winters," I say, and then I don't say anything else. I just wait for the understanding to snap across his face.

It's there instantly. He is a reporter, after all. Even if the police weren't allowed to release my name to the press as a minor, everyone knew. "What can I help you with, Sophie?"

"Can I sit?"

He nods, gesturing to the stool in the corner of the cube. I balance as best I can, my lower back, still red and sensitive from the shots, flaring hot with pain. "I found some notes of Mina's." I open my bag, grab the printouts I'd made of the excerpts from Mina's time line, and hand them to him. "I was wondering if she ever mentioned to you that she was looking into Jackie Dennings's disappearance."

Mr. Wells's lips press together tight, then disappear as he scans the three pages I've given him. "This is . . ." He looks up. "This was Mina's work?"

I nod.

"Is there more?" he asks.

"No," I say. It comes out of my mouth, all instinct. I slip into that part of me that can bullshit so easily. It knocks too close to the addicted pieces, the ones I've beaten into submission, and I can feel them stir.

He shakes his head. "I'm sorry, but Mina never brought Jackie up. And she would have if she was interested in the case. It was one of the first stories I covered for the paper. I suppose she just never got around to it?"

I think about Mina saving the articles on Jackie's disappearance. No way she wouldn't have noticed that Wells had written a lot of them. "Maybe," I say. "Anyway, that's all I wanted to know." I get up off the stool, leaning on his desk to keep my balance. "Did you have any theories?"

"About Jackie?" Mr. Wells leans back in his chair, threading his hands to cradle his head as he thinks. "The detective in charge was convinced it was the boyfriend."

"What about you?"

Mr. Wells grins, his enthusiasm over an old story almost infectious. It reminds me of Mina, of the hunger in her, to *know* . . . to *tell*. "Sam James is a good detective—" he starts.

"Detective James was in charge of Jackie's case?" I interrupt.

"He was," Mr. Wells says, frowning.

"Right," I say quickly. "Anyway, sorry. You were saying? About Jackie?"

"Matthew Clarke is a solid suspect," Mr. Wells says.

"But you don't think he did it."

"Can't really say. It's a decent theory, considering the lack of motive elsewhere, but the evidence just isn't there."

"Did Matt have a motive?"

"You're awfully interested in this," Mr. Wells says.

I shrug. "I guess I just thought . . . it was important to Mina, you know? Working here, for you. She was always talking about how much she learned from you. I thought maybe if I did some research on the stuff Mina was doing, it'd help me, I dunno, move on. It's been hard, since, you know . . ." I trail off, resisting the urge to widen my eyes, because that'd be pushing it.

Mr. Wells sets the copy of Mina's notes on the desk, his expression softening. "I understand," he says. "Look, the Dennings case, it's a dead story. Whatever happened to that girl, it's doubtful that after all this time it'll ever be known. That's the nature of things. You're better off just letting it go."

I nod, like I'm agreeing with him instead of searching for

a way to bust both cases wide open. "I should get home," I say. "Thanks for taking the time to talk with me. I appreciate it."

I'm almost out of his cube when he stops me. "Sophie, what happened at Booker's Point that night?"

I look back at him over my shoulder, and it's there again, that gleam in his eyes that reminds me of Mina. She'd had that look that night. She'd been practically vibrating from it, the excitement humming beneath her skin, close enough to the truth to taste it.

"Off the record?" I ask, because I'm not stupid.

He grins approvingly. This guy has to have all his girl interns wanting to jump him. Probably some of the guys, too. "I'd prefer a comment *on* the record."

"I'm sure you would," I say. "Thanks again for your time."

I don't turn around to confirm it, but I can tell he's watching me the entire time I walk away.

46

I dig in the dirt, making small furrows. "Will you hand me that flat?" I point to the seedlings I nursed under fluorescent lights for weeks, waiting until they were strong enough to transplant. I was pretty proud of them; they were the first I'd grown under the lights Dad had bought for my birthday.

Mina sets her book down and gets up off the wicker chair so she can move the flat closer to me. She balances delicately on the edge of the redwood bed, eyeing the soil suspiciously. "What are these going to be, again?"

"Tomatoes."

"Seems like a lot of trouble for tomatoes," Mina says. "Couldn't you just get the plants at the garden center? Or one of those plastic upside-down-hanging planters to put them in?"

"These are different. They're purple."

"Really?"

"Yes, I ordered the seeds specially."

Mina beams. "You could've just gotten me flowers."

I set a seedling carefully into the dirt. "Where's the fun in that?"

"We can make purple pasta sauce," she suggests.

"As long as you're doing the cooking."

"Oh, come on—remember that vegetable soup you tried to make?

There was only a teeny tiny fire that time. You're getting better."

"I think I'll stick to what I'm good at." I dig a third hole, lift another seedling out of the tray, and set the fragile roots into their new home.

"Aren't you glad I made you get a hobby?" Mina asks, grinning. "When you become a world-famous botanist, I can say I'm responsible whenever I brag about you."

"I think out of the two of us, you're going to end up being the world-famous one," I say, laughing.

"Well, that goes without saying," Mina answers. "I'll make sure to thank you when I win my Pulitzer."

"I'm honored."

Mina goes back to her chair and book, and I go back to my tomatoes. She flaps the neck of her tank top back and forth. "It's so hot," she complains.

I grind my good knee into the dirt, spacing the seedlings evenly apart, neat rows of three across, four down. "The twentieth's coming up," I say finally. "You okay?"

Mina shrugs, eyes glued to the page. The sun beats down my back, and I wonder if I've gone too far.

For a moment, I think that's all I'm going to get out of her. But then she looks up at me. "I'm going to spend the day with Mom and Trev. She wants to go to Dad's grave in the morning."

"Do you . . . do you go out there a lot?" I ask. I'm curious, all of a sudden, and she seems willing to actually talk about it for once. I know that Mr. Bishop is buried in Harper's Bluff, that he grew up here and that's the main reason they moved back after his death. And the only reason I know that is the first time Mina and I got drunk, she'd slurred it out against my shoulder and cried and didn't—or just maybe wouldn't—remember the next morning.

47

Trev's late by almost twenty minutes. I've almost given up hope he'll show when the doorbell rings. My parents are out on their weekly date night, so I let him in the house and we stand awkwardly in the foyer for a moment. I don't know what to say to him now that he knows.

"Let's go upstairs," I say.

He follows me up the stairs, and I pause at the top, my back aching at the injection points. When we get to my room, he hovers in the doorway as I walk over to my desk and sit down.

He closes the door behind him and stands at the edge of my bed, waiting.

"Kyle filled you in on Mina's notes?" I ask.

Trev nods. "We looked at the time line and some of the articles she saved."

"There are three interviews," I say. "Mina talked to Matt Clarke, Jackie's grandfather, and her little sister, Amy, all in December. Mina dropped the case after talking to Amy, because she got those threats. Something made her go after it again in February, but I'm not sure what."

"She was always bad at leaving things alone," he mutters.

"She probably figured the risk was worth it."

It's almost a relief, his frustration. It makes me feel less guilty about my own.

"Did she ever mention Jackie to you?" I ask. "Even in passing?"

"Not since you guys were freshmen. She was really into figuring it out back then. Remember? It was kind of creepy."

"She wanted to know what happened. People were still talking about it when I got out of the hospital and back to school. She was curious," I say.

"She was too curious," Trev says, and his voice cracks on the words. "She was fucking reckless."

"You can't blame her," I say, and it comes out low and shaky. "Yes, she was stupid not to tell anyone what was going on. But it isn't her fault. It's *his* fault. He killed her, whoever the hell he is. And he's going to pay."

Trev looks at me with shiny eyes, and I can see it happen, the way he pulls himself together, seems to grow a foot, his shoulders squaring. "Play Matt's first. We were friends. Maybe I'll catch something."

I click on Matt's interview, keying up my speakers. There's a bit of static, and then:

"Okay. You ready, Matt?"

The moment her voice fills the room, I'm flooded with it, the pain and relief that comes from hearing her again. Trev sinks onto the edge of the bed, his fingers knotted, eyes closed.

Hearing her, it's not the same.

But it's all we have.

"How did you and Jackie meet?" Mina asks.

I force myself to focus on Matt's answer. He has a deep, slow voice, and he pauses between his sentences, like he's thinking carefully about each word. *"Our moms were friends,"* he says. *"She was always around, you know? Girl next door. I asked her out in eighth grade, and that was it."*

"That's a long time to be together," Mina says, and I can almost hear the encouraging smile in her voice.

"Yeah," Matt agrees. *"She was special."*

"It must have been really hard for you when she went missing."

There's a long silence, only broken by rustles and a clinking sound. *"Yeah. It was horrible for everyone. Everyone loved Jackie."*

I look anywhere but at Trev as the recording continues. Mina asks Matt about school, about his and Jackie's friends, about Jackie's involvement in youth group and soccer; ordinary, unassuming questions that won't make him suspicious. Slowly but surely, she gets him to open up to her, until she's asking about the weeks before Jackie disappeared, about Detective James and how he'd treated Matt during the questioning.

"That guy's an ass," Matt scoffs, an edge in his voice. *"He thought he had it all figured out. I wanted to let him search my truck, but my uncle Rob kept saying they had to get a warrant. Detective James spent so much time thinking I did it, he didn't look anywhere else, and the case got cold. Everyone always says that the first three days are the most important when someone goes missing."*

"But he let you go."

"He didn't have anything on me," Matt says.

On the recording, a phone rings. *"Just one more question before you get that. You and Jackie—you guys were, you know, intimate, right?"*

There's another long pause while the phone rings and rings. I can picture Mina sitting there, baldly asking Matt if he'd had sex with his girlfriend, that calm smile on her face, like she wasn't crossing some line.

"I don't think that's any of your business," Matt says. *"And I think we're done now."*

"Of course," Mina says. There's a rustling sound, and then the recording cuts off abruptly.

I look over at Trev, and my heart jackknifes in my chest at the sheen in his eyes. "We don't have to listen to any more," I say quickly.

His face hardens and he says quietly, "Play them."

I press Play.

Mina's interview with Jackie's grandfather is focused on Jackie's childhood. She doesn't ask any questions about the case, but once Jack Dennings starts talking about Jackie's teen years, Mina keeps steering the interview back to her relationship with Matt.

I can hear the whistle of the six o'clock train downtown as I grit my teeth and click on the final interview—the one with Jackie's sister, Amy. As it begins to play, I realize the file's less than a minute long. Both Matt's and Jack's interviews were more than fifteen.

"What's that?" a girl's voice asks.

"I was going to record the interview," Mina says. *"That okay?"*

"No," Amy says. "I told you, I'm not supposed to talk to you. Turn it off."

"Okay," Mina says. There's a shuffling sound, and then the recording cuts off abruptly.

Trev frowns. "That's it?"

"I guess." I do a quick global search of Amy's name to see if Mina had transcribed the interview somewhere instead of recording it, but all that comes up is the time line document. "She didn't put the interview in here."

"What do you think they talked about?"

"Well, when I talk to Amy, I'll ask her. She's friends with Kyle's little brother; I'm gonna try to nail down her schedule."

"You do that, and I'll call Matt," Trev says.

"Are you still in touch?" Trev had never spent much time with Mina or me at school. I knew who his friends were, but I'd never been around them much.

"I've seen him a few times since I left for college. Playing soccer with the old team, you know."

"How bad was Matt into drugs?" I ask. "Are we talking a little pot, or pills or . . ."

"Meth," Trev says.

"Shit."

"Yeah. But that didn't happen until after Jackie disappeared. Or at least, none of our group knew about it. I mean, he was definitely getting to a place where people were worried. His dad left when we were freshmen, and Matt got into a lot of fights after. The whole thing with Jackie just kind of pushed him over the edge."

"Do you think he could've killed her?"

Trev gets up from my bed, walking over to my window and pushing my blue curtains aside to look down at the front yard. "Back then, I would've said no way."

"What about now?"

Trev doesn't say anything for a while, just stares out my window, his jaw tense. "I have no idea," he says. "Maybe they were in love. Maybe she hated him. Maybe he killed her. I'm not really trusting my ability to judge people right now."

I look away.

"I should go," Trev says. "I'll call Matt."

"See if we can meet him tomorrow," I say. "Maybe he said something to Mina off the record or talked to someone else about Mina's interest in Jackie. Or maybe he did it."

As I talk, I lean forward on my desk so I can push myself up and out of my chair. My back is killing me. After the shots, it's always worse for a day or two before it gets better, and I can't hide my sharp intake of breath when I get to my feet too fast.

Trev turns at the sound, but I make it to my bed and ease myself down belly-first before he can move to help me.

"You okay?" he asks.

"I'll find Jack Dennings's address," I say, ignoring the question. "We can go see him, too." I'm beginning to feel desperate about all of this. I don't even know how to solve the murder I witnessed, let alone a three-year-old cold case.

I close my eyes. I've been staying up late rereading articles about Mina's murder and Jackie's disappearance. Every time I make an effort to sleep, I'm back at Booker's Point with her, and I can't think about that. So I don't sleep. Not when I can help it.

But I can't fight it much longer.

There's a hand. Warm against my shoulder.

Trev's hand.

I tilt my head to the side so I can see him. He's watching me, sitting beside me, and I don't look away.

There's a realization that's settling in him, something I think he's suspected but tried to deny for months, if not years. An acceptance that's not begrudging, but hesitant. I can see it in his face, feel it when he touches me.

"Your back hurts?" he asks.

I tuck my hands underneath my chin and nod. He rests his hand on my shoulder, and that constant pressure, that bloom of heat, is another reminder of how present he is. How gone she is.

"Need anything before I go?"

I shake my head. I'm afraid to speak. Afraid I'll do something stupid, like press into his touch.

I can't do that to him—to myself, to her.

I won't.

"Do you think she's up there?" I mumble. The words are half-lost in the pillow, and he has to tilt forward to hear them. "Watching us from heaven?"

"I do." He brushes hair off my forehead with his free hand, and the backs of his fingers graze my temple.

"Must be nice."

"Sometimes." Trev keeps stroking my hair, a light touch

that spreads through me like a warm blanket. "Sometimes it's hell, thinking of her watching everything and not getting to be a part of it."

We stay like that for a while, with her memory wrapped around us. I'm half-asleep, eyes closed, when he leans over and presses his lips against my forehead.

His footsteps echo as he leaves my bedroom and I tell myself I'm crying from the pain.

48

"You know, the whole point of being on a sailboat is to sail," Trev says.

Mina laughs, and I can feel the vibration of it through my skin. She's resting her head on my stomach, and the two of us are lying out on the deck of the *Sweet Sorrow*, Trev at the helm. Both of them are reading. Trev's got some paperback mystery that he sticks in his pocket when he needs to get up and man the sails. Mina's been absorbed in the same hardcover about Watergate for a week, taking precise notes in her journal. She props it on her knees, highlighting passages as she goes.

I am content to lie here and listen to them call back and forth to each other, their familiar, good-natured bickering more soothing than anything else could be. We've been dead in the water for an hour, Trev too absorbed to chase what little wind there is.

"I don't see you pulling the rope things to get us going," Mina says.

"It's called the rigging, Mina. And I'm at a really good part." Trev holds his book aloft.

She squints at the title. "I finished that last week. Want to know who the murderer is?"

"Don't ruin it for him," I protest.

"See, Soph's on my side. Two against one."

Mina rolls her eyes and turns a page.

I fall asleep eventually, lulled by the sun and the rocking of the boat—and by the pills I took before I got in the car this morning.

When I wake up, the sun's sinking fast, and Mina has moved up to sit with Trev. I watch them for a moment, their dark heads bent together, legs dangling off the side of the boat. And I catch the end of Trev's sentence, still half-asleep and hazy. ". . . worried about her?"

"It's those stupid pills they have her on."

I freeze. They're talking about me.

"She needs them. She's in pain."

"I know, but lately . . . Never mind. I'm being stupid."

"Hey, no." Trev puts his arm around her, pulling her into him. She rests her head on his shoulder. "I get it. You're worried. We all worry about her."

"*You* worry about her," she says pointedly. There's resentment in her voice, and resignation.

A long silence. Trev pulls away from her, and they stare at each other. "Does that bother . . . Is that a problem?" he asks.

My heart thumps. I should cough, call out one of their names, anything to draw attention to the fact that I'm awake. It'd be the right thing to do.

But I stay where I am, eavesdropping in the worst possible way on the two people I love the most. I wait for her to answer. A part of me can't help but hope that this will be *the* moment—when she finally tells him, when he finally realizes the truth.

"Of course it's not a problem," Mina says, and it's so smooth, the way she says it, like there aren't years of denial and heaps of lies and boys who touched our bodies but never had a chance at our hearts.

"You sure?" Trev asks. "I know she's your best friend. If it's weird—"

"Oh, whatever," Mina says lightly. "You've never been able to hide things. It's why you suck at poker. Everyone knows. Even—"

"Sophie," Trev says. He's glanced over his shoulder, caught sight of me. "You're awake."

I'm looking out at the water, away from the two of them, but my cheeks heat up. I'm still not sure what I ever did to inspire that need, that love in them both. I'm not honest and steady like Trev or bright and burning like Mina. I'm just me, with dirt underneath my fingernails and a weakness for love and drugs. Somehow, though, I've managed to tie us all in knots, and I don't know how we can break free.

"We should get back." Trev is up and pulling at the rigging while Mina stays where she is.

I can feel her watching me.

But when I look at her, she's turned toward the docks, blocking me out.

Cowards, both of us.

49

My mother's in the kitchen the next morning, waiting for me.

"Where are you going?" she asks over her coffee cup.

"Breakfast with some friends." I'd texted Kyle and Rachel the night before, and they're meeting Trev and me at the Gold Street Diner before we head over to talk to Matt.

"Do those friends include Trev?" Mom asks. Her eyebrows practically disappear, they rise so high. "Your father said he was here yesterday."

I grab the coffeepot and pour some into a travel mug. It's only a ten-minute drive to the diner, but I'd slept badly. "Yeah."

"Does Mrs. Bishop know?"

I dump too much sugar into the cup, popping the lid on it. "Mrs. Bishop's in Santa Barbara. Anyway, Trev's twenty. I don't think he needs her permission to hang out with anyone."

"Sophie." Mom's got a worried look on her face. "You and that family . . ." She stops.

Mom isn't forgiving. After the crash, she'd tried to separate me from both Mina and him, and it hadn't worked then, either.

"What about me and 'that family'?" I demand. "I grew
up with Trev. I'm not going to throw that away."

"I know how that boy feels about you," she says. "Are
you still on birth control?"

Anger spikes inside me. It isn't any of her business. I
hate that she automatically assumes this is all about sex;
like with me, that's the only thing it could be about.

"I'm not sleeping with him," I say. And I wait until the
relief pulls across her face. I wait, because I want to hurt her
like she's hurt me. "Not anymore, at least," I add.

Mom flinches. I tell myself I don't care, that this is what
I wanted, but I regret it almost instantly.

"I'll be back later." I walk past her and out of the kitchen
before she can say anything.

I lock the front door behind me and swing my bag over
my shoulder, my coffee in my free hand. Trev's getting out
of his truck as I walk down the path.

"We're meeting Matt in an hour at his apartment," Trev
says. He pauses, his eyes darting to his truck. "You want to
drive to the diner?"

I know it makes him nervous to drive with me, so I say,
"Sure." I catch the keys when he tosses them and climb into
the driver's seat. Trev slides in next to me, buckling his seat
belt as I turn the key in the ignition.

"I forgot to tell you last night—I talked to Mr. Wells, the
reporter in charge of Mina's internship."

Trev's been carefully looking out the window, concentrating on the trimmed hedges and tidy older houses that
fill my neighborhood. But at the mention of Mr. Wells, he

turns to face me so fast, I'm afraid he might strain something. "Tom Wells?" he demands.

"Yes." I turn off my street and head toward the railroad tracks.

"Don't talk to him," Trev says, and it sounds like an order.

"Why? What's wrong with him?"

"He was bugging Mom, after Mina . . . after it happened. Showing up at Mass, trying to get her to talk, wanting to do a profile on Mina. I told him to leave us alone, but then he started calling the house, saying he had some of Mina's stuff from her desk after the cops searched it. He wouldn't stop until I came and got it."

"I just went over there to ask him if Mina had talked to him about Jackie," I say. "He said she didn't. But he tried to get me to talk about Mina on the record."

Trev's hands clench and unclench rhythmically; I can see it out of the corner of my eye as the truck rumbles over the railroad tracks and I turn onto a side street lined with dingy industrial buildings. The road's rough here, bad asphalt that the county's never bothered to replace, and the truck jerks back and forth when I hit the potholes.

"I didn't talk to Wells about anything important," I assure him.

"I know you didn't," he says, and relief unfurls inside me that at least he still knows that hasn't changed. He still trusts me with some things.

"What did he give you?" I ask as I pull into the parking lot. The diner in front of us is a squat little building made up of two big rooms with the bathrooms on the outside instead of in. It's painted an eye-smarting shade of yellow, with wind chimes made out of old silverware dangling from the porch.

"It was just a bunch of half-filled notebooks, some pens, and a few pictures. I didn't really look carefully through it," Trev admits. "I haven't . . . It was right after, and Mom was still . . ." He stops, looking away from me. "It was hard," he says finally. "Afterward. You were gone, and I was so mad at you, and Mom was . . . I didn't have anyone. And I just—I couldn't. I kept the door to Mina's room shut and I put the package in the garage and tried to forget about it."

I want to reach out and grab his hand or raise my own to squeeze his shoulder, like he'd do for me. But I'd probably make things worse.

All we ever do is hold it in. It's the only way to keep going.

"Kyle and Rachel are waiting for us," I say.

Trev nods. We get out of the truck and head into the diner. It's noisy inside, the counter lined with old-time regulars on their stools, sipping black coffee and reading the local paper. The dining room is crammed with tables and mismatched chairs, with just inches between for the waitress to navigate. Rachel and Kyle are sitting in the corner next to the picture window.

"You must be Trev." Rachel smiles. "I'm Rachel."

"What happened to your eye?" I ask Kyle as Rachel and Trev shake hands. He looks up from his coffee, his right eye swollen and purple.

"I punched him," Trev says.

"What?"

Rachel laughs. "Seriously?" she asks Kyle.

"It's not a big deal," Kyle mutters.

Trev shrugs and sits down. "He deserved it."

"Okay, no more punching," I say, shaking my head. Punching wasn't going to solve anything. "Let's just all get along. We all want the same thing."

After we order our food, we get down to business.

"I asked Tanner about Amy," Kyle says. "He told me that she has soccer practice tomorrow from five to six. I figured you could talk to her then."

"I just hope she'll talk to us," I say. "If she didn't want Mina recording her interviews, I don't know why she bothered to do one in the first place."

"Her family probably just doesn't like reporters," Trev says with a scowl.

"Do you want me to go with you to see Matt?" Kyle asks. "He knows me pretty well because of Adam."

"Trev's coming," I say. "But thanks. I think we've got another job for you." I nudge Trev with my elbow. "Do you think it'd be okay if Kyle and Rachel went over to your house? They can go through the package from the *Beacon*. Maybe there's something in Mina's notebooks."

"That's a good idea," Trev says. "If you want to dig around the garage, you can. It's the only place I haven't finished searching yet. There's still a lot to go through."

"I've got time," Rachel says. "You in, Kyle?"

Mouth full of coffee, Kyle nods.

"I'm friends with your brother. And Kyle Miller."

"Oh yeah." Matt's smile widens. "Come on in."

Matt's place is neat and clean. Two brindle pit bulls jump and wiggle up to me, trying to lick my face as we walk through the doorway. He calls them off and opens the back door for them. I search as subtly as I can for any sign that Matt has relapsed. The house smells like smoke and there's a china bowl with burn marks almost overflowing with cigarette butts, but when I look down, I don't see any roaches, just yellow filters. There are no beer bottles or caps, no mysterious baggies in plain sight, no pipes—not even a bottle of Visine or NyQuil.

All of it could be hidden somewhere. When getting high is the only thing you can think about, you get pretty smart about keeping it a secret.

"How's your mom doing?" Matt asks Trev.

"You know." Trev shrugs. "It's better for her, being with my aunt, I think."

"That's good. What about you?"

Trev shrugs again. Matt reaches out, claps Trev on his shoulder. "I'm sorry, man." He looks at me. "Hey, you guys want something to drink? I've got soda and water."

"I'm okay," I say.

"So what's up?" Matt asks after we've settled on the peeling vinyl couch. He sits down across from us in an armchair.

"Well, it's kinda weird," Trev says. "I'm going through Mina's stuff; I want to have it packed up when my mom comes home. I found this list of names in her desk, and yours was on it. I was wondering what the list was about. I didn't know you guys were friendly."

"We weren't," Matt says. "Not really. She didn't tell you about the story she was doing on Jackie?"

"No," Trev says.

"It was for the *Beacon*. She said she was doing a profile for Jackie's birthday and asked me for an interview. I said okay and talked to her. When I never saw anything come out in the paper, I just figured she hadn't finished it before . . ." Matt trails off uncomfortably.

"What did she want to know?" Trev asks.

"Normal stuff. How Jackie and I had started dating, what our plans had been."

"Did she ask you about the case?" I ask.

"Nah," Matt says. "Mina knew I had nothing to do with it. Detective James is an asshole on a power trip."

I keep my expression neutral, thinking about how Mina had Matt as Suspect Number One on her list.

"What else did you guys talk about?" I ask.

"Um, she asked how long we'd been together. We talked about soccer, how Jackie ran for student body president junior year. She must have bought a case of glitter glue for all those signs we put up."

Trev grins. "I forgot about that. She freaked out when she ran out of pink."

Caught in the memory, Matt laughs, then sobers suddenly, running a hand through his black hair. "Sometimes it's like she was here just yesterday," he says. "She always made me laugh, even when everything else sucked."

Absently, he digs something out of his pocket, flipping it over in his fingers, and I see it's a six-month sobriety chip.

"Six months is awesome." I gesture at the chip.

His fingers tighten around it. "You in the program?"

"I've got a little over ten months."

"Good for you," he says. "The meetings are a big help, but it's still hard sometimes."

"Yeah, it's tough. But you know, it's just one—"

"'One day at a time.'" He finishes the slogan and looks up at me with a rueful smile. "That's all we've got, right?"

"Something like that." I smile back, letting it be my excuse to stare into his eyes. Had it been him that night? It's so hard to clearly remember the killer's voice, to remember exactly the shape of his eyes through that mask. Three little words punctuated by gunfire, and I . . . I can't be sure.

But I can be sure of one thing: addicts lie.

Matt rubs his fingers over the edge of the chip, like he's drawing strength.

"Did you happen to mention to anyone that Mina was doing a story on Jackie?" Trev asks.

"I think I told my mom," Matt says. "She thought it was nice that the *Beacon* was doing a feature on Jackie. Mom loved Jackie." His green eyes go bright, and he grips the chip tightly, swallowing hard. "It's just tough," he says, "thinking about her. Not knowing what happened."

"Do you think she ran away?" I ask him.

Matt shakes his head, his eyes still moist. "Nah, Jackie loved her family—she'd never leave them, especially Amy. Jackie was excited about college. We even talked about us getting an apartment near Stanford, me going to community college. She wouldn't have run—no reason to. Someone took her." He breathes deep, his chip clutched tightly in his hand. "And all I can do is pray she's out there somewhere, that she'll get away if someone's got her, that she'll come back home."

"You think she's still alive?" The second it's out of my mouth, I know it's a mistake. He looks like he's about to burst into tears; pushing this way won't do any good.

"I hope so," Matt says. "More than anything."

There's an uncomfortable stretch of silence when I don't know what to say. He could be lying, laying it on thick to mislead us. He could be telling the truth—he could really believe that she's alive after all these years, because he can't stand to imagine the alternative.

"We should go," I say. "I don't want to take up any more of your time."

"You cool, Matt?" Trev asks. "I can hang out."

"No, no, it's fine." He waves us off. "Just . . . bad memories."

"Thanks for talking to us."

Matt nods and walks us to the door. "See you around." He smiles, but his eyes aren't in it. The door shuts behind us, and I hear the sound of the bolt sliding into place as we head to the stairs.

"Well, what do you think?" Trev asks when we get to the truck.

"He's tall enough to be the killer," I say, stepping up into the cab. I fasten my seat belt and turn the key in the ignition. "I know he has guns. Adam goes hunting with him all the time."

"Just about every guy has a gun around here," Trev points out as I back out into the street. "I have a gun."

"You have your dad's old pistol. Have you ever even shot it?"

"Sure. It'd be stupid to have a gun I didn't know how to use. I taught Mina, too."

"When was this?" I don't remember Mina ever mentioning it.

"When you were in Portland. She asked me to. She . . ." Trev frowns. "She asked me right around Christmas."

"When she was getting the threats."

"So why didn't she take it with her that night?" Trev asks, and there's this angry note in his voice that makes me flinch. "She knew where it was, how to use it. She could've protected herself."

"She didn't bring the gun because she didn't suspect whoever she was meeting," I say.

We slow to a halt at the stoplight at the end of the street, and out of the corner of my eye, I can see a muscle in Trev's jaw twitching. It's eating at him, that Mina knew she was in enough danger to want to learn how to shoot but had kept her secrets too long.

"Matt doesn't think much of Detective James," I say, because I hate how well Trev can blame himself. I need to steer him away from this.

"Neither do you," Trev points out.

I roll my eyes. "That's because Detective James gets

an idea in his head and won't budge from it. How much progress has he made in all these months chasing after non-existent drug leads? If he'd done his job the first time, Mina wouldn't have had to go after the guy who took Jackie. He's failed to catch the same killer twice. That's his fault, too."

"Look, I'm pissed at him, too, but eventually, we'll take all of this stuff to him. We'll have to get along."

"He's an ass."

"Well, let's say that Matt is responsible," Trev says. "What's his motivation for getting rid of Jackie?"

I flip the turn signal at the stop sign, looking both ways. "Did they fight?"

"Sometimes. I think she was pissed he was smoking so much pot. She was trying for a scholarship so her parents wouldn't have to pay for college. Spent a lot of time working out, running drills, studying so her grades were good enough. She wanted him to keep up."

I raise an eyebrow. "So, what—he kills her 'cause she's bugging him about weed?"

"Maybe it was an accident," Trev says. "She disappeared out on Clear Creek; that's getting into the woods. Maybe they went hiking or they were fighting and she fell?"

"Then why wouldn't he just call the rangers and tell them it was an accident? Accidents happen in the Siskiyous all the time. No, someone took Jackie and killed her and probably dumped her somewhere. That's why no one's ever found her body."

"This is so messed up," Trev says under his breath.

"I know," I say. We sit in silence for a long moment. "You

still up for going to talk to Jack Dennings?"

"I can't let you go alone," he says, which isn't really an answer, but I'll take it.

"Then get my phone out. I have the directions on it."

We're quiet on the drive to Jack Dennings's place out in Irving Falls. Trev fiddles with the radio, finding an old-school country station, and Merle Haggard's worn voice fills the cab of the truck as I focus on the road.

I don't know what to say to him when it's about normal stuff. So I keep quiet and roll down the window, trying to get some relief from the heat, but the hot air blasts me, blowing my hair back in my face. The truck's AC has been broken for as long as I can remember, and though it's not even noon, it's in the triple digits already. Sweat collects at the small of my back, and I pull my hair off my neck with one hand, slinging it over my shoulder.

He watches me out of the corner of his eye. I pretend not to notice. It's easier.

The air cools as we keep driving. Climbing up and out of the valley, we're surrounded by mountains on both sides, thick with pines, the houses set in the far reaches of the woods where privacy is paramount. About twenty miles ahead is the waterfall the town is named for, but Jack Dennings lives on the outskirts, a real backwoods sort of man.

"This is it," I say, slowing down at the life-size iron turkey nailed on top of the wooden mailbox. We weave through the thickets of digger pines and barbed wire fencing that line the dirt road, and it twists and turns for a few miles before we come across the house, set far back in the taller trees. It's a simple little one-story rancher, stretched out low on the hilly terrain.

Trev and I get out of the truck and walk up to the door to knock. Dogs bark frantically inside, but there's no answer. After a minute, Trev steps back and shades his eyes against the sun. He gestures to the old two-tone Ford parked underneath an oak tree. "Maybe he's around back?"

I follow him, a foot behind as we circle around the house. There's a neat vegetable garden with sunflowers planted around the border, and beyond that a huge chainlink enclosure, brimming with lush green plants.

Then I hear it.

A click.

It's familiar.

Dread surges through me. I'm blocking Trev. Maybe I can save him, like I should've saved her.

I spin around, instinctually, toward the noise, and for the second time in my life, I'm looking down the barrel of a gun.

50

Detective James is tall, at least six and a half feet, with slick dark hair and a worn plaid shirt. He sits on my mom's red couch, and the cup of coffee looks tiny in his large hands.

My mom places her hand on my shoulder. "Sophie, this is Detective James. He has some questions for you."

I'm ready to answer them. He's safe. He's police. If I just tell the truth, everything will be fine. He's going to find her killer.

I have to repeat it a few times in my head before I can venture further into the room.

"Hi," I say. "Do you want me to sit?" I ask.

"Hello, Sophie." He stands up briefly to shake my hand and nods, short and clipped. His face is grim, like he's seen it all and then some.

I sit down in my dad's armchair across from the couch, folding my good leg underneath me. I stretch out my bad one, the flex brace on my knee only letting me get so far. My mom hovers in the doorway, arms folded, her eyes on the detective. I can hear Dad moving around in the kitchen, staying close so he can eavesdrop.

Detective James pulls out a notepad. "Sophie, can you tell me who attacked you and Mina?"

"No. He was wearing a mask."

"You'd never seen him before?"

I frown. Did he not hear me? "I don't know. He was wearing a ski mask."

"But it was a man?"

"Yes. He was tall. Over six feet. That's really all I can tell you about him. He had a big coat on; I'm not sure if he was heavy or thin."

"Did he say anything?"

"Not at first. He . . ." I can feel my face scrunching as I try to think, and it pulls sharply on the stitches swirling across my forehead, ending at my hairline. "He said something. After he hit me. Right before I passed out, I heard him. He said something to Mina."

"And what was that?" Detective James asks.

I have to think about it, pick it apart through the tumult of fear and pain and panic that had surged through me in that moment. "He said, 'I warned you.'"

The detective scribbles something down on his notepad. "Had someone been threatening Mina? Had she been fighting with someone? Having problems with anyone?"

"I don't know . . . I don't think so. I—"

"Why don't you tell me why you girls were out at Booker's Point?" he interrupts. "Your mom says that you told her you were going to a friend's place—Amber Vernon—but Booker's Point is a good thirty miles away from her house."

"We were going to Amber's," I say. "But Mina had to take a detour to the Point. She was meeting someone for a story."

"A story?"

"She has an internship at the *Beacon*." I stop, my lips pressing together tightly. "Had," I correct myself. "She *had* an internship."

"She didn't tell you who she was meeting?" The skeptical note in his voice makes my mother bristle, the lawyer coming out in her face.

"No. She wouldn't tell me. She said she didn't want to jinx it. She was excited, though. It was important to her."

"Okay," Detective James says. For almost a minute, he's silent, writing on his notepad. Then he looks up, and my mouth goes dry at the look on his face—someone zeroing in for the kill. "Booker's Point is well known as the place to go for drug deals," he says. "It would be understandable, for someone with your history, to return to bad habits."

"We weren't out there for a drug deal," I say. "Test me again. Go get me a cup right now to pee in. I don't care what anyone's saying. Kyle's lying. Mina was meeting someone for a story. Ask her supervisor at the paper what she was working on. Ask the newspaper staff. Go through her computer. That's where you'll find your killer."

"And the drugs in your jacket?" Detective James asks. "Were those part of Mina's story, too? Or did they just appear out of nowhere?"

I open my mouth, tears flooding my eyes, but before I can say anything, there's Mom, striding to the center of the room. "I think that's all for tonight, Detective," she says firmly. "My daughter's been through a great deal and she's refused pain medication. She needs to rest."

He opens his mouth to protest, but my mom is already hustling him out with the power of her stare and the authoritative click of her heels.

I'm left alone in the living room, my parents talking in low voices in the kitchen, so I slip upstairs before they notice.

I curl up on my bed, and a few minutes later my mother comes into my room. My mattress sinks down as she sits next to me.

"You did well," she says. "You didn't incriminate yourself. But this is just the first interview. There'll be more as the investigation proceeds."

I look straight ahead, unable to meet her eyes. "I didn't relapse," I say. "I know you don't believe me, but I didn't."

"It doesn't matter what I think," she says. "It matters what the police think. You could be in a lot of trouble, Sophie. You need to be aware of that."

I turn over on my back and finally look at her. "What matters is that they find Mina's killer. They can't do that if they think it was a drug deal. Because that's not what happened. I don't care if they charge me with possession—I only care about finding the person who did this."

Mom flinches. "Well, *I* care what happens to you," she says curtly. "I am doing everything I can to keep you out of trouble, Sophie. You're seventeen; you could be tried as an adult. No offering drug tests, do you hear me?"

"I'm clean," I grit out.

"Promise me." Her fear has crept inside the room with us, thick and heavy. Her mouth, shark-bite red, trembles, and her fingers twist together. Mommy will always protect me, even when I'm destroying her.

"I promise," I say.

It's the only way, because I know my mother. She'll never believe me, but she'll do whatever it takes to keep this from ruining my life.

It's the first thing I've done that isn't about Mina.

It's for me, and for Mom, who'd claw her fingers bloody fighting for me.

It feels like a betrayal.

51

It's happening again.

I've wondered every day how it could have been differ-ent: if I had been faster, braver, if he hadn't gone for my bad leg first, maybe I would've been able to stop him.

And now there's another gun in my face and I want to be brave this time. More than anything, I want to be brave.

But I can't stop my bad leg from folding beneath me.

I go down hard. My knees scream in protest. There's blood in my mouth; I've bitten through my cheek. I can't look anywhere but at the shotgun barrel. Can't even focus enough to make out the blurry figure holding it. All I know is that it's happening again and I can't do anything to stop it. I'm not blocking Trev anymore, and the panic makes me scramble forward, toward the gun. I can't be responsible for his dying, too.

Someone's yelling. Something brushes against my shoul-der, forcing me away from that night and back to reality. Trev's moved past me.

"What the fuck?"

It's Trev. Trev's yelling. Angry and loud in a way that's shocking, because he has the slowest fuse in the universe.

Things start to sharpen, my heartbeat slowing in my ears as my eyes focus.

He takes another step until he's completely in front of me. I want to grab his legs, yank him away. "Get that out of her face!" he yells.

"Who are you two?"

I try to focus on the voice, on the white-haired man holding the gun.

"I said put the gun *down*!" Trev looms in front of the man, using his height, his broad shoulders, and the strength that he won't unleash until it's needed. There's no fear in his voice, ringing out clear, an unmistakable order.

It's crazy.

It's stupid. And I love him for it.

The man, bent, scrawny, with leathery skin and a razor-blade mouth, lowers the barrel a few inches. "What the hell are you two doing here?"

"I'm Mina Bishop's brother. We wanted to talk about an interview she did with you a few months ago."

The suspicion melts from the man's face, and he lowers the gun. "Sorry 'bout that," he croaks, wiping his forehead. "You never know, out here." He nods toward the cage of plants. "Kids come out all the time, try to steal my medicine."

"We're not here to jack your weed," Trev says as he kneels down on the ground next to me. "Soph," he says gently, and I can see in his face how bad I must look right now. He holds his hand out, waiting for me to take it.

Both my legs shake as I get up, and I rub at my cheeks with my sleeve.

"I didn't mean to scare you that bad, girlie," Jack Dennings says to me.

"Yes, you did."

He smiles like I'm being funny. "I'm sorry to hear about your sister," he says, nodding at Trev. Trev nods back, his shoulders still tense. "What did you want to know about Mina talking with me?"

"All we want to know is what you two talked about," Trev says.

"Jackie's childhood. I showed Mina the trophies she won." Jack smiles, and this time there's sadness at the edges of his mouth. "She was a natural. Got a soccer scholarship and everything. Was gonna be the first in the family to go to college." He taps the rifle against his leg, eyes softening. "She was my first grandchild . . . such a good girl."

"And did you tell anyone Mina was interviewing people close to Jackie?"

"Nope. I don't get into town too much these days. Though I think Matt Clarke knew about it, because that's where Mina said she got my phone number."

"Are you close to Matt?"

Jack Dennings spits on the ground. "Not likely. Boy wasn't good enough for my granddaughter. He took a bad turn when his daddy left. Quit sports, started fighting, doing too many drugs. Didn't want that for her, told her that, but she was a headstrong one, my Jackie."

"You ever think he was responsible for Jackie going missing?" Trev asks.

Jack's eyes narrow. "You sound like your sister," he says.

"Did she think Matt did it?"

"Don't know, didn't ask."

"Do *you* think he did?" I demand.

"Let me put it this way," Jack says. "You gotta be sure, and I'm not. So Matt gets to go along, live his life."

"And what happens if you *are* sure?" I can't help but ask.

Jack Dennings smiles wide. He's got a gap in the back of his grin, missing a few molars. "When that day comes, that boy's gonna be bear food in the forest before his momma even misses him."

I shudder, too on edge to stop it, because I can see how much he means it.

Because something inside me understands him.

"Okay, thanks," Trev says. "We'll be going now."

"You don't come back, you hear?" Jack orders. "Don't be getting any ideas."

"Your plants are safe, sir," Trev says wryly.

He slips into the driver's seat without asking, and I hand him the keys, not taking a deep breath until we're on the move, driving down the highway. Trev shuts off the radio and watches me out of the corner of his eye, one hand on the wheel, the other curved out the window.

One mile. Two.

I'm drowning in the quiet.

We don't speak the entire forty minutes it takes to get back to my house. And when he pulls up to the curb and I get out, he follows. He follows me down the driveway, through the back gate, along the raised beds he built for me, up into the tree house that he'd repaired countless times.

I scrunch myself in the corner, and he sits across from me, the silence as bruising as a hailstorm. I think about the last time I was up here with him, how I don't regret it, even though I probably should.

There are still gingham curtains, crudely sewn, hanging from one of the windows. They flap gently in the midafternoon breeze, their lace edging ratty and yellowed.

"Do you remember when we met?" I ask him.

He looks up, startled. He rubs his thumbs over his bent knees, straightening one leg out slowly. The hem of his jeans brushes my calf.

"I do," he says. "Mina had been talking about you for weeks. I remember being glad she'd made a friend, that she was talking and laughing instead of crying. You were so quiet at first, you held yourself so still, sort of like Mina's opposite." He laughs. "But you were always watching her. I knew I could count on you, that you'd help her. Looking back, I feel so stupid, not realizing the two of you . . ." He lets out a huff of breath, not quite a laugh, not quite a sigh. "It's weird to think she and I had the same taste in girls. Is that why she never told me?" Trev's hands knot together. "Because of you?"

We both know the answer, but I can't bring myself to say it. "I wanted to tell you about me," I say instead. "But I couldn't without telling you about her. I'm wrapped up in her, Trev. I never learned how to love anyone else because she was there and we were *us*. We were always just us, and I couldn't break that without breaking me. Without breaking her."

"She wanted to hide," he says. "And you went along with it, because you always did."

"She was scared," I say, as if I need to defend her.

But I know I don't, not to him. He's telling the truth, too. Mina led, and I followed. She hid, and I was her shelter. She kept secrets, and I guarded them. Mina lied, and so did I. Sometimes we were downright ruthless to each other. For once, it isn't some cotton-candy idea of her; it's who she was, in all her maddening, heart-squeezing truth.

"What about you?" Trev asks abruptly. "Were *you* scared?"

"Loving her was never scary. It was never wrong. It was where I fit. But I wasn't raised the way you two were, and she thought I had a choice. Because I didn't like only girls. Because I had . . ." I can't finish that sentence.

But he does it for me. "Because you had me."

I nod, the only thing I can manage.

And he's right—I had. Trev's been waiting for me all this time. Between boyfriends, breakups, fights, and more than two years of an addiction I managed to hide until it ate me up, he's been there, waiting. I know exactly what that kind of love requires.

Because I'd been waiting, too.

Just not for him.

I wrap my arms around his shoulders, press my forehead against his temple.

His hands cup the back of my neck; our foreheads slide together, noses brush. I know he won't kiss me, know he'll never make a move again. This is up to me and me alone.

I know I can't kiss him, know I have to draw the line here and now, because I can never love him like I loved her, and he deserves that. Deserves better than me and the empty imitation I can offer.

So I swallow back the tears and the words in my throat, the ones I can't say, that I wish I could.

If it hadn't been her, it would have been you.

52

I can't stop crying as I slip through the back door of the Bishop house. "Mina? Mina, are you here?"

When she doesn't answer, I open her bedroom door without knocking. She's sitting on her canopied bed, legs crossed.

She doesn't ask me what's wrong.

She's been waiting for me.

We stare at each other, silent, and I suddenly understand why she looks so guilty. Why she has to force herself to meet my gaze.

She *knows*.

She's the one who told my parents where to find the drugs. And the prescription triplicates I'd stolen from Dad's office.

The betrayal swamps me. I want to punch her. Grab a handful of her hair and pull until it rips out in my hand. Punish her the way she's been punishing me all along. Is this her new solution—get me sent away so I won't be a temptation?

"I had to tell them, Sophie," she says.

"No."

"I had to." She gets up from the bed when I start to back away from her. "You don't listen to me. You won't talk to me. You need help."

"I can't believe you did this!" I'm almost out of her bedroom, horror coursing through me.

"I had to!" She chases after me and yanks me back into her room, slamming the door behind me, locking us in.

My balance, always precarious, is thrown off and I stumble, knocking into her.

"You told me you were getting off those pills," Mina hisses, all hints of apology or guilt erased now. Her fingers bite into my arm, and I squeeze her wrist tight where I'm holding on to her, because this is what we're good at: hurting each other.

"I lied," I say. I drawl it out right in her face.

She goes white, letting go of me so fast, I'm reeling. "How could you do this?" she demands. "Stealing from your dad? That's not you. You could have killed yourself, taking so many pills!"

"Maybe that's what I wanted."

Mina makes a sound, inarticulate and feral. Then she pushes me.

She puts her weight into it, pushes me like she would a steady person. No more careful touches, no arm looped through mine. Now is the time to make me fall, twist me up, ruin me for good.

I topple, but I bring her down with me, reaching out at the last second and dragging her to the carpet. My hands are in her hair, and I pull. Her nails dig into my shoulder.

"Don't you dare say that," she gasps. "Take it back."

"No." I buck beneath her; she's half sprawled on top of me. I can't breathe around the feeling. Her hands press down on my shoulders, pinning me to the floor. My back aches, my leg twisted at a bad angle, but her eyes burn into mine. She won't look away now. I can't, because I've never seen her this way before, like this is the most dangerous thing she's ever done. She leans down, so close I can feel her breath against my skin. Her hair spills across my shoulder, brushing my neck.

"Take it back," she says again.

I lick my lips and shake my head. My final dare.

Mina breaks, and the space between us is finally gone.

She kisses me, and even now I'm amazed that it's her instead of me who concedes.

"Take it back," she whispers into my mouth, and my breath hitches, my body hitches, rises up to meet hers when her palms slip underneath my shirt, touching the fragile skin around my belly button.

I trail my hands down the sides of her face, kiss her hard, tongue and teeth. This has never been soft or sweet; we've always been more than that, sharpened by time and want, our secret war finally won.

I start to say *please*, but I really want to say her name, pressed against her lips, mouthed along her collarbone, so I do, murmuring it like a mantra, like a thank-you, like a blessing.

Her hand pushes farther up my shirt. She brushes her knuckles against me, underneath my bra, and I let my body arch into her.

We take forever, kissing for minutes at a time, clothing shed piece by piece, until finally her fingers slip into my underwear and I moan against her neck, jerk beneath her hand as the feeling flutters through me, as her fingers circle and seek and I can't breathe through it, I can't breathe at all as I tense and shake and pulse around her.

After, when it's her turn, when she trembles below me, soft, slick skin and warm hands, her breasts pressed against mine, my mouth, trailing down, down, down, salt and silk and her whispering my name, I'm awestruck.

I want to remember everything because it's the first time.

Later, I'll remember everything because it's the only time.

53

By the time Trev leaves, I feel wrung out. I walk out to my garden but end up lying down in the grass between the two beds, following the sun's progress as it fades behind the Trinities.

I'm almost dozing when someone bangs on the back gate. My eyes snap open and I struggle to my elbows as Rachel calls, "Sophie, are you here?"

"Hey, coming." I get to my feet slowly, my back hurting from lying on the ground for so long.

When I finally get the gate unlocked, I pull it back to find Rachel clutching a plastic baggie to her chest. There are smears of dust across her forehead and arms and a scratch on her leg. She charges forward, waving the bag. "I found them!" she says. "It took forever. Kyle had to ditch me for work around two, but I kept at it. Mina hid them in a big box of Barbies stashed in a mountain of junk. I nearly got buried underneath an avalanche of Christmas crap."

"She hid them in a box of Barbies?"

"Actually, she hid them in Barbie's car, folded in the little trunk. Mina was tricky. I almost didn't check there."

My hands shake as I take the clear plastic baggie from

her. Inside, two pieces of white printer paper are folded, so I can't make the text out. "Did you read them?" I ask. "Touch them? What about fingerprints?"

"Way ahead of you." Rachel digs in her bag, coming up with a pair of pink dishwashing gloves with daisies on the cuffs. "I used these. I doubt there's anyone's fingerprints but Mina's, but it doesn't hurt to be careful."

It takes me a couple of tries to get the gloves on my trembling hands. "Did you show Trev?"

"He still wasn't back when I found them. I brought them right over."

"Seriously? He dropped me off, like, an hour ago."

Rachel shrugs. "He wasn't there. Maybe he got home right after I left."

"Probably," I say as I open the baggie and pull out the first note, folded in quarters. I unfold it square by square, until the black ink, his words of warning, appears:

SNOOP ANY MORE AND YOU'LL GO MISSING TOO.

I read the words over and over, and press my thumb hard into the bottom of the paper—so hard it crumples.

I want to rip it apart.

I want to rip *him* apart.

I take deep breaths, in and out, in and out, before reaching for the second note. I unfold and smooth it flat next to the first:

FINAL WARNING. IF YOU DON'T WANT ANYONE HURT
YOU'LL LEAVE IT ALONE.

I frown when I see four addresses typed below the killer's threat: Trev's apartment in Chico, the Bishop house on Sacramento, Kyle's house on Girvan Street—and my address, the only one that's circled over and over in red.

The paper crumples in my hand; I can't seem to unclench my fist. My fingers are sweating in their pink rubber prison, and my heart beats fast. I turn to look over my shoulder. Dad's in the kitchen, doing the dishes; I can see the top of his head through the little window above the sink. I can't help but think about it for a second, about him or Mom having to open the door to the police for the third time.

For the last time.

I don't want that for them. I've put them through as much hell as they've heaped on me. Probably more.

But it can't matter. I can't let it matter. What matters is finding Mina's killer.

"Hey, wanna unclench there?" Rachel asks. She shoots a look at the balled-up note in my hand until I relax my fingers. "That's evidence! Anyway, there's one more thing." Rachel gestures at the baggie. I reach inside it and pull out a business card.

MARGARET CHASE

WOMEN'S HEALTH

(531) 555-3421

"Oh, you've gotta be kidding me," I say. "Did you call it?"

"I was waiting for you," Rachel says. "But you know, it

doesn't take a brain surgeon to make the logical assumption here. You *know* why girls go to Women's Health."

I key the number into my phone. My mind's racing as it rings and rings. Finally, it clicks over to voice mail. *"You've reached Margaret Chase, adoption coordinator for Women's Health. I'm on vacation and will be back at my desk on July eighth. If you leave your name and number, I'll get back to you when I return. Thanks, and have a great day."*

I hang up, staring down at the phone, my suspicion confirmed.

"I was right, wasn't I?" Rachel asks. "Jackie was pregnant."

"Margaret Chase is an adoption counselor," I say. "And in Mina's interview with Matt, she asked about his and Jackie's sex life. He got all offended."

"Okay . . ." Rachel says, sitting down on the edge of one of the raised beds, gesturing for me to join her. I take the bed across from her, sitting on the ground with my back against the wood for support instead of trying to balance. "Let's think about this. Say Jackie gets pregnant. . . ."

"And she wants to give the baby up for adoption," I continue, looking down at Margaret Chase's card. "She's got college. She couldn't play soccer with a baby. So, she tells Matt—and what then?"

"A few possibilities," Rachel says. "Matt could have wanted her to get an abortion. She refuses, so he kills her. Though that seems kind of extreme, especially if she was gonna give the baby up. But a seventeen-year-old with a burgeoning drug problem probably doesn't want a baby around. And he's probably not making the most rational decisions."

"What if he did want the baby, though?" I look down at the two notes sitting in the baggie in front of me. At the way the most important people in Mina's life are there in black and white, a threat to the heart of her. The only kind that would've gotten her to really back off. "Family's important. And Matt's dad walked out on him and Adam. Maybe he freaked at the idea of giving the baby to strangers. Killing Jackie might not have been planned. It could've been an accident. They could've fought about the baby and things got out of hand. He pushed her and she hit her head or something like that."

"Is he an angry guy? What was he like today when you talked to him?" Rachel asks.

"He seemed . . . tired," I say. "Sad. He said that he believes Jackie's still alive."

Rachel raises an eyebrow.

"I wish I'd known all this stuff before I talked to him." I look down at my phone. It's almost six thirty.

I think about Matt in his apartment this morning, holding on to the six-month chip like it was a lifeline. David had given me a schedule of Narcotics Anonymous meetings, and I'd reluctantly keyed them into my phone's calendar. I pull it up. The Wednesday meeting is at the Methodist church—it'll be ending soon. I bet anything he's there right now. Even if he's using again, he might go just to keep up appearances.

"Hey," I say to Rachel. "Want to take a drive?"

• • •

The meeting is letting out when Rachel and I pull into the church parking lot. People walk down the steps, mingling at the bottom, a few pulling out cigarettes as they chat.

"Stay close, okay?" I ask her. I'll need some backup in case it gets ugly.

"Stick around where I can see you," Rachel counters.

"Deal. Be right back."

"Remember: *subtlety!*" she calls after me.

There's a tall man with his back to me talking to Matt as I approach. When I get to the steps, I realize it's his uncle. I remember what Adam had said, about family having to make sure Matt went to meetings. I can't imagine it, sharing like that, and letting your family listen.

"Sophie." Coach smiles at me. "Your dad is so happy to have you back. How are you feeling?"

"Hi, Coach, Matt." I look up at the church. "I'm doing good. Feeling kind of stupid right now—I must've misread the meeting time. I thought it said seven."

"No, it starts at six," Matt says.

Coach's cell phone rings. "I've got to get that," he says, squeezing Matt's shoulder. "Good job today," he says in an undertone. "Sophie, it was great seeing you. Tell your dad I'll get back to him about the game next Thursday."

"I will," I say as he steps away toward the parking lot to take his call.

Matt smiles down at me. "I'm sorry you missed the meeting, but there's another one tomorrow at the Elks Lodge."

If I were Mina, I'd smile back and twirl my hair. I'd ask innocuous questions, make him feel comfortable, lull him into my net.

But my edges are too sharp. I want this done.

"I'm actually not here for a meeting. I'm here to ask you if you got Jackie pregnant."

Matt's smile vanishes, along with most of the color in his face. "What the fuck are you talking about?"

"Look, I could be all nice like earlier, dodging around the questions, but you're a tweeker. Lying is what you do. So—you . . . Jackie. Did you get her pregnant?"

I stare hard at his face, trying to see the answer in it because I know his words won't tell me. But there's only fury pulsing off him. He looks over his shoulder, where his uncle is standing just out of hearing distance.

"You need to get the hell out of here." He steps toward me when he says it, and I hear a car horn blast from the parking lot—Rachel letting me know she has my back.

"Was Detective James right?" I ask, never taking my eyes away from him. He won't meet them, and his shoulders shake underneath the baggy polo he's wearing. "Did you do it? Did you take her? Kill her? Was the baby why?"

"You are so out of line," he says. "Get out of here."

"Or what?" I ask. "Are you going to hit me in the head with a piece of rebar again? Try to finish me off this time?"

He backs hastily away from me, all the fight suddenly gone. "You're a crazy bitch," he says. "And you need to leave me the hell alone."

He stalks down the steps toward Coach Rob, and I stare at his retreating back, at the line of his shoulders, trying, *trying* to recognize something from that night—something, *anything* in the way he walks or sounds. Rachel comes running up to me, breathing hard.

"Are you okay? What happened?" she asks.

I keep staring after Matt until he turns the corner. "I wasn't subtle," I say.

54

"Why are you so late?" Mina demands as I get out of my car. She's perched in the back of Trev's truck on a plaid blanket she's spread carefully over the peeling paint. Her legs swing off the edge of the tailgate, a daisy flip-flop dangling from her foot. In front of us, the lake stretches out for miles, nothing but blue water reflecting sky and mountains. The sun's starting to fade, and we have at least a half hour before the fireworks begin.

I get the plastic bag I've stashed in my backseat. "Fourth of July traffic," I say. "Is Trev here?"

"No, I borrowed the truck," Mina says. "What's in the bag?" She makes a grab for it, and I step back so she can't get it. She pouts, her strawberry-red lips sticking out. "Mean."

I just smile and set the bag out of her reach before boosting myself up beside her.

Mina sinks down, lying on her back in the truck bed, and I follow suit. We pass a bottle of Boone's Farm back and forth, the fruity sweetness clinging to the back of my throat as Mina traces clouds with her fingers, rings glimmering in the dying sun. She describes shapes to me, each more fantastic than the next.

"Soph, do you ever think about what's going to happen when we leave?" she asks.

I tilt my head to the right so I can look at her. My hair and hers, blond and brown, are twined together on the blanket, and she's careful not to meet my eyes.

"You mean for college and stuff?"

Mina nods, still staring up at the darkening sky. The crickets are starting to sing, and their chirps echo across the water, blending with the frogs and some distant laughter from a houseboat out past the harbor.

"It'll be weird, right?" Mina asks. "Not to see each other?" When I don't answer, she turns to look at me, rolling from her back to her side, our faces inches apart. "Won't it be?"

"I don't like thinking about it," I say.

Mina bites her lip; I'm close enough that I can smell the strawberry gloss. "Sometimes it's all I think about," she says, so quiet I almost don't hear her. She sighs and reaches out, tucking a strand of hair behind my ear. Her hand lingers for a moment on my skin, settling into the little crook under my jaw where my pulse thumps.

There's a *pop-pop-pop* in the air, breaking the spell. Sparks light up the night sky in a dazzling cascade of red, white, and blue. The reflection of the fireworks on the water stretches out until it feels like we're surrounded by light.

"It's starting!" Mina sits straight up and hops out of the truck, clapping her hands like a kid, and I smile as she watches the show, as transfixed as I am by her.

After the final firework has been shot off, the night settling into hints of smoke and ash, Mina stands there, eyes fixed on the sky, waiting, like there'll be one more just for her.

While her attention is on the sky, I reach back and pull out the plastic bag I stashed earlier. When she turns around, I'm sitting on the edge of the tailgate, a lit sparkler in hand, my offering to her.

She beams at me, and I beam back.

Instead of taking it, she wraps both hands around mine, and we stay there, me sitting on the tailgate and her standing in front of me, the sparkler showering light between us, popping and hissing in the air. Shadows play across her face, the light illuminating her in fits and starts, and I've never felt more sure, and she's never looked more beautiful.

Long after the sparkler's fizzled out, Mina's ash-smeared hands hold mine between her palms.

"I don't know what I'd do without you," she whispers.

I hook my thumb around hers, and our matching rings click against each other, the unspoken promise of forever . . . someday.

55

When I get home, I page through Mina's notes, trying to find any mention of Jackie's possible pregnancy. But either she hadn't had the time to write it down or she hadn't finished figuring it out, because there's nothing in the time line or her notes to suggest she even suspected it.

I close my laptop after I've searched all the files. I'm almost positive an unplanned pregnancy is the reason Jackie disappeared. I wish it were July, so Margaret Chase was back from vacation. I don't have much hope that she'll confirm my suspicions—there are rules about sharing that kind of stuff—but maybe if I go into the clinic and talk to her, I'd be able to tell from her reaction. Just to be sure.

"Sophie?" My mom taps on my door before opening it.

I jerk in surprise, and the notebook in my lap falls to the floor. "Yeah?"

"Just checking on you. I made dinner, if you want some."

"Thanks, but I already ate."

"With Trev?" she asks.

"No, I went to Angry Burger with Rachel."

"Your father said Trev was here earlier."

"He dropped me off after we were done hanging out," I say, and her lips pinch together.

"I see. Well, then, good night."

"Night."

As the door closes behind her, I open the notebook in my lap again. The plastic bag containing the warning notes is pressed between the pages.

I'm scraping up on the edges of something . . . something that will make all this clear. It buzzes underneath my skin, makes me want to pace, to keep moving, forward, upward, no matter what.

Is this how she felt? This tantalizing reach for answers that had her addicted and reckless?

I can almost understand it. It's just another kind of high.

I press my hand over the notes, safely enclosed in the plastic. What would Detective James do if I brought them to him now? Would he think I wrote them myself? Would he laugh in my face?

Tomorrow, I have to ask Trev what we should do. After we talk to Amy Dennings. Maybe it'll be enough, the threats coupled with Mina's notes about the case. Detective James would have to listen to Trev. He'll have to pay attention to new evidence, even if it messes with his drug deal theory. And he'd worked Jackie's case—he might be able to draw connections that none of us could see.

I close the notebook, tucking it carefully in my desk drawer before shutting off my light.

I sleep, but all I dream about is chasing after Mina, her laughing, and me never quite catching up.

•   •   •

The next day, I drive to the soccer field at quarter to six and sit on the hood of my car, waiting for Trev. He shows up five minutes later, and we walk across the wide green lawn, the summer sun beating down on our shoulders. The girls are still out on the field, with some parents watching on the sidelines as Coach paces, shouting encouragement or correction.

"Do you know what she looks like?" Trev asks. "She has dark hair, I think."

I shade my eyes against the sun, looking over the sea of heads to pick out the brunettes. We hang to the side until practice finishes and the girls disperse. A girl with a pixie cut jogs up close to us to grab her bag, and I smile at her and ask, "Hey, I'm looking for Amy. Is she here?"

"Yeah, she's over there with Casey." The girl points to two girls huddled together. The dark-haired girl is laughing, and the other, a short redhead, squirts water at her from her bottle while Amy shrieks and dodges back.

"Thanks."

"Hey, you're Coach Bill's daughter, aren't you?" the girl asks. "You used to play."

"I used to," I say.

"Your dad's cool. Way easier than Coach Rob."

I can't help but smile. "I'll tell him you said that," I say to her. "Thanks again."

By the time Trev and I make it across the lawn, the redhead has walked off, leaving Amy by herself, stuffing her gear into her bag.

"Amy?" I call.

She turns, her long brown ponytail swinging over her shoulder. I can see the resemblance to Jackie: the upturned nose, the sweet expression in her blue eyes. "Yeah?"

"I'm Sophie," I say. "This is Trev. Can we talk to you for a second?"

"What's this about?" She casts a sideways look at Trev that lasts a little too long. "Do I know you?" she asks him.

"I was friends with your sister," Trev says. "I think we met once or twice when you were little."

"Oh." She crosses her arms, looking us up and down. "Is this about Jackie? Because I don't talk about her. Especially with strangers."

"You talked to my sister about her," Trev says. "Mina Bishop?"

Her eyes widen. "You're Mina's brother?"

He nods.

"Look, I'm sorry about what happened to Mina," she says.

"Thank you," Trev replies, and there's a mechanical feel to it. I wonder, suddenly, how many times he's heard this from people. Apologies and awkward silences must be his reality now. I wonder if he's as desperate to leave this town as I am, even as I know he'll never desert his mom. Not now.

"But whatever this is about . . ." She looks over her shoulder. "My mom's right over there. I've really got to go."

"Mina did an interview with you, didn't she?" I ask. "About your sister's disappearance? She was doing a story about it."

"No," Amy says, but she's not a good liar. Her cheeks burn red even before the lie's off her lips.

"Amy, I have Mina's notes," I say. "She might not have recorded all of your interview, but I have the first minute of it. I know you two talked."

Amy's chin juts out, a mulish expression settling over her face. "We didn't. I realized it was a mistake, so I left after I asked her to turn off the recorder." She looks over her shoulder again, toward the cars that are pulling into the parking lot as her teammates pack up their gear and join their parents. "I have to go," she says.

"We're sorry for bothering you," Trev says, and he smiles gently at her, that comforting, safe smile of his—and, like almost every other girl in the world, she responds to it.

"It's okay," she says. "But I have to go."

"I know," Trev says. "I just need to ask you one more thing, then I won't bother you anymore. Did you tell anyone that Mina was doing interviews about Jackie?"

"No," Amy says. "I didn't tell anyone. Why does it even matter? It was just a stupid newspaper story."

"I'm just trying to figure some stuff out," Trev says.

"Well, I can't help you with it." Amy slings her bag back over her shoulder. "Bye." She takes long, loping strides away from us.

She's hiding something.

"Give me a minute," I tell Trev. Then I go after her. "Amy!" I call. "Wait a second."

"Seriously, this is, like, harassment," she says, spinning around. "What do you want?"

"Was Jackie pregnant?"

I'm standing right in front of her, but I could be half a mile away and see the truth. She sucks in a breath, sharp and fast, her chest heaving with it.

"I don't know what you're talking about," she says, once she manages to slow her breathing a bit.

"Bullshit," I say. "She was pregnant, wasn't she? And you knew."

Amy looks over her shoulder like she's scared the group of girls thirty feet away will hear us. Then she grabs my arm, squeezing tight enough to bruise. "Shut up."

"Did you know all this time?" I ask, shaking off her grip. "Did you withhold it from the police? Why would you do that?"

Amy's cheeks get red again. The color spreads down her neck, up her ears. "Seriously, shut up. Do you want someone to hear you?"

But I'm ruthless. I have to be.

"How did you find out she was pregnant? Did Jackie tell you?"

"I'm gonna start screaming in a second," Amy threatens. "My mom's right over there waiting for me." She points at the group of grown-ups who are talking with Coach and some of the girls by the parking lot.

"No, you won't," I say. "If your mom comes over, she'll hear what I'm saying, and I'm pretty sure you don't want that. Because I'm pretty sure she has no idea about this, does she? Answer my question: how did you know your sister was pregnant?"

"God, I thought Mina was bad," Amy spits out. She comes closer to me and lowers her voice. "What is with you people? Can't you just leave us alone? Do you think I feel good about this? I was eleven when Jackie disappeared. I barely knew what a pregnancy test was, or what it looked like. I didn't think it was important when I found it. By the time I realized what it meant, Jackie'd been missing for two years. My parents—they don't need to wonder about a grandkid, okay? They already have enough unanswered questions."

"Did you tell Mina Jackie was pregnant?"

"Why is that even . . ." Amy stops. Her mouth hardens; when she squares her shoulders, I see determination in her. "Look, Mina was nice, okay? I refused to talk to her for a long time, I was a total bitch to her, and she was still nice to me. She wore me down." Amy digs the toe of her cleat into the grass, avoiding my eyes. "She promised she wouldn't tell anyone. That it was off the record."

"Mina kept your secret. She was good at that."

"Are you going to keep it?" she asks, the tremble in her voice almost under control.

"No," I say, because I won't lie to her.

She glares at me. "Why not?" she demands.

"Because whoever took Jackie killed Mina," I say. "She wasn't just doing a newspaper story, Amy. She was trying to figure out who took her—trying to crack the case—and she died for it. Right in front of me. So I can't keep quiet, okay? Because this . . . this isn't a little thing. This is *motive*."

Amy's mouth drops open in surprise. She steps back from

me, her cleats digging hard into the soil. "You mean . . . you think . . . Matt. You think Matt took her. That he killed her because of a baby?"

"I'm not sure yet," I say. "But it's a possibility."

"And you're gonna . . . what? Catch him? How the hell are you gonna do that? If what you're saying is true, the police didn't find enough on him to arrest him for my sister. He already shot someone in front of you, and the police didn't catch him then, either. What are you gonna do that they couldn't?"

"At least I'm aimed in the right direction," I say. "Detective James bungled Mina's murder case. He was in charge of Jackie's case, too. Who knows what he overlooked back then? No one is looking in the right places. I can at least try."

"If it's Matt . . ." She stops, like she can't even say it. Like the hope for answers is too much. "If it's Matt," she says again, stronger this time, "do you think he'd tell us? Do you think they could make him tell us where he put her? So we could bury her?" Her voice cracks on the last question, and I realize that she harbors none of the hope that Matt claimed to have. That there's something worse than having a grave to visit.

"I'm going to try," I say, because I hadn't been lying to David that day in therapy. I want to be able to keep my promises.

There's a prolonged honk coming from the parking lot, and Amy jerks, looking over her shoulder. The group of parents has scattered, and a woman with blond hair is leaning out of an SUV, waving at Amy. "That's my mom," she says. "I have to go." She grabs her bag, slinging it over her shoulder. "You're not just some crazy drug addict, right?" she asks. "Because even the freshmen hear stories about you."

I let out a breath, half laugh, half shame. "I am a drug addict," I say. "I'm in recovery. But I'm not crazy. Not about this. I promise."

"Okay," she says. "Just . . . be careful, then."

"Thank you," I say. "For telling me the truth."

"Don't make me regret it," she says. She hurries away across the field before I can answer. I watch her for a moment before Trev comes up behind me.

"What was that about?" he asks.

"Jackie was pregnant," I say. "Amy just confirmed it."

"Seriously? *Jackie?*" Trev looks shocked. "That means Matt—"

"Yeah," I say. Trev frowns, not following me as I start toward the parking lot. I stop and turn back to him. "What?"

"How did you find this out?"

I dig inside my purse, coming up with the plastic baggie containing the threats, handing them over to him. "Don't take them out of there. Rachel found them in your garage. And there was something else with them: a business card for an adoption counselor at Women's Health."

Trev's quiet as we walk back to our cars, the threats clutched in his hands. I wonder if he's mad that I didn't call him as soon as Rachel had shown them to me, but before I can ask him, we get to the parking lot.

Trev's truck is parked ahead of mine, so we get to it first.

There's a piece of paper tucked under the wiper, but I notice the other cars' windshields are clear. "What's that?" I reach up for the paper, and then stop.

It's not an ad or a coupon like I expect.

It's a piece of printer paper, with a photo taped to it and some words below.

"Trev." I stare at the image. At the words.

BACK OFF OR IT HAPPENS TO HER TOO.

The photo's an inkjet printout, grainy and poor quality, taken from a distance. It's Trev and me, standing in front of the truck, just like we are now. I'm shading my eyes against the sun; Trev's bending toward the door handle. I'm wearing the black shirt I had on yesterday and I can see the edge of Matt's apartment building in a corner of the photo.

"Shit," Trev says. He looks around, as if he's expecting whoever left it to be hanging about, watching us. The parking lot is empty except for the girls loading up equipment into Coach's truck.

"He's following us," I say, and my fingernails bite into my palms as I clench my fists, the thought heavy in my stomach. "This . . . this is good. This is proof." Trev grabs for the paper. I stop him. "No, don't touch it. We need a napkin or something."

I root around in the truck bed until I find a rag and carefully pick up the note by a corner, my fingers shielded by the cloth. "Got it." I look up at him with a big grin. "Now all we have to do is . . ."

Trev shakes his head.

"What?" I ask.

"It's time to call the police, Sophie," he says. "Now."

I let out a long breath. "Okay," I say. "You're right."

"Why didn't you tell me you found the other notes last night?" he demands.

"Because I knew you'd want to go to the cops, and I wanted to talk to Amy first," I say.

"You could've been hurt," Trev says. "He's watching us! Why are you so calm?"

"I had to make sure I was right about Jackie's being pregnant. And anyway, you were here the whole time. I knew you wouldn't let anything happen to me."

He laughs, a bitter sound, and it twists at my stomach, ties it into knots. "You really believe that, don't you?"

"I do," I say. It's one of the two universal truths of my life. Something that I've always been sure of, since that night in the hospital when he'd begged my forgiveness.

"I should be the last person you think that about."

"I know you. You don't make the same mistake twice."

"Christ, Sophie," he hisses, like I've said something horrible. He glares at me. "We're going to the cops."

"No," I say.

"Sophie, I swear to God—"

"I'm not saying no to going to the police. I'm saying no to my going *with* you. If I'm there, Detective James won't listen to a word either of us says."

I'd thought this through carefully. But it hadn't taken me long to realize Trev had to do this solo.

"You're her family. If you show up there by yourself, he has to listen. Tell him you found those warning notes and the thumb drive in Mina's room, started investigating, and then got *this* note on your car yesterday. He'll believe you— but not if I'm with you. If I'm there, it'll screw everything up. He doesn't trust me. It has to be just you."

Trev grits his teeth. "Okay," he says. "Then I'll go. And you stay home and wait for me to call you."

"I can't. I promised Rachel I'd go to a party."

"A party? Seriously?"

"Kyle invited Rachel, but she doesn't want to go without me. If you hurry over to Detective James, you can meet me out at the lake. We'll go through everything the cops say. You can even challenge Kyle to picnic table beer pong if you want."

That gets a reluctant smile out of him. "Fine," Trev says. He digs his keys out of his pocket and heads toward the driver's side of the truck. "No beer pong, though."

"Thank you."

He looks up grimly. "Thank me when this is all done."

He follows me home, just a few feet behind my car.

56

"Do we have to do this now?" I ask, fiddling with the iPod hookup in my car. "We're going to be late."

"I know, I know, I suck," Mina says as she takes the Old 99 exit. "It'll be quick. Thirty minutes. Then we'll go to Amber's."

It's been storming all week, but it's clear now, and you can see the stars so much better away from the town lights. I think about rolling my window down and sticking my head out, but it's too cold.

"You still not gonna tell me what this is all about?" I find the playlist marked *Sophie* and page through the songs.

"Not yet," Mina trills.

"You and your weird superstitions," I say, rolling my eyes and grinning.

Mina sticks her tongue out. "They're not weird. But this is going to be *huge*. I'm not going to jinx it now, when I'm so close."

"You're crazy."

"Hey, I'm not the one with a shrink on speed dial."

Silence fills the car. Her mouth twists back and forth.

"Too soon?" she asks.

"No."

She shoots me a look.

"Okay, maybe a little," I admit.

"I'm a bitch. I'm sorry."

"No, it's okay. It's the truth. How bitchy can that be?"

"Pretty bitchy."

I've been home from Portland for two weeks. After almost six months with Macy, clawing my way clean and free, I was finally sure enough to come home.

But finding steady footing has been hard. Six months ago, I'd have happily burned any bridges I could for a handful of pills, but now I've got the reality of the damage I've done—to myself, to Mina, to Trev, to my parents.

Mina and I aren't the same anymore. There's a tense undercurrent to all our conversations. Out of the corner of my eye, I catch her watching me, but every time I look at her straight on, she pretends she hasn't been staring.

I wish she'd just say something. Anything to stop this agonizing push and pull we've fallen back into.

Mina's phone rings. She checks it, sighs, and throws it in her purse. It's the third time she's done that in the last twenty minutes.

I raise an eyebrow.

"I don't want to talk about it," she says.

"Okay."

We're quiet for a while. Songs cycle through the playlist, and Mina drums her fingers against the steering wheel as the headlights cut through the darkness.

"Soph, you know that fight we had last week, when we had dinner with Trev and Kyle?" Mina's voice is level; she keeps her eyes on the road, but her cheeks blush a steady pink.

"Yes," I say, and I feel like I'm walking on eggshells and hot coals all at once. Is she really going there?

Mina twists a strand of dark hair around her finger, still not looking at me, even though I'm staring so hard she has to feel it.

"You remember what you said? About choices?"

"I remember," I say carefully. I'm afraid to say any more.

"We should talk about it."

"Now?"

She shakes her head. "Not yet. But soon. Okay?"

"Okay."

"You promise?" She turns away from the road, and I'm startled to see a rare streak of vulnerability in her face.

"I promise."

She's got to hear it, how much I mean it.

It's the first (last, only) promise I break to her.

57

"The handwriting matches the notes I found in the garage?" Rachel asks as we drive in my car toward the lake, Kyle in the backseat.

"Yeah," I say. "Check my phone. I took a picture of it. And see if Trev's texted me yet."

"Nada," Rachel says as she opens my photos, squinting at the image of the note. "He took a picture of you guys?"

"That's creepy," Kyle says, taking the phone from her to look. "He's stalking you. Are you sure you didn't see anyone?"

"All the parents were picking up the soccer team. I wasn't paying attention to what was going on in the parking lot. He could've easily pulled up next to Trev's truck, dropped the note, and driven off while we were talking to Amy."

"Maybe he left fingerprints," Kyle suggests.

"The police will dust all the notes, but I doubt they'll find anything. They didn't find any fingerprints at the crime scene."

"So, we think it's Matt, right?" Rachel asks. "Unless Jackie was sleeping around, he's the dad of the baby. And the baby has to be the reason she disappeared."

"It makes sense," I say. "And I made him angry after the meeting, bringing up the possibility of a pregnancy."

"He looked like he was gonna hit you," Rachel says.

"Well, he didn't," I say.

"Jesus," Kyle says.

"What?" Rachel asks.

Kyle just shakes his head. "I've known him forever," he says. "As long as I've known Adam. He got us our first beers back when we were freshmen. It's just . . . it's fucked that we even have to think like this about people we know."

Rachel and I exchange a look. "It's not for sure," Rachel says.

"Yeah," Kyle says, but he sounds far from convinced.

"Okay, we need a happier subject," Rachel insists.

"Well, this is probably my final night of freedom," I say. "As soon as the cops call my parents about the threats, they're gonna freak and lock me in the house."

"Not really happy," Rachel says. "But you're not Ms. Sunshine, so A-plus for effort."

"I'd suggest you do something wild, but isn't that against the rehab rules?" Kyle asks.

"We could go skinny-dipping," Rachel suggests, and while I can tell she's half joking, Kyle perks up at the idea.

I smile outright now, because he can't tear his eyes off Rachel. "Sure. Let's do that," I say. "Kyle, you can't come. I don't want to see your bits."

"Like I want to see yours," Kyle shoots back as Rachel giggles.

I look down at the phone in my lap as we pull into the

parking lot of Brandy Creek. Still no text from Trev.

What's taking him so long? It's been three hours.

I feel a flash of nervousness as I see all the people on the beach. The bonfire is already crackling, coolers set out, music blasting. I turn the car off and get out. The reluctance must show on my face, because Rachel nudges me with her elbow. "We don't have to go down," she says.

I shake my head. "No, let's," I make myself say.

I have to figure out how to come out of this with some kind of normal. Otherwise I'll backslide. I'll fall so fast and so hard that I won't be able to pull myself out again.

Ten months. Five days.

I toss my phone into my purse and walk down the beach with Rachel and Kyle.

There are some pockets of strained silence as we make our way through the group of familiar faces. Kyle's hugging people and smiling at girls, introducing Rachel as I follow behind, my eyes cast down. A shyness I haven't felt in forever suffocates me.

"I'm gonna get some water," I tell Rachel, zeroing in on one of the coolers tucked farther down the beach. It's less mobbed over there.

She nods and waves me off with a look of understanding, though I can feel her tracking me, making sure I'm okay as I break from the crowd. I look over my shoulder and watch her for a second, see the way she smiles at Kyle in the firelight. He's already ditched his shirt, now tucked into his back pocket.

"Watch it," says a sharp voice.

I run smack into someone and stumble backward, my footing unsteady in the sand.

Amber doesn't even reach out to try to help me. She stands still, her arms folded, as I teeter, trying to keep my balance. When I'm finally steady, she stands there, disapproval radiating off of her.

"Hi, Amber."

"Sophie," she says, and I'm impressed—she could freeze ice with that voice. "I can't believe you thought it was okay to show up here."

I feel tired all of a sudden. I don't want to do this. Not here. Not ever. "Let's just avoid each other." I start to move past her.

"You know, I never got what she saw in you. You wrecked yourself. And then you brought her down with you."

I stop. We're drawing attention now, and my skin crawls at all the eyes on me. "Let's not talk about it. I don't want to fight."

"Don't tell me what to do," Amber snaps. "I don't have to listen to you. You shouldn't be here. You should be in jail."

"Hey!" Rachel comes up, scattering sand everywhere, her shoulders tense. "Leave her alone."

Amber's mouth twists in disapproval at Rachel's funky bubble skirt and the necklace she's made out of Scrabble tiles. "Freak," she mutters.

Rachel's face lights up; her eyes flick up and down Amber's body, taking in her perfectly tousled beach hair and sparkly eye makeup. "I'm taking that as a compliment," she says.

Kyle comes up behind Rachel, looming over her like he's our personal bodyguard. He crosses his arms, brown eyes narrowing. "Sophie and Rachel are here with me. Don't talk about stuff you don't know shit about, Amber. Leave us alone."

Amber's eyes widen when Kyle defends me, then she deflates. "Whatever. You wanna stomp on Mina's grave with the person responsible, Kyle, you go ahead." With another disgusted look at me, she tosses her hair over her shoulder and stalks off.

I let out a long breath. "Thanks."

Kyle runs a hand through his hair, eyes on the sand. "She was being a jerk."

"Come on, just ignore her," Rachel says. "Let's get something to drink."

"I should check my phone. I left it in the car." It's a lie, but I want to be alone.

"I'll come with," Rachel offers, but I wave her off.

"It's fine. Trev probably texted me. I just want to check. Be right back." I need a few minutes by myself. There are too many familiar faces here.

Before either of them can protest, I'm walking away as fast as my bad leg allows. I'm halfway up the beach, concentrating on navigating through the sand and getting my phone out of my purse when I hear someone calling my name.

"Sophie! Hey!" Adam comes jogging up. There are wet spots on his faded T-shirt, and his hair's dropping into his eyes. "Kyle sent me after you. He didn't want you to go anywhere solo." He looks down at the phone in my hand. "Thought you were getting your phone." I flush, but Adam smiles. "Hey, it's okay. Amber was being mean. I'd want to get away, too. Can I come with you, at least, so Kyle doesn't get mad at me?"

"I'm just going to my car; not that exciting."

"I'll tag along. Hey, you want?" He offers me a bottle of Coke, which I grab from him. I twist it open and take a drink as Adam gestures for me to keep going. He follows, hands in the pockets of his board shorts. I don't look down at my phone, even though I want to check to make sure I didn't miss any texts. "How's your garden?" he asks as the beach fades into pavement.

"Good. Thanks again for helping me with that soil. What about you? How's your summer?" The one light in the parking lot is about to die. It's quieter up here, the noise from the beach fading as we walk farther away. I unlock my car and dump my purse onto the front seat. I flip my phone over so I can see the screen. There's a missed call from a number I don't recognize. My heart skips a few beats before starting to pound in my ears.

Is this it?

"I'll be right back," I tell Adam. I walk a few steps down the path before entering my voice mail code. I take another drink, expecting Trev's voice on the message, but it isn't his.

"Hi, Sophie, this is Tom Wells from the *Harper Beacon*. I've been thinking about our conversation last week. I'll hope you'll get back to me; I'd really like to talk about your side of this story. On the record. Give me a call back."

I frown and delete the message.

You still talking to the detective? I text Trev before putting my phone on vibrate and pocketing it so I'll feel it. I can't stop the thread of worry working through my brain. I tell myself instead that it's a good sign he doesn't have time to text me.

"You mind if we hang out here for a sec?" I ask as I walk back to Adam. He's sprawled against my car trunk, his soda in his hand. "Things out there are kind of . . ."

"I get it," Adam says.

I hoist myself carefully onto the trunk, my legs swinging. Adam boosts himself up beside me.

"Who was on the phone?" Adam asks.

"Oh, I'm just waiting for Trev to text me. He's supposed to come by later."

Adam raises an eyebrow. "You guys finally getting together?" He laughs when he sees the look on my face. "What? Everyone always talked about you two like it was this predestined thing. Why do you think I never asked you out?" He wiggles his eyebrows at me, making me laugh.

"*You* wanted to ask me out?" I grin and take a sip of soda. "When was this? Before or after Amber?"

"Before," Adam shrugs, grinning. "I had a big crush on you in second grade. Trev's lucky."

I don't bother to hide my smile. "Well, I'm not dating Trev," I say. "Trev is . . ." I try to figure out a way to put it. That feeling that went beyond friends, beyond family, but wasn't the right kind of love. "Trev is Trev," I say finally. "And dating . . . dating is not for me. Not right now, at least."

"I get that. You've got a lot going on," Adam says. "Concentrating on being healthy is important. You're going to meetings, right? Uncle Rob said you were at the church the other day."

"Been talking about it with my therapist," I say. "He thinks it might be good for me."

"It's interesting," Adam says. "I go sometimes with Matt so he won't ditch. I dunno, listening to all those stories . . . It's like people fuck up all the time, but I think it helps to admit it, you know? To ask for forgiveness? Most of the time, you get it. People are really good at forgiving, if you just ask for it."

"Some things, though, you can't forgive," I say. "Sometimes you do or see things that are so bad. . . ." I take a long sip of soda, thinking about Matt, about how he'd probably killed Mina, Jackie, and his baby. I think about Trev, and how everything he wanted had been stalled by our secrets. I think about Rachel, finding me on that road, broken and bloody, and never showing any fear. I shake off the thoughts, pasting a smile on my face. "Anyway, Matt's doing good with the meetings now, right? He looked really healthy when I saw him."

"Definitely," he says. "And, I mean, he did a lot of things that were bad. Made a lot of mistakes. My mom wouldn't talk to him for six months. But Uncle Rob got him clean, got him to work the program, prove to her he was serious."

"It's nice that you have him looking out for you," I say. I pat the phone in my back pocket absently. Trev should've texted me by now. Was he still at the station?

"Yeah," Adam agrees. "He stepped up when Dad left. Helped Mom out with money and stuff. He did so much for me—there wouldn't be half the recruiters coming to see me play if it weren't for him."

"That must be crazy to think about," I say. "All those people, coming to see you. I'd freak out."

"Yeah." Adam grins nervously. "But in a good way, you know?"

"You've worked really hard," I say. "You deserve it." I wish Trev would text me. I take another long drink of soda. My mouth's dry. I feel too hot all of a sudden. I swing my good leg back and forth and frown when it hits the bumper.

"You excited about senior year?" Adam asks.

"Kind of." I blink, rubbing at my eyes. I struggle to swallow, and when I try to take a sip, I miss, spilling soda everywhere. My arm feels weird and heavy.

"Easy," Adam says, taking the bottle out of my limp hand and sliding off the trunk.

I blink again, trying to clear my throbbing head.

"Sorry, Sophie," he says quietly. "I like you. Always have. You're a nice girl."

The words take a second to work themselves into my brain. I can't concentrate; my eyes droop. I feel like I've just done six shots of tequila in a row. "You . . . what? I don't . . ."

I try to get up off my elbows, but my arms and legs are like Jell-O. I can barely feel them.

Drugged. The word floods into me, a too-late realization that breaks through the sluggishness.

"Oh God," I mumble with numb lips. "No." I try to get

up again and slide off the trunk, but he's there, holding me up. His face is inches away from mine; I can see a spot on his jaw that he missed shaving.

"No!" I push at him, a solid wall of muscle, as he crowds me against the car. I need something. The bear spray. It's in my purse. I have to get it out. . . . If I can just reach it . . .

"Sophie, don't fight it," he says, and he's so gentle when he holds my wrists together, it scares me more than if he had punched me in the face. I kick out with my good leg, but my bad one is so rubbery that it won't take my weight, and I sag against him farther.

"I'm sorry, I really am. I didn't want to do this the first time. I tried to warn you but you just won't stop," Adam says. I push at him again, trying to tilt my body to the side as he loops some hard plastic around my hands, pulling at the end of the zip tie, binding my wrists together. "You have that reporter asking questions, you went to Matt, you went to Jack, to Amy. You're too nosy, Sophie. Just like Mina."

I open my mouth, cottony and dry from the drug, to scream, but he's too fast for me. He claps a hand over my lips and shoves me as I struggle against him—when had he opened the door?—and I fall onto the backseat of my car, dizzy as he lets go of my mouth to yank the keys out of my pocket.

"It was you." I croak out. I have to say it. I need to hear it.

Leaning over me, he says, "It was me." A quiet confirmation, an almost relieved revelation, the last words I hear before he slams the car door shut and I pass out.

58

"Seriously, this is creepy. What are we doing here?"

Mina leaves the keys in my car so the lights will stay on. I get out, shutting the door as Mina props herself up on the hood. Her hair is illuminated by the headlights. She looks unearthly, almost glowing, and I'm struck by it for a moment, half forgetting that I've asked a question.

"I told you, it's for the *Beacon*."

"Mina, the only people who come out here are tweekers and couples who don't mind screwing in a backseat."

I skirt the edge of the cliff. The drop down is an endless gape of darkness. My leg's stiff from being in the car. I stretch it out, nearly overbalance.

"It'll just take a few minutes. Get away from the edge, Soph."

"I'm feet away from the edge." Okay, maybe only about a foot, but still, plenty. "What is so important about this story? Amber's going to be pissed that we're late."

"I'll tell you later. After I figure . . . After I write it. Seriously, get away from there. I just got you back from your aunt; I'm not gonna let you fall off a cliff. Come over here."

She snaps her fingers, and I stick my tongue out but walk away from the edge so I'm closer to the car. "You should at least entertain me until your Deep Throat or whoever shows up."

"I'm so proud of you for that reference." Mina places a hand against her chest dramatically, wiping away pretend tears with the other.

I kick dirt at her and she squeals, scrambling farther up the hood until she's pressed up against the windshield. "Okay, I'll tell you," she says solemnly. "But you have to promise not to breathe a word." She looks to her left, then her right, before leaning forward and hissing: "Alien takeover is imminent."

"Oh no! The little green men are coming!" I fake a gasp, and she beams at me for playing along.

I hear the crunch of footsteps before she does, in that last brief moment when everything is still okay.

Mina's sitting on the hood, so her back's to him. I'm facing him, and at first, it's too dark to see something's wrong.

Then he steps into the beam of the headlights, and I realize two things in quick succession: the person—a man—coming toward us is wearing a ski mask.

And he has a gun pointed at Mina.

"Mina." I choke on her name. I have no air; it's all been sucked out of my lungs. I grab her arm, drag her off the hood of the car.

We have to get away, but I can't run—I won't be fast enough. He'll get me. She needs to leave me behind. She needs to run and not look back, but I don't know how to tell her this; I've forgotten how to speak. I almost fall as her shoulders knock into mine. Our hands grasp as her mouth drops into an *O*, her eyes fixed on the man as he advances on us.

This is happening. This is actually happening.

Oh God, oh God, oh God.

He stops just a few feet away, saying nothing. But he points to me and gestures with the gun, his meaning clear: *Get away from her.*

Mina's nails dig into my skin. My leg shakes; I lean against her, and she takes some of my weight.

"Oh my God, oh my God, oh my God," Mina whispers between quick, staccato breaths.

"There's cash in our purses." I falter over the words. "Keys are in the car. Just take it. Please."

He stabs the gun at me again, quick and angry.

When I don't move, he strides forward. He seems impossibly huge in that moment, coming toward us. Terror seizes me so quickly, so harshly, so unlike anything I've ever known, that if I could, I'd shrivel beneath the weight of it. Mina whimpers and we stumble back, still clinging to each other, but he's too fast. I've been so distracted by the gun that I don't see what he has in his other hand before it's too late.

The rebar connects with my bad leg, smacking the twisted bone. I yell, a wretched, cut-off sound, and I collapse belly-first onto the dirt. My fingers scrabble at the ground, dig in. I need to get up. . . . I need . . .

"Sophie!" Mina starts toward me, and then she screams as the rebar swings into my line of sight and glances off my forehead. My vision blurs, my skin splits open. Pain, white-hot, stabs through my skull, wetness trickles down my face, and the last thing I see, hear, feel, is him raising that gun, speaking muffled words behind a mask, then the sound of two shots, fired one after the other, and a warm splatter: her blood. It's her blood on my arm.

Then there's nothing. No shooter. No blood. No Mina.

Just dark.

59

My eyes are heavy. It takes a huge effort to open them. I blink, trying to focus on the gray blur in front of me.

Upholstery.

We're driving.

Adam's driving. Speeding down the twisting road that goes around the lake.

Adam killed Mina.

And he's going to kill me.

I have to stay awake. I blink rapidly, struggling to sit up.

Everything tilts crazily, making me dizzy, but maybe if I get upright, I won't feel like puking.

Ten months. Five days.

Ten months. Five days.

I can do this. I'm a drug addict. I'm supposed to be good at this. I just have to fight the high. This is nothing.

It has to be nothing. I have to think—I need to get out alive. They'll never know it was him, they'll never catch him, if I don't.

"Come *on*," says Adam angrily.

Breathing quietly, I sneak a peek at the front seat. Sweat's pouring off his forehead as he punches Send over and over winding down the mountain road. We're almost to Pioneer Rock. I can see the light from the ranger's station across the lake out the back window.

"You know this is crazy," I tell him. "You took my car. People at the party are going to notice both of us are gone. Kyle sent you to watch me; he'll notice."

"Do you really think Kyle sent me after you?" Adam says. "Come on, Sophie. You're smarter than that. Now, you're gonna tell me who's been helping you. I know about Trev. What's the redhead's name? Did you mix her and Kyle up in this? And the reporter? What did you say to him?"

I have to breathe deeply to keep from panicking. Remind myself that Trev is probably still with the cops. That Rachel and Kyle are safe in a crowd of people.

It's just me who's dead.

"What are you gonna do, Adam? Kill all of them, too?" I ask shakily. "You aren't thinking this through. You thought it through before. I know you did. You were prepared last time. You brought the rebar and the pills so you wouldn't have to kill me. That was smart. It worked, didn't it? But you're not ready this time, so why don't you just think for a second?"

"Shut up." Adam wipes fresh sweat off his face with a shaking hand. But as soon as he touches the gun again, his fingers steady, like the feel of it comforts him. "You're gonna tell me everything you know. About Jackie. About Mina. And about who knows what you know. I'll make you."

There's no reasoning with him. He's going to kill me no matter what.

We round a curve, passing by another sign: PIONEER ROCK VISTA POINT (1 MILE).

I can't waste another second—I need a plan. Now.

If I can't calm him down, I might as well make him angry. Make him lose control, slip up. I need a window of opportunity.

"I'm not telling you shit," I say, with a lot more strength than I've got. "You're a fucking murderer, and so is your brother. Your whole family—there's something wrong with you."

In profile, I can see Adam's pretty-boy face twist, the mean gleam in his eyes a stark contrast. His hand tightens on the gun. "Fuck you," he growls between gritted teeth. "You don't know shit about my family. We look out for each other. We rely on each other. We'd kill for each other. That's what family does."

It fills me, the anger, trampling every other feeling in its power. He took away the most important person in my life and he's sitting there with a gun, ready to kill me, lecturing me about *family*. I want to throw myself at him. I want him writhing on the ground, want him to feel what she felt. I want him bleeding while I watch and laugh and refuse to call the ambulance until it's too late.

I want him dead. Even if I have to do it myself.

The idea surges through me, giving me strength, and I push up on my knees on the backseat and lurch forward, clumsy with the drug and adrenaline. I manage to loop my bound arms around his neck; the edge of the zip tie bites into his windpipe, and I pull back with all the force I've got.

His cut-off gasp, stifled instantly by the zip tie, is the most perfect sound.

He jerks the wheel, an involuntary movement that nearly sends us into a tailspin down the mountain. Choking, he fights back, scrabbling to hook his free hand between my wrists as we swerve across the narrow two-lane road. Any second, we'll veer off the pavement, down the red clay cliff on one side or tumbling into the lake on the other—and I don't care. *I don't care.* I hope we crash. It'll be worth it, as long as he's dead, too.

"Soph—" he gurgles, frantically clawing at me with his free hand, his blunt nails digging into my skin.

I lock my arms, muscles straining as I pull back as hard as I can. He's wedged a fingertip between the zip tie and his neck, and my arms are trembling with the effort of resisting him. He's so much stronger than I am, but if I can just hold out . . .

The gunshot splits the air, and the windshield implodes in a shower of shards. I flinch from the flying glass, jerking back, and suddenly Adam's hands aren't on the wheel anymore. One's holding the gun and the other's pinning my wrists, and the car's spinning, too fast, too close to the safety rail. I have one second, one hysterical breath to take in before metal screeches and sparks, and we're through the guard rail and racing down the slope, trees and boulders blurring as our speed picks up and I know it's over. The end.

Third time's the charm.

60

I wake to the sound of Mina dying. A death rattle.

"Mina, oh my God, *Mina*." I crawl over to her; it's like I'm moving underwater.

She's lying on her back a foot away, bathed in the light from the car's brights and the blood, *her* blood, has already stained the dirt around her. Her hands rest against her chest, and her eyes are barely open.

There's blood everywhere. I can't even tell where the bullets went in. "Okay, okay," I say, words that have no meaning, just to fill the air, to drown out the sound of her breath, the way it comes too fast and shuddery, wet at the end, like her lungs are already filling.

I rip my jacket off, press it against her chest where the dark wetness keeps spreading. I have to stop the blood.

"I'm sorry," she breathes.

"No, no, it's okay. Everything will be okay." I look over my shoulder, half convinced he's lurking somewhere, waiting to finish us off.

But he's gone.

She coughs, and when blood trickles out of her mouth, I wipe it away with my hand. "I'm so sorry, Sophie," she whispers.

"You don't have to be. It's okay." I press harder into her chest with both hands. "It's okay. It'll all be okay."

But the blood bubbles up against my fingers, through the denim of my jacket.

How can there be this much blood? How much can she lose before . . .

She swallows, a convulsive movement, and when she breathes out, more red stains her mouth. "Hurts," she says.

When I reach out with one hand to smooth the hair off her forehead, I leave a trail of blood behind. All I can think about is that time in third grade. She fainted when I cut my arm open so badly I needed stitches; she didn't like blood. I want to hide it from her now, but I can't. I can see it in her eyes, that she knows what's happening, the thing I can't accept.

"It's okay," I say again. I swear it, when I have no right to.

"Sophie . . ." She lifts her hand, clumsily drags it toward mine. I twist our fingers together, hold on tight.

I won't let her go.

"Soph—"

Her chest rises with one last jagged breath and then she exhales gently, her body going still, her eyes losing their light, their focus on me dimming as I watch. Her head leans to the side, her grip slowly loosening in mine.

"No, no, no!" I shake her, pound against her chest. "Wake up, Mina. Come on, wake up!" I tilt her head back and breathe into her mouth. Over and over, until I'm drenched in sweat and blood. "No, Mina! *Wake up!*"

I hold her tight against my shoulder and scream in the darkness, begging for help.

Wakeupwakeupwakeuppleasepleaseplease.

No help comes.

It's just her and me.

Mina's skin gets colder by the minute.

I still don't let her go.

61

I smell the smoke first. Then charred metal and gasoline, the tang filling the air, sharp in my nose. There's a rhythmic ringing in my head, growing louder and louder. I blink, but something spills into my eyes, moisture that I smear off my face.

I squint down at my bound hands, trying to focus as the wetness drips down my chin, splattering red on my arm.

Blood.

It hurts. I realize it between one shaky breath and another. Everything hurts.

Oh, God.

My legs. Do they work?

I push forward with my good one, and it hurts, *it hurts*, and I never thought it'd feel so good to hurt that much, but pain is good. Pain means I'm not paralyzed. That I'm still alive.

Is Adam? I try to push myself up to see, but the ringing in my ears grows louder as I lean forward through the gap between the seats. I tilt my head up, trying to get a good look at him, slumped over the steering wheel. His dark hair is matted with blood on one side, and his chest is rising and falling steadily.

I have to get out of here before he comes to.

My mind's made up in a second. I hook the edge of the zip tie around the jagged edge of the broken window, sawing it back and forth until it snaps. My hands free, I grab the door handle, trying to push it open, but it's jammed.

The ringing sound's getting louder, like someone's turned up the volume on me, and underneath the insistent tones, there's a moaning.

Adam begins to stir in the front seat, and I try the opposite door handle, my heart pounding as more blood dribbles down my cheek. This door's also too mangled to open, so I heave myself up and out of the broken window. The fit's tight, and glass digs into my stomach as I push myself forward, but I keep going, pitching headfirst, almost somersaulting out of the car. I hit the forest floor with a thump, my shoulders tightening as pain flares down my back.

The car had gone straight down the embankment, the hood crumpled like ribbon candy. Smoke is rising off the engine, choking me, and I cough weakly, something sharp knifing through my ribs.

I stumble up to standing, unsteady on shaky legs, and look around. We've ended up in a flatter area, but there are trees looming everywhere. Deep forest spreads ahead of me on all sides. I want to get the gun and my phone, but I don't see either of them in the car, and I don't have time to look—I've got to go. Leaves and branches crackle underneath my feet. The full moon is climbing in the sky, its light illuminating the forest.

I have to move. I forge ahead, my bad leg dragging in the

dirt, catching on rocks and branches, leaving a trail a mile wide, dotted with blood. Even with the moonlight, it's hard to see. I stumble, falling to my knees, my palms scraping the dirt as I push myself back up.

Climbing the embankment isn't possible. Not like this, not with my bad leg, and not with my good one, which is trembling almost as badly.

Hiding's the only option.

The trees thicken as I limp farther into the woods as fast as I can, weaving between the pines as the smoky smell from the crash starts to fade into the dark scents of earth and water, a stronger tang of copper sharpening the breeze. My stomach's wet; my shirt's heavy with blood, slapping against my belly with each movement. I don't have to look down to see the darkness of blood spreading. The cuts on my stomach are shallow but long; they sting with each breath I take, along with the pain in my ribs. But I keep moving. I have to keep moving as fast as I can.

For what feels like forever, it's just me and my harsh breathing and each step crushingly loud in my ears, hurting, hurting, hurting, and wondering if it's going to be my last. If I'm going to fall.

I collapse behind a group of boulders before my leg gives out, panting at the effort it takes to lower myself to the ground. My eyes droop shut, and I force them open again.

I have to stay conscious. I have to focus.

I have to stay alive.

I curl myself up, my knees tucked up near my chin, trying to make myself as small as possible, pressing against the solid rock. It hurts, makes me bite my lip hard, but I power through it, my ribs throbbing with each breath.

When I hear the footsteps, quick and solid through the brush, my heart leaps, my muscles seize up, and everything in me says *run, run, run*. It's a death sentence, I know that, but I'm hardwired for fight or flight, even though I can't do either.

I quiet my breathing and focus on the footfalls—are they coming toward me or heading away?

The crunching suddenly stops. I bend farther into myself, every muscle shrinking, as a deep voice in the distance, laced with panic, breaks the silence of the forest. "Adam? Adam? Where the fuck are you?" More footsteps, closer now.

Heading toward me.

Now there's a snapping sound, someone thrashing through the underbrush.

Two sets of footsteps, coming from different directions: one sure and steady, the other stumbling, injured.

Matt and Adam. I curl up tighter, dread settling in my bones.

"Adam!" They've found each other. They're still a good twenty feet away, but I can hear them.

"Did you see her?" Adam's slurring his words. He must be really hurt.

Good. I hope he bleeds to death.

"See who? What the hell happened? That car . . . Your head! We need to get you to the hospital!" Matt's voice, urgent, almost angry, sounds strange.

"*No!* We gotta find her! She knows everything. We gotta stop her before . . . before . . ."

"What are you talking about? Let's go!"

"*No, listen.* She *knows.*"

"Knows what? Who? Come on, let's move it!"

The footsteps start up again, and the voices are getting closer. Too late for me to move now. I cringe against the rock, wishing it'd swallow me up.

"I didn't tell anyone." Adam's babbling, his words jumbled together. "All these years, I never told anyone. But I saw her get into your truck that day. I know what you did to Jackie. But I didn't tell anyone; not even Mom or Matt. I thought it would be okay. But then Mina started asking questions. I had to stop her—I *had* to."

"What are you talking about?" Matt's voice growls, incredulous.

Wait.

No.

The footsteps are coming closer now as my sluggish brain trips over Adam's confession, tracing it back.

I didn't tell anyone; not even Mom or Matt.

It isn't Matt on the other side of the rock.

If this isn't Matt . . .

If it wasn't Matt's baby . . .

We'd kill for each other. That's what family does.

That's what Adam did. The realization jolts heavy in my stomach, and I can't stop the sharp gasp for breath as it hits me.

"What was that?"

Before Adam can answer, there are boots moving on the ground. Those sure and steady steps that can't be Adam.

His boots. Coming toward me.

He's too fast. I try to get to my feet, but my bad leg collapses under me. I scrabble at the rock. I need a handhold to pull myself up. I need to run. I need to try.

But it's too late.

He rounds the corner of the group of boulders I'm crouching beside, and when he turns his head and sees me, something like relief sparks in his eyes.

"Sophie," he says, like it's a normal day. Like I've been lost in the woods and he'd been sent to find me. "You're hurt." He reaches out, and he looks so *concerned* when he touches my face.

My head smacks against the boulder in my effort to get away. My good leg kicks out, twitching as every muscle locks up, screaming *runrunrun*. Pain throbs through me so badly, I lose my breath.

He smiles at me. That you-can-do-better smile that he used to shoot us when we'd miss a goal. "It's okay, Sophie," Coach Rob says. "I think it's time we have a talk."

After Mina stops breathing, I can't let go of her. I know I have to. I need to get up. Find help.

I have to let go.

I whisper to myself, rocking, her back pressed into my chest, her head cradled in the crook of my neck, my arms around her. "C'mon. C'mon." But it's almost impossible to unclench my fingers. To grasp her shoulders and lay her down on the ground. I tuck my jacket beneath her head. I wish, in a frantic moment that's so sharp it leaves me gasping, that I had something to cover her with. It's cold outside.

I brush a strand of hair off her forehead, smoothing it behind her ear. Her eyes are still open, hazy now, staring but not seeing the endless sky.

My hand shakes as I close them. It feels so wrong, like I'm taking away the last part of her.

I stagger up off my knees and drag myself, stumbling, toward the car. The door's open, and the keys and our phones are gone.

Help. I need to get help. I repeat it over and over in my head. I have to drown it out, the voice that screams *Mina, Mina, Mina,* over and over and over.

I take one unsure step. Then another. And another.

I walk away from her.

It's the hardest thing I've ever done.

His hand slides from my cheek to my throat, applying the barest amount of pressure.

A warning.

"Don't move," he tells me quietly. "Adam," he calls, raising his voice, and Adam rounds the corner to stand behind him. There's blood all over Adam's face, and he's cradling his right arm like it's broken.

I lunge, because it still burns inside me, how much I want Adam dead. It'll never go away. It'll probably be the last thing I feel.

Coach catches me by the throat and he squeezes, his fingers biting into my neck as he shoves me back against the rock, crowding against my body in a way that makes a whole new kind of fear bloom inside me.

"I told you not to move," he says, and again, it's his coach voice. Like he's disappointed in me for missing a goal.

I whimper. An involuntary sound that wants to be a scream, but I don't have the power for it.

"Why didn't you kill her that night, too?" Coach asks Adam. He doesn't even look at him; he's staring at me, eyes scanning my face like he's trying to memorize it. That and the punishing press of his body against mine keep me frozen and silent. "It would've been easier."

Adam swallows, looking down at his feet. "But she didn't do anything. I didn't want to—it was Mina who was the problem."

"You created a whole set of new problems by leaving a witness," Coach says. "Not smart, Adam."

"I'm sorry," Adam mutters. "I was just . . . I wanted to help you. I thought I had it covered."

Coach sighs. "It's okay," he says. "We'll figure it out. You don't have to worry." His hand tightens on my throat, and I can barely get a breath in. I start coughing, making my ribs move against each other all wrong, a grating, painful sensation that makes me dizzy. "I'll take care of it," he says. "You have your gun?"

I have to bite down on my tongue to hold back the panic caught in the back of my throat. My head's spinning; I'm not getting enough air.

"In the car, I think."

"Go get it. Then come right back."

"But—"

"*Adam.*" Coach turns to look at him impatiently. "My job is to look out for you. Your job is to listen to me. What do we say?"

"Family first."

"That's right. So let me take care of this. Go get the gun."

I can hear the rustle of brush as Adam walks off. Coach waits until he's gone before turning his attention back to me. His hand loosens on my neck, moving lower.

"*No.*" The word rips from my lips, because I'm terrified of what he might do. But he leaves his hand resting on my shoulder, pinning me to the boulder.

"They'll figure it out," I pant, wanting more air, not being able to get it. "They'll get you. You can kill me, but they'll get you. It's over."

"It's not over until I say it is." Coach's fingers flex into my shoulder, five points of pain radiating through me. "I won't let you ruin my nephew's life."

But I'm going to.

And with that understanding, despite the panic, a beautiful sense of calm falls over me. It's probably shock or trauma more than an epiphany, but I don't care. It feels too good after all the fear.

Adam's blood is all over my car. Even though Coach will kill me, this is the end for them. Trev and the police will figure it out. He'll make sure they pay.

I lift my head with some effort. My vision wavers; I'm running on adrenaline and I'm gonna crash soon, but I want to be looking into his eyes when I say it. "I'm going to ruin both of your lives. I don't have to be alive to do that. Too many people know what I was doing. By now, the police are looking for me—and for Adam. They'll find my car. They'll find my body, wherever you dump it. You know my mom—you think someone like her will stop at anything? My dad thought you were a friend, but he'll see through you. My aunt is a bounty hunter; finding people is her job. Trev has all the evidence—he'll never rest until it's done. Until you're done. You were right, Coach: family does come first. And my family will bring yours down."

"I'm not going to discuss this," Coach says, like I've brought up something mildly annoying.

"You're a murderer. You killed Jackie and her baby. You probably raped—"

The shift in his demeanor—so in control, so steady and normal even while he's got me pinned—is lightning fast. He slams me against the boulder and I cry out as he presses close. My spine feels like it's being crushed by his weight. "Don't you ever say that," he hisses. "Should I have let Matt drag her down with him? I saw the way he was going. I *loved* that girl. And she loved me."

My eyes widen at the implications. "You—did you— were you and Jackie . . . *together*?" The disgust drips from me. He's my *dad's* age. It's almost worse if she'd loved him. If she'd trusted him.

He doesn't say anything.

"You didn't even have to force her to go with you, did you?" My voice cracks. It hurts to talk. My throat's bruised from his hands. "I bet it was easy. Just told her you wanted to talk about the baby, and she got right in your truck."

He stares at me, his hands loosening on my shoulders, transfixed by my words, by the exposure of the secret he's been keeping for so many years. I recognize that look, know it all too well. When you're kept by a secret, the first time you hear it spoken out loud is mesmerizing.

Over Coach's shoulder, through the shadow of the trees, I see a pinprick of light. It moves steadily back and forth, like someone's looking for something.

Looking for me.

Trev.

Coach doesn't see it; he's lost in the past. "I told her to get rid of it, but she didn't want to. She didn't understand what it'd do to me. She just . . ." He lets out a rough exhale, angry at a girl who just wanted to live.

His hands tighten on my shoulders, pinning my arms and lifting me off my feet. I scrabble frantically with my hands, trying to grab something, anything. My fingers brush against some loose pebbles, scattering them, and then snag a bigger, rougher piece of slate, unable to get a good enough grasp to lift it.

I lick my bloody lips. The light is getting closer, and there are more now—I count four, sweeping steadily toward us. If Coach sees them, hears the footsteps, he'll kill me before they can stop him. I have to keep him talking, keep him distracted.

He looks me in the eye, big, cold pools of dark, and my stomach lurches at the smoothed lines of his face, at how relieved he looks.

He's made up his mind.

"She was going to give it up," I gasp out. "Did you know that? That she was talking to an adoption counselor? She was gonna do what you wanted." It's a gamble, but it's the only card I've got left.

Coach's grip on me falters for a split second. It's just enough for my fingers to reach the loose piece of slate, and I swing it high, slamming it into his head as hard as I can.

He grunts and lets go of me, and I duck beneath his outstretched arm as he lunges forward, trying to catch me.

I manage only a few steps before my leg gives out and I collapse on the ground. I shout as loud as I can, even though it hurts so much I think my eyes will pop out of their sockets. I crawl forward, hoping they'll reach me before he does. I can hear shouting now; it's close, so close. Please just let them find me. . . .

Coach slams into me from behind, flattening me before roughly flipping me over. I yelp; my shoulders take the worst of it. My head slams against the ground as he pins me again with his body, grasping my hands with one of his, forcing them to the ground above my head. I want to shrink away from him, from the pain as his other hand clamps over my mouth, stealing my air.

I manage to open my mouth underneath his hold and bite down hard on his palm, shaking my head back and forth like a dog. The flesh between my teeth tears and he shouts, yanking his hand away as blood arcs from it.

"Stupid *bitch*!" He reaches forward with both hands, curls his fingers around my throat, and squeezes.

Kneeling on my stomach, he's pressing whatever air's left out of my lungs as he cuts off the rest at my throat. Gasping for air where there is none, I try to twist out of his grip, but he's too heavy, and I'm still yanking uselessly at his arms as things go gray around the edges.

My lungs burn as I start to drift, my hands fall away, and the world fades.

The police are here. It's over. I can be done now. And maybe . . . just maybe she was right all along about the heaven thing.

Bang.

Coach jerks, and as he slumps to the side and falls off of me, I suck in air in huge gulps, choking on it. Suddenly, the darkness of the forest is obliterated—everything's too bright, like someone's just turned on a spotlight. I blink dazedly up at the sky. There's a whooshing sound above my head. I feel a sudden breeze on my face and see the pines bending and swaying from the chopper hovering above us.

"Sophie!" Someone's grabbing me, dragging me across the dirt. I bat at the hands on my wrists, trying to fight again. "Sophie! It's okay! You're okay!"

"Where's Adam?" I croak. "He has a gun."

"It's okay," the guy says again. I'm having trouble focusing on the blurry person in front of me, I'm shaking so badly. "We got him. It's okay," he repeats, and then turns his head and yells out, "Can I get some EMTs down here?!"

"Where's Coach?" I mumble. My throat hurts, like someone's dragged a razor through it. Everything hurts. I push at the cop who's holding on to me, trying to sit up. There's a branch digging into my back. "Is he dead?"

"Sophie, you need to stay still. Wilson!" He spots somebody in the distance and calls him over. When the blurry figure trots up, he barks, "Where are my EMTs?"

My eyes drift shut. It feels so good to close them.

"No, no, Sophie, stay awake." Fingers dig painfully into my jaw, yanking my head up. I struggle to open my eyes, blinking, finally focusing on the face in front of me.

It's Detective James. He looks scared. It's weird—cops shouldn't look scared.

"'S'you," I say. "Told you . . . told you I was clean."

"Yeah, you did," he says. "Stay awake, okay? Keep talking to me."

"Don't let them give me anything," I tell him, my eyes shutting again.

"Sophie! Stay awake!"

But I can't. It's too hard. "No drugs," I say. It's important. I don't want them. Not like last time. "Don't let them. . . ."

I fall into blackness between one breath and the other, and nothing is painful and everything is fine and I can feel her, somewhere, somehow . . . and it doesn't hurt. It just feels right.

Waking up in the hospital is familiar. The beeping of the machines, the scratch of the sheets, the smell of antiseptic and death.

"Mina," I murmur, still half-caught in a dream. My hand's being held, carefully, reverently. I know it's not her, but for a moment I keep my eyes closed and pretend.

"Hey, you with me?"

I turn my head to the side. Trev's sitting there. "Hey." I swallow, and then immediately regret it. My throat's on fire; it makes me splutter for air. Trev helps me sit up, rubbing my back.

"So I guess you got my text," I say when I can breathe again. My voice is barely a husk of sound.

"I did," he says. "Jesus, Soph, you scared the crap out of me."

"I'm sorry," I say. I lean my head against his shoulder. His T-shirt feels ridiculously soft against my bruised skin. "I'm really glad you got it, though."

He chokes out a laugh, squeezing my hand. "Yeah, me too."

"You okay?" I ask.

He looks at me, then down at my hand that he's holding. "No," he says. "I'm not okay."

I want to pull back the blankets to let him crawl into bed with me, but I don't. He'll keep it together, because that's who he is. That's what he always does. But we take a minute, just one, of silence, where I hold his hand and hope that it's all right, that it helps in some small way, because both of us have to be strong for her just a little longer.

"Where are my parents?" I ask finally, when his grip loosens. I pull back from him, leaning against the pillows, our fingers still entwined.

"They're talking to the doctors. I snuck in."

"How long has it been?"

"Day and a half. You should go back to sleep. Everything else can wait until tomorrow."

I can't rest or wait, even though every muscle in my body aches and my head is killing me.

Trev's thumb rubs my fingers gently.

"They won't let them out on bail, right?" I blurt out. It's silly, but last time I woke up in the hospital, I woke up to people not believing a word I said. I can't help but be scared of that happening all over again. "Detective James shot Coach—is he still alive?"

"Got him in the shoulder. He'll live to be charged. Adam's already confessed," Trev says, his jaw rigid. "He cracked the second they started questioning him. You were right: he killed Mina and planted the drugs so everyone would think it was your fault. Coach Rob says he didn't know Adam was doing any of it. He's lawyered up. Won't say a thing about Jackie. But it doesn't matter. There are enough charges to lay on him . . . on both of them. They're gonna be in prison for a long time." The satisfaction in his voice is so thick, I can almost taste it.

"Adam saw her," I say. "When he was fourteen. He saw Jackie get into Coach's truck that day. And he never told anyone. Oh, God—Kyle." I look up at Trev. "Adam is—was—his best friend. How is he?"

Trev shakes his head. "Kyle's in shock. The whole town's in shock. I think every girl who ever played soccer is getting grilled by her parents about Coach and if he messed with any of them. He's lucky he's in custody; he wouldn't last a day loose in town."

I shudder, wondering if there are any more girls Coach had "loved." Ones who were lucky enough not to get pregnant.

"My mom keeps asking me how this could be," Trev says. "How no one could know what was going on between him and Jackie, and I don't know what to tell her." He looks up at me with so much pain in his eyes, I need to look away. "He sent us a fucking fruit basket after Mina died, Sophie. I remember writing the thank-you note for it, signing Mom's name."

I swallow, hoping I'll feel less sick. All it does is make my throat hurt more.

"Bastard," I say. I see the same rage simmering back at

me in Trev's eyes. But the word doesn't begin to encompass what we feel toward them. I'm not sure I want to examine it too closely, how clear everything was in those moments when the zip tie had gouged into Adam's neck, cutting off his breath.

Prison is enough. They can both rot there.

I have to repeat it to myself, like it'll convince me that it's a fair trade.

It's not.

It never will be.

But we have to live with the loss. Shape our lives around it.

Trev's hand tightens over mine, and I squeeze back, trying to be reassuring. But there isn't enough reassurance in the world for the two of us. There's no more hiding. Mina is gone, and it's just him and me, who we are and what we did and what lies ahead.

That's the most terrifying thought of all.

"And Matt?" I ask. I feel horrible for confronting him at the church the way I did. If it were me, finding out I came from a family of killers, that they took the love of my life away, I'd be halfway to an OD by now.

"I tried calling. The phone's disconnected. They probably unplugged it because of the reporters. We did the same thing when Mina—" He stops, because there's a tap on my hospital room door and then my mom comes in.

"Sweetheart," she says when she sees I'm awake. Trev lets go of my hand and gets up. "No, it's all right, Trev," she says. "You can stay if you'd like."

"It's okay. I've gotta tell Rachel and Kyle that Sophie's awake," he says. "Check in with my mom. I'll be back later."

My mom sits on the bed next to me, watching me with red eyes. "I'm so glad you're awake. Your dad ran home for a few minutes," she says. "He said you'd want your yoga pants when you woke up. How are you feeling?"

"Tired. Hurt."

"I didn't let them give you any opiates," she says. "I'm sorry, honey, I wish I could—"

"No," I interrupt. "Thank you. I don't want any of that stuff."

She holds my hand between both of hers. "I wish I could make you hurt less," she says.

"It's okay," I say. "I'm fine. I'll be fine. It's over now."

I need to hear that out loud. I need it to sink in, but it hasn't yet.

In a little while the nurse shoos my mom out and turns the lights off, ordering me to rest. I've got three broken ribs, a bruised throat, and enough stitches holding my stomach and face together to feel like Frankenstein's monster; fortunately, most of the injuries are superficial. But even those hurt like hell when you can't have anything stronger than an aspirin.

I don't sleep yet. It hurts too much and I'm afraid of what I'm going to dream about. Afraid that the second I close my eyes, I'll be back in that car, back in Coach's grip, back at Booker's Point.

I can't stop pressing my fingers against the raw skin of my wrists where the zip tie had dug in.

All I can think about is Mina and how I wish I were like her, because then I could believe she's looking down at me right now, happy that we figured it out, brought her and Jackie some justice.

But I can't believe that. All I can do is feel what I feel: a vague sense of relief, dulled by shock and the spacey haze that's stolen over me.

Now it's only me keeping the monsters at bay: I have no mission, no crusade, nothing else. Mina's memory will sustain me for only so long. It scares me, how easy it could be to fall back down that hole I've worked so hard to climb out of.

Ten months. One week.

I want Aunt Macy. I grab the cell phone my parents left for me and punch in her number with shaking hands.

"I'm on my way right now," she says when she picks up. "I'll be there in a few hours."

I let out a shuddery breath. "It's over," I say into the phone.

"Yes it is. Remind me to kick your ass later for putting yourself in so much danger," Macy says, the relief in her voice robbing the threat of all of its power. "This almost-dying thing is getting to be a habit with you. Not good."

"I guess I just take after you," I say.

Macy laughs shakily. "Hell, I hope not."

I'm quiet for a long time, listening to the buzz of Macy's radio, the occasional honk of an eighteen-wheeler as it passes her car. She's on the highway, driving to me. Just the sound of it soothes me in a way nothing else could.

"I'm scared," I say, breaking my silence.

"I know you are," she says, her voice ringing out over the traffic noise. "But you're brave, babe. You're strong."

"I want . . ." I stop. "I really want to shut down right now," I confess. It's sharp in my gut, that need to numb myself, to bury every worry about the future, avoid all the hard choices I have to make.

"They didn't give you anything, did they?"

"No," I say. "Mom wouldn't let them. I don't want any."

"That's smart."

We're quiet again, and eventually I fall asleep, the phone cradled against my ear.

Around two in the morning, the click of the door closing wakes me. I sit up, expecting the nurse, but it's Kyle.

"What are you doing here?" I ask.

"Charmed the nurse into letting me in." Kyle sits down at the foot of the bed, dropping a handful of candy on my lap. "I raided the vending machine."

He looks as bad as I feel. His eyes are all puffy and red, and he's careful not to meet my eyes as he pushes a pack of licorice toward me.

I sit up, tearing the bag open and popping a piece in my mouth. "I don't know what to say," I tell him.

Kyle makes a sound in the back of his throat, an almost childish whimper. "Are you okay?" he asks. "I shouldn't have let you go off alone. You were just gone for a second and then we couldn't find you."

"I'll be fine. It's not your fault. I thought Adam was okay. I walked right into it."

"This is so fucked up, Soph," he says, his voice rough. He rakes his hand through his floppy hair, making it stick up. "He was one of my best friends. We were on the same soccer team since we were, like, six. And he . . . he took her *away.*"

Kyle swallows, fiddling with an open bag of M&M's. He starts to group them by color, eyes focused on his task instead of on me.

"I hate him," I say. It feels good to say it out loud again. It rushes underneath my skin, the fact that now I *know.*

"I want to fucking kill him," Kyle mutters as he makes a neat pile of the green M&M's before moving on to the blue.

"I tried," I confess quietly.

Kyle pauses, turning his head just a sliver toward me, his brown eyes determined. "Good," he says, and the word echoes between the beeping of the machines. For some reason, it makes me breathe easier.

"I'm glad you didn't die," Kyle says.

"Yeah, me, too," I say, and it's the truth. It feels good for it to be the truth.

I shift in the bed, wincing when the movement jostles my ribs.

Kyle stares at my IV bag like it's gonna tell him what to do. "Want me to get the nurse?"

I shake my head. "They can't do anything. No narcotics, remember? Anyway, I don't want to sleep. I'll be fine."

I sound sure, even to my own ears. I know the truth: that months in David's office are waiting for me. That I'm going to have to work at it, through it. That there'll be nightmares and freak-outs and days I jump at the slightest thing and days I want to use so badly I can taste it and days all I want to do is cry and scream. That David is probably going to be on speed dial, and it's going to suck and hurt, but hopefully there'll be some light at the end of the tunnel, because there usually is.

"I'm sorry I've been so shitty to you," Kyle says.

I take a red M&M from his pile. "I've been shitty to you, too," I admit.

For the first time since he came into the room, he looks up, his expression serious and measuring. It makes my mouth go dry.

"What?" I ask, half hoping he'll break the gaze.

But he doesn't. "I know I promised I wouldn't talk about it," he says. "What she told me, about her, about the two of you. But I'm gonna break that promise, this one time." He stares me down, and there's a gentleness in him I've never seen before.

"She was in love with you," he says. "And I don't think she got to tell you, did she?"

My heart lurches, seizes inside my chest, fluttering to life at the words I've always wanted to hear. I shake my head. Tears spill down my cheeks.

"She loved you. She wanted to be with you. That's why she told me about herself. She said she'd made her choice. It was you. I think it was always you."

I look away from him, out through the blinds at the lights of town, and he stays quiet, a comforting witness, letting me cry.

Letting me finally let her go.

64

"Watch out!" Mina stomps into the puddle. Muddy water splashes against my back, drenching me.

"Oh my God!" I shriek, spinning around. "I can't believe you just did that."

She beams over her shoulder, rain dripping down her forehead. She's abandoned her umbrella on the sidewalk, and she's standing smack-dab in the middle of a room-sized puddle. When she tilts her head to the sky, opening her mouth to let in the rain, my stomach swoops. "Come on. Play with me."

"You are such a brat sometimes," I tell her, but when she pouts, I grin and kick water her way, wading in after her. In the deepest part of the puddle, the water reaches my ankles. My feet squelch in the mud as we splash each other, helpless with laughter. We fling mud like we're seven again. I rub it into her hair, and she darts around me like a seal, quick and sleek.

For once, she falls first, right on her ass in the mud, and instead of getting up she holds her hand out, pulling me gently down with her. Just the two of us and the mud and rain, side by side, like we're supposed to be.

Mina sighs happily, her arm looped in mine. She leans her head against my shoulder.

"You're crazy. We're gonna catch pneumonia."

She squeezes my arm, snuggling closer to me. "Admit it. There's nowhere else you'd rather be than here with me."

I close my eyes, let the rain fall on my face, let the weight of her press into me, her warmth seep into my skin. "You got me," I say.

65

"How are you feeling today?" David asks.

I bite my lip. "I'm okay."

"We had a deal, remember?" David says. "It's been six sessions. It's time, Sophie."

"Can't we just talk about the woods instead?"

"The fact that you'd rather talk through being attacked again than talk about Mina is exactly why we need to start talking about her," David says. "It's okay to start small."

"I'm . . ." I stop, because I don't even know how to finish that sentence. "I haven't been able to go out to her grave," I say instead, because it's the thing that's been waking me up at night, in between nightmares of hiding in the forest again. "I thought I'd be able to. Go out there, I mean. I thought that after we caught who killed her—*if* we did— it'd be easier. Like a reward. I know that's stupid. But it's what I thought."

David leans back in his chair, thoughtful.

"I don't think that's stupid," he says. "Why do you think it's so hard for you to go see Mina's grave?"

"I just . . . I miss . . ." I struggle for strength, for composure, for any control, but I am safe here, and I have to say the words. They need to exist somewhere, because they were never said in the right place at the right time.

"We were in love. Me and Mina. We were in love."

I lean back on the couch, hugging myself. I meet his eyes, and the approval I find there, the confirmation, makes the tightness in my chest ease.

"I guess that's why it's so hard," I say.

AUGUST

When my dad comes out of the house, he finds me on the deck, curled up in one of the Adirondack chairs. The sun's setting on my flower beds, and I turn my head toward him, slipping off my sunglasses.

Dad took a few weeks off after I was attacked. And even now, night after night, I hear the rhythmic thumping of the basketball against concrete as he shoots hoops in the driveway while the rest of the world sleeps. Sometimes I sit at the kitchen window and watch him.

Now he sits down in the chair next to me and clears his throat. "Sweetie, I need to tell you something."

"What happened?" I sit up straighter, because his mouth's a flat, unhappy line.

"I just got a call. The forensic team finally found Jackie's body on Rob Hill's property." He rubs a hand across his jaw, his stubble almost completely silver now. He's not sleeping much, and neither am I. Both of us look it.

"Oh," I say. I don't know what else to do. It's weird, but finding Jackie's body feels like a good thing, because I can't help but think of Amy, of not knowing. Of not having a grave to visit.

"So that's it, right?" I ask. "They'll put him away for good?"

"It'll be hard for a jury to overlook that kind of evidence."

I pull my feet up onto the chair, hugging my knees, ignoring the way my bad leg twinges. Sometimes I need to do this, pull into myself, when I think about Coach. When I think about hiding behind that rock, waiting for him to find me. Kill me.

"Sweetie . . ." Dad begins, but then he doesn't say anything else, just continues to watch me.

I wait.

"Is there . . . is there anything you want to talk about?" he asks finally.

I think about it for a second. Telling him. All of it. Me and Mina. Me and Trev. The tangle I found myself in, no way out but drugs, for so long. A part of me wants to. But a bigger part wants to keep it to myself, foster it inside me for a while longer.

"Not right now," I say.

He nods, takes it as a dismissal, and when he moves to get up, I reach over and grab his hand. I push the words out of my mouth—I have to start somewhere.

"Dad, someday, I'll tell you everything. All of it. I promise."

He squeezes my hand, and when he smiles at me, the sadness in his eyes fades a little.

A few weeks later, I stand outside the cemetery gates alone as the funeral procession passes by. I watch from the gates as they bury Jackie, unable to venture inside. In the distance, I can see the group of mourners gathered around the grave. A girl breaks from the crowd at the end.

Amy doesn't say anything. She walks to the bottom of the hill and faces me, close enough to the fence that I can see her clearly. She presses her hand against her heart and nods her head. A silent thank-you.

I nod back.

SEPTEMBER

"Please tell me your mom's stopped freaking out about this," Rachel says, dipping her fries into barbecue sauce. A few drops splatter on the practice test she's grading.

"Neither of them is really happy about it," I say. I've been shredding my napkin into little pieces, and they flutter across the table when Rachel turns the page. "I may have played the 'I was attacked by psychos' card to get them to agree."

"It's well earned," Rachel says. "Twice in one year."

I grin and lean over the table, trying to see what she's writing. "How'd I do?"

She scribbles my score on the top of the paper, circling it with a big red heart. "Ninety-five. Congratulations—if this were the actual test, you'd be the proud owner of a GED."

"Let's hope I do as well on the real thing," I say.

"Someone's ready to get out of here."

I shrug. "I'm just . . . I'm over school, you know? I want

to move forward, or whatever. I like Portland. I like living with Macy. I'm just lucky she wants me to come back."

"Well, I'll miss you. But I think I get it. Plus, now I have an excuse to visit Portland. I am very fond of roses."

"We can go to the Botanical Garden," I promise. "And I'll be back for the trials and stuff."

I'm not looking forward to testifying, but I know I have to. They need to pay for what they did to Mina. To Jackie.

I rub my knee. When Matt came to see me a few weeks after it happened, I'd tried to apologize to him. He could barely look me in the eye, and we'd both ended up crying. I'd gotten him to wait, called Trev to drive him home, and Matt had gripped his sober chip and my hand like a lifeline until he arrived.

There's this long road ahead. It's never-ending, because you don't get over losing someone. Not completely. Not when she was a part of you. Not when loving her broke you as much as it changed you.

I fear it, that long road, just as Matt must. For months, the urge to use has been buried beneath my need to find Mina's killer. Now I need to be strong for myself.

"Change is good, right?" I ask Rachel.

"Right," she agrees.

OCTOBER

Mom and I still don't talk much—though we never have, so it's not a big deal. Sometimes we sit together at the kitchen table, her working on legal briefs, me going through seed catalogs for plants suited to Portland's weather. But it's always quiet, the flip of pages, the scratch of her pen the only sounds.

One night she folds her hands over her briefcase and waits until I raise my eyes to meet hers, and I know, with more than a little dread, that she's finally ready to talk.

"I should have stopped and listened to you when you told me you were clean." It sounds like she's rehearsed this in the mirror, like she'd written it down and crossed things out, painstakingly trying to get the words right, like it's a speech instead of a confession.

I'm quiet for a long time. It's hard to even think about what to say. Her words can't change what she did; they can't erase those months I spent trapped at Seaside, forced to figure out how to grieve on my own. But I can't change that no matter how wrong it was. She did it only because she was trying to save me.

She will always try to save me.

That, more than anything else, is what makes me apologize.

"Look, I get it. I do. I lied and I kept everything from everyone and I just . . . I wasn't very good, and I'm sorry—"

"Honey." Mom's face, always so composed, crumples, worry lines appearing out of nowhere. "You've been through so much."

"That can't be an excuse," I say. "There can't be any excuses. Every single therapist you've sent me to will tell you that. I'm an addict. I'll always be an addict. Just like I'll always be crippled. And you've never been okay with either. I am. It took me a long time, but I am. You need to be, too."

"I'm okay with who you are, Sophie," she says. "I promise. I love who you are. I love you no matter what."

I want to believe her.

Mom reaches out and takes my hand, tilting it so the rings—Mina's and mine—shine in the lamplight. She doesn't touch them, seems to understand that she shouldn't, and I'm grateful for that small gesture. For the strength of her fingers, smooth and comforting, wrapped around mine.

"When you were in Oregon, Mina would come by. I used to find her up in the tree house. Or she'd sneak into your bedroom to do homework. We'd talk sometimes. She was scared you wouldn't forgive her for telling us about the drugs. I told her that she shouldn't worry. That you were the type of girl who didn't let anything stand in the way of loving someone. Especially her."

I look up at her, surprised at the warmth in her eyes that's almost encouragement. Mom smiles and brushes her cheek against mine. "It's a good thing, Sophie," she says softly. "Being able to love someone that much. It makes you brave."

I squeeze her hand tightly and I choose to believe.

NOVEMBER

"You sure you want to do this?"

I stare down at the black notebook in my hands. When

Trev brought her diary to me, turned up by the police during a second search of the house, I didn't even want to touch it. I could barely stand to keep it in the house. So a week later we drove to the lake and built a fire on the beach, waiting for night to fall and delaying the inevitable.

"Do you want to read it?" I ask him.

He shakes his head.

My fingers stroke the smooth black cover, tracing the ridges of the binding, the edges of the pages. It's like touching a part of her, the core, the heart and breath and blood of her in purple ink and cream-colored paper.

I could read it. Finally know her through all her layers and secrets.

Part of me wants that. To know. To be sure.

But more than anything, I want to keep my memory of her untainted, not polished by death nor shredded to pieces by words she meant only for herself. I want her to stay with me as she always was: strong and sure in everything but the one thing that mattered most, beautifully cruel and wonderfully sweet, too smart and inquisitive for her own good, and loving me like she didn't want to believe it was a sin.

I drop the diary into the fire. The pages curl and blacken, her words disappearing into smoke.

The two of us stand quiet and close until the fire dies out. Our shoulders touch as the wind carries away the last of her secrets.

It's Trev who finally breaks the silence. "Rachel told me you got your GED. That means you're going back to Portland."

"Yeah. Right after my birthday."

"Know what you're gonna do yet?"

"I don't," I say, and it's wonderful, not to know anything without dreading the feeling. To not have a suspect list in my head. To not think about what's next except for an open road and a little house with a yoga studio and a vegetable garden in the backyard. "College, I guess, eventually. But I think I'll take a year off, get a job, figure some things out first."

He smiles, all lopsided. His eyes go bright.

"What?" I ask.

"She would've loved you like this," he says.

I don't think it'll ever be easy to think about it, about all the chances Mina and I missed, the beginning, middle, and end we never had. Maybe we would've fizzled out instantly, her fear getting the better of her. Maybe we would've finished with high school, with fights and tears and words that couldn't be taken back. Maybe we would've lasted through college, only to end in quiet, strangled silence. Maybe we would've had forever.

"You could stay," he says, looking down. "I could build you that greenhouse you always wanted."

My smile trembles at the edges. "You know I love you, don't you?" I ask him. "Because I do, Trev. I really do."

"I know you do," he says. "Just . . . not the way I want you to."

"I'm sorry."

And the thing is, I am. In another life, if I had been a different girl, if my heart had gone traditional instead of zinging off after the unexpected, I might have loved him like he wanted. But my heart isn't simple or straightforward. It's a complicated mess of wants and needs, boys and girls: soft, rough, and everything in between, an ever-shifting precipice from which to fall. And as it beats, it's still her name that thrums through me. Never his.

When I kiss him, a quiet meeting of lips that's there and gone, it feels like good-bye.

66

At lunch on the first day of second grade, I'm eating with Amber and Kyle when I notice the new girl at the far end of the courtyard, sitting alone at a picnic table in her purple dress. Mrs. Durbin had put her next to me in class, but she hasn't said a word all day. She'd kept her head down even when she was called on.

She still seems sad, so I grab the rest of my lunch and walk over to her.

"I'm fine," she says when I get to her table, before I can even say anything.

Her face is wet. She scrubs at her cheeks with a fist and glares at me.

"I'm Sophie," I say. "Can I sit?"

"I guess."

I slide onto the bench next to her, setting my lunch down. "You're Mina, right?"

She nods.

"You're new."

"We moved," Mina says. "My daddy went to heaven."

"Oh." I bite my lip. I don't know what to say to that. "Sorry."

"Do you like horses?" Mina asks, pointing to my sticker-covered lunch box.

"Yeah. My grandpa takes me riding on his land."

Mina looks impressed. "My brother, Trev, says that sometimes they bite you if you don't give them sugar."

I giggle. "They have big teeth. But I give them carrots. You have to make your hand flat." I hold my hand out, palm up, to show her. "Then they won't bite."

Mina does the same with her hand, and our fingertips bump. She looks up and smiles at me.

"Do you have brothers?" she asks. "Or sisters?"

"No, it's just me."

Her nose wrinkles. "I wouldn't like that. Trev's the best."

"Sophie!" Amber waves at me. The bell's about to ring.

I get up, and there's something about Mina, about the way she's been crying and how she looks like she's lost, that makes me hold my hand out to her again. "Come with me?"

She smiles, reaches out, and takes my hand.

We walk into the rest of our lives together, not knowing it'll end before it's truly started.

On my eighteenth birthday, I drive to the cemetery at dusk. It takes me a while to find her; I trek across wet grass, weaving between headstones and angel statues to a shady, secluded spot.

It's plain, polished gray marble with white engraved letters:

Mina Elizabeth Bishop
Beloved Daughter and Sister

I wish this could be like in the movies. That I was the type of person who could reach out and trace the letters of her name and feel peaceful. I wish I could speak to this hunk of marble like it was her, feel comforted that her body is six feet below, believe that her spirit is watching from above.

But I'm not that girl. I never was. Not before or after or now. I can live with this knowledge—a simple gift to myself, quiet acceptance of who I'm becoming from the pieces that remain.

I kneel down next to her and pull the string of solar

Christmas lights out of my bag. I drape them on her headstone, trailing the strands down both sides of her grave.

I stay until nightfall, watching the lights begin to twinkle. My hand rests on the ground above her. When I get up, my fingers linger in the grass.

I walk to my car and never once do I look back.

Mina's night-lights will endure. Year after year, Trev will replace them when they dim. And I know that someday, when I'm ready to come home, they'll light my way.

ACKNOWLEDGMENTS

This book would not be possible without so many people's support and faith that carried me through its creation. Writing can be a solitary thing until the village it takes to publish a novel welcomes you into their fold. And I was lucky enough to be welcomed by the best village of all.

Thank you to my agent, Sarah Davies, for everything. You changed my entire life, and I'm not sure I'll ever be able to thank you properly for what you've taught me.

For my editor, Lisa Yoskowitz, thank you for your understanding of the characters and the love story I wanted to tell. You raised me and my work to new heights.

Thanks to Amber Caraveo, whose patience and instincts helped the book blossom in such lovely, deadly ways.

Thanks to the wonderful team at Disney • Hyperion, who put so much care and creative spark into all aspects of the book. Special thanks to Kate Hurley, my copy editor, whose sharp eye I am indebted to, and Whitney Manger, who designed me an absolutely beautiful cover.

For my parents and the rest of my amazing family. But especially for my mother, Laurie. Thank you, Mom, for reading every single thing I've ever written like it mattered, even my second grade opus "Two Fast Doctors."

So much gratitude must go to my dedicated, brutally honest critique partners: Elizabeth May and Allison Estry, who make my manuscripts bleed in the best ways. And thanks to Kate Bassett, for beta-reading and cheerleading.

Thanks to the Fourteenery, for hand holding, hilarity, and always blaming it on Melvin.

For Franny Gaede, who is truly the Walter to my Hildy.

A shout-out to the girls of the Crazy Chat. You ladies know who you are. Thank you from the bottom of my broken teen girl heart.

To those who helped shape me: Georgie Cook, Ellen Southard, Arnie Erickson, Carol Calvert, Ted Carlson, Antonio Beecroft, John Dembski, Michael Uhlenkott, Peggy S., Lynn P., and the entire crew over at SSHS circa 2001–2004.

And to my gramz, Marguerite O'Connell, who told me when I was little that I must always start my stories with something attention-grabbing. Hopefully I lived up to her advice.